About the Author

Tina J. Gordon was born in New York City. She was an educator for many years. Currently she is a blogger with serious food and travel addictions. She lives on the coast of New Jersey and is working on a new novel.

BLOG: teethetrav.travellerspoint.com
WEBSITE: TinaJGordon.com
TWITTER: @TinaJGordon

ISBN 978-0-9966060-0-4

Cover design by Allison Reich

Hardscrabble Way

PART 1

CHAPTER 1
May, 2012

I rolled over and checked the floor to see if anything was moving, just as I did every morning. The first morning we lived in our tent I found a trail of ants leading to one giant cluster, a moving mass of little black bodies.

"Delia, is that you?" My mother whispered from her cot.

"Mom?"

Silence. I breathed as quietly as I could. Waiting, I tried to decide if I should speak again. Maybe she was dreaming.

I had no idea what time it was, but it felt early. We had no electricity, so we had no clock. My cell phone had been turned off months ago.

I tried again. "Mommy?" I didn't know where that came from. Neither Rachel nor I had ever called our mother mommy. We called her Emily. Rachel started it when she first learned to talk. In the beginning, Daddy said she copied him. But Emily was always more of an Emily than a mommy so the habit stuck and was passed on to me when I was old enough to speak.

"Delia, are you here?"

"Are you hungry? Do you want something to eat?"

She sat up. The sheet fell away from her body and she stretched, her thin arms reaching high overhead. She looked at me and smiled. Emily looked...for a few seconds, she looked like she did before. Maybe this was going to be a good day.

"I am, actually. Are there any more buns?"

I got her a sticky bun and a container of Sunny D from the cooler. The cooler kept the ants, bugs, and other disgusting things I didn't want to think about away from our food. I sat and watched her eat. I wished she would take the bun out of the tent, but I didn't want to say so and upset her. Ever since the ant invasion on our first morning we put down tins with poison called ant traps, but still. I didn't want to put temptation in their path, so I never ate in our tent.

My mother looked at me. "It's not so bad here, is it Delia?" she asked, licking the stickiness from her fingers. I stared at her fingers, hoping she wasn't leaving crumbs.

"No. It's not." That was the truth, in a sense. Living here was better than being sent to a foster home. I knew it was better than the welfare motel. The only good thing that came from living in the motel was meeting Gloria. She was the one who brought us to tent city and saved me from getting separated from my mother and sent to live with strangers.

"You would tell me, wouldn't you? I need you to be honest with me, baby. You don't have to protect me, you know. I'm feeling much better."

"It's okay here. For now, anyway." I stared at my mother, trying to decide if she was telling me the truth. It seemed like she was doing better. At least some of the time.

The tent city known as Hardscrabble Way *was* okay. At least for the summer. When it got cold outside, I wasn't sure we could manage. But that was months away, and for now we were fine. I liked living in a community. Chief Cheyenne made us feel welcome as soon as we got here. Cheyenne is not his real name, and he's not a chief or even Native American. When Gloria said he was a character, I wasn't sure what she meant. When we met him, I completely understood. He was dressed in khaki pants and a sleeveless vest with a dozen zippers going every which way, and he looked as though he belonged in a jungle, right down to the safari hat he wore. He carried a clipboard with a thick stack of papers attached to it. When he talked he referred to the board often, as if he was looking things up. He wore a lanyard with a whistle around his neck. Circling his waist was a wide canvas belt with hooks. A megaphone dangled from one large hook, a canteen hung from another, and various tools such as a Swiss army knife swung from other smaller hooks. As he showed us around the tent city, he told us parts of his story. When he started the enclave that he called

Hardscrabble Way, he decided to give himself the title of Chief and called himself Cheyenne. He told us that without a trace of self-consciousness. He used to be a stockbroker and had a big house and a lot of money. He never mentioned if he had a family. The Chief, unlike most of the people in the tent city, walked away from his other life. He didn't bother to explain why. I wondered if he had told anyone the whole story.

"Why this?" Gloria asked when we got our orientation tour. "Why start a tent city on the outskirts of Philadelphia?"

"The homeless do not choose to be homeless," he said, as if that explained everything. Maybe it did.

There were between thirty-five and forty large, canvas tents on the curving path where someone had stuck a wooden sign with painted letters: **Hardscrabble Way**. I also saw about a dozen teepees, a small pop-up camper, and a tent that was one part latrine, and one part shower. The toilet was chemical. I wasn't exactly sure what that meant, but it kept things sanitary, according to Chief Cheyenne. The water for the shower was heated by propane and there was a strict schedule to use the shower. You could use the latrine whenever, but you had to supply your own paper. Every family in the community had to agree to contribute twenty dollars a month to run the generator, buy propane, and other supplies. Singles paid ten. It was up to you what to do about cooking. Propane or charcoal grills were allowed only on the outside of tents and no hotplates (the chief had to tell me what a hotplate was, I had no idea) or stoves of any kind were allowed in the tents. They were a fire hazard. I asked him what people did in the winter to stay warm. Cheyenne told us that most added insulation and plywood inside using the tent as a frame. So essentially they built a little house inside their tent. They also used small propane heaters. I couldn't envision Emily or Gloria doing this, but cold weather was months away. We could figure that out later. Cheyenne did say that some people left during the coldest months. I wanted to ask him where they went, but I didn't.

He told us there was a chapel, a small tent where you could pray. A Reverend named Willy came once a week in a purple bus and held a service. He supplied donated propane tanks, as well as clothes and canned foods. If someone got sick he drove them to a free clinic where they could see a doctor.

At one point the Chief looked at his clipboard and asked, "Did I mention I don't let families with small children stay here? Too risky." Cheyenne looked at me. "You're thirteen, right? That makes you the youngest one here right now."

Cheyenne supplied the tents for a fee, if you didn't have your own. He asked Emily and Gloria if they were a couple and if they would be sharing a tent. "When I met you last week, you didn't mention a partner," he said to Gloria. She explained to him she and my mother were friends, not partners, and that we would prefer to live in two tents. "Either way works," he said. I was relieved by his accepting attitude. I was more relieved he didn't ask questions about our sudden appearance. We didn't have to explain our sudden flight from the welfare motel. The fewer people who knew we were hiding, the better.

"Thank you for letting us in," Gloria said. "We're filled with gratitude."

"I'm glad we have room. Sometimes I have to turn people away. That's tough. I limit the numbers. Keep it to under seventy. I try to stay under the radar so the system doesn't shut us down." He pulled some papers from his clipboard. "Just follow the rules and you'll be just fine. Did all three of you read the contract?"

We had, so we each signed off on the papers that Chief Cheyenne handed us. He took them back and clipped them back on his board.

"I don't know what we would have done without you," Emily said. She was tearing up and I hoped she didn't lose it in front of the Chief. I didn't want to have to tell our whole awful story to a stranger.

" 'One man gives freely, yet gains even more...A generous man will prosper...' That's from Proverbs," Cheyenne said.

After he helped us pick spots to pitch our tents, the Chief turned to us and said, "As soon as you can, get pepper spray and a Swiss army knife. For each of you. Also, tick and mosquito repellant. The kind with deet. It'll take your nail polish off, but it's the only kind that works."

We stared at him.

"Lyme. Dengue fever. West Nile. I'm an ex-Marine. Pays to be careful."

"What about the pepper spray? And the knife?" I asked.

"Protection," he said. "We patrol and it's safe enough here, but we've had a few incidents. I tell everyone to sleep with some defense under their pillows. Especially the women." He reached into one of the many pockets in his vest and pulled out a roll of zip lock baggies. Handing one to each of us he said, "These are your Go Bags. Put your documents in them and keep them with you at all times. Birth certificate, driver's license, passport if you've got one. Anything ever happens— fire, flood, avalanche, tsunami, you grab these and GO!"

I looked at my mother and then at Gloria as we watched Chief Cheyenne walk away to get our tents. This wasn't summer camp. I don't think any of us knew what to say. But there was no turning back, at least not for me and Emily. Unless we were willing to turn ourselves in and face our social worker Joy Pierce and her horrendous plan to separate me from my mother.

~~

Larry lived in one of the big tents. I met him the first night we moved in. There was a big screen television and a DVD player someone donated that was hooked to a portable generator. Anyone who wanted to could gather and watch movies from nine to eleven Wednesdays and Saturdays, if the weather was good. At eleven it was lights out to save energy.

Emily had fallen asleep. She was exhausted after the drama of fleeing the welfare hotel and Joy Pierce. The scare had the opposite effect on me. I couldn't sit in the tent. Lucky for me it was Wednesday. I stopped at Gloria's tent to see if she wanted to come see what was playing, but she was making a list of places she was going to look for work in the morning.

"You look lost, kid," Larry said to me when I wandered over to the TV area. There were about a dozen people sitting in assorted chairs.

"Can I sit here?" I asked, pointing to a camp chair next to him.

"Sure. I nibble. I don't bite. I'm Larry. First night?"

I nodded.

"Tough. You with your family?"

"My mother." I hoped he wasn't going to ask me a million questions.

He must have read my mind. "Last question. You got a name?"

"Cordelia. But everyone calls me Delia."

"Cordelia, huh? Someone must like Shakespeare."

I was impressed. Very few people knew my name came from Shakespeare.

"Is your Daddy named Lear?" He smiled. Cordelia was King Lear's daughter.

"No. Mark. Mark Williams. He died. My mother loves literature. She chose my name."

"Sorry, kid. No wonder you look lost. I didn't mean to stir things up. Look, the movie's starting. You like *The Godfather*?"

"I've never seen it."

I might as well have said I never ate ice cream. Larry looked at me. "You've never seen *The Godfather*? What kind of education have you had, child? I've seen it at least thirty times. You are in for a treat. Have some popcorn." He reached his arm over and put a bowl in my lap. "And don't say a word until the movie's over. You are about to have a mandatory cultural experience."

We sat side by side under the stars sharing popcorn and watching Marlon Brando and Al Pacino in silence. My broken heart shattered again when Michael Corleone sat next to his father in the hospital and said, "I'm with you, now." I wished I could have been there for Daddy. I wished I could have told him how much I loved him. Maybe he knew.

When it was over Larry asked me, "Something, huh kid? Classic. What'd you think the theme was?"

I reached down deep, remembering the times we talked about theme in Ms. Louis's language arts class. We'd had long, good discussions about the theme of *To Kill a Mockingbird*. Larry took my pause for lack of understanding.

"Theme is...," he started to explain.

"I know what a theme is," I interrupted. "I was thinking." Then, choosing my words carefully I said, "It's about family and loyalty. It's about taking care of your family no matter what you have to sacrifice. Michael gave up the life he wanted to take care of his father and the family. That's the theme."

Larry raised his eyebrows. He nodded his head slowly. "You're okay, kid."

"How many times have you seen that movie, Larry?" a woman called out as she walked over to us. She was dressed like a gypsy.

"I've lost count. Annie, this is Delia. She and her mom just moved in."

"How many times do I have to tell you? It's Crazy Annie, jackweed. Hey, Delia. Welcome to Hardscrabble Way." I had to force myself not to stare. I'd never seen anyone who looked like Crazy Annie. She had long, purple dreadlocks and wore lipstick to match. Every finger was decorated with a different ring and she wore a long sparkly caftan. She had no eyebrows and her skin was, well, it was impossible to tell what color skin she had. Or how old she was.

Larry continued his introductions. "And this is Irish Jimmy, the drunk. Not to be confused with Greek Jimmy the gangster. We stereotype unabashedly around here. That's Haysoos over there. Not Jesus. Haysoos. Over there is Sarge. He's a war Vet. Served in Iraq a couple of times. Doesn't talk much. These are new arrivals; Cher and her fiancé, John. They're noobs."

"What's a noob?" I asked.

"A newbie. Newly homeless."

"Me too," I said.

"Sucks," John said. Cher looked like she might cry. Looking at Cher, something made me think of my sister. Maybe it was because Cher didn't look too much older than Rachel. Neither did John. I wondered if my sister was safe. Six months ago we had all been living together. Six months ago I had a home, a sister, a mother, and a father.

"I know," I said. "It does suck." There wasn't much else to say.

"I'm not a drunk anymore," said Irish Jimmy, the drunk. "But it's okay to call me one. It keeps me sober and reminds me how I got here."

"Where's your mom?" Crazy Annie asked me.

"Sleeping. She hasn't been feeling well."

"You're Gloria's friends, right? The hairdresser I met this afternoon? She promised to condition my dreads for me. I'm going to paint her tent in return. We barter here. You know what that is?" Annie asked.

I nodded. I did know what it meant, but I thought bartering, trading one thing for another, had gone out with the pilgrims. "You're a painter?" I couldn't tell if she meant she was an artist or someone who painted walls.

"I prefer sculpting. But I was classically trained, so I paint, too. I'll show you some of my work tomorrow if you'd like. Come by my tent in the morning."

"I'd love to. Thanks. Night, Annie."

"That's Crazy Annie, if you don't mind." Her voice went cold.

She didn't seem crazy. I wondered what her story was. Everyone here had one. Once upon a time they had all been somewhere. Living lives with a roof over their heads, shopping, eating, going to school or work, but never in their wildest dreams ever imagining that someday, somehow, they would become homeless. When you're little and people ask you what you want to be when you grow up, no one ever says "homeless." So how did so many people end up here?

CHAPTER 2
September, 2011

How many people do you know lose everything, become homeless, and have a parent die before they even make it to high school? The year I became a teenager we lost our money, our house, and I had to leave my school and my friends. I never saw any of it coming. No one sees their future, of course. I have a vivid image in my head of the last day I was happy. Maybe happy isn't the right word. Maybe I was just oblivious. On that September day, I was oblivious to the possibility that circumstances could change me whether I was prepared for them or not.

I was the flier. I was the cheerleader on the top of the pyramid who whizzed through the air, got caught, tossed into the sky to flip in mid-air and then land, planting my feet on the ground. I got to be the flier because I was tiny. Something I always hated, by the way. But it paid off. I was five feet tall and just under a hundred pounds. This was the first game of the last year I would cheer for Bala Cynwyd Middle School. My plan was to be the eighth grade Scholar Athlete this year. I neglected my friends so I could study and go to my lessons, practices, and meets. Being good at school and cheerleading gave me a sense of purpose. When I was cheering, I felt necessary. My cheerleading squad was the only place I felt like myself. Even though I wasn't close to any of the girls, I had a sense of belonging to something. When I wasn't cheering, I felt like nothing. My goal for next year was to be good enough to be a flier on the high school cheerleading squad. If I didn't grow too much. I knew I couldn't control my growth. I had no inkling about how little control I had over the rest of my life.

On that carefree September day in the beginning of eighth grade, I remember exactly how I felt. My arms were spread out from my body and I was perfectly balanced. I had never felt as confident as I did right that minute. I waited for a long moment. My adrenaline was pumping and I was like a high wire walker

11

about to step off the platform and walk out onto the cable without a safety harness or a net beneath me to catch me if I fell. More than anything, I wanted the sensation to last. Everyone down below was looking at me, holding their breath. I was thirteen and I was in charge of my own destiny.

The sky seemed bluer up there, standing on the shoulders of the other girls. Clear, deep blue with wisps of white clouds hanging like curtains moving slowly in a breeze. I was calm. I was ready. I breathed in and the air was chilled. Crisp. Cleansing. I didn't want this to end yet. I paused, knowing the feeling when I jumped would be even more mind-blowing. The final thing I did before I vaulted was to gaze around the stands searching for my parents. I kept hoping that if I was good enough, just once someone would come to cheer for me.

I leapt. I was plummeting into the air. Soaring, my body was surrounded by deafening music, pounding drums, and cool air. The sensation of speed exhilarated me as I began to fall. People were frantic; I heard screaming. There was simply nothing else I could do that would compare to this. Without cheering, without flying, I didn't exist. I was nobody. Then, everything went quiet and I couldn't see anything. Once I jumped I had no fear. If I died during a stunt, it didn't matter. For me, the moment was irresistible.

I tucked, rolled, straightened, and landed on a tangle of arms. They tossed me up; I twisted and landed on my feet, my arms in a V over my head. The crowd went insane and I was grinning from ear to ear. I loved cheerleading more than anything in the world.

The first thing I did after I landed was look up and search for my parents again. I knew no one was there. Daddy was working, and my mother, well—Emily was just off somewhere being Emily. Week after week, I told myself if only my family would come to see me cheer, I'd show them I was a better daughter than my sister Rachel. I was the perfect daughter. The good one. Back then, I thought I would never want anything more than their approval. Now I know I couldn't have been more wrong.

~~

I keyed in the security code on the front door and yelled, "Emily! Is there any food? I'm starving!"

"In here," she called from the kitchen. "How did you get home? You want a tuna sandwich?" My mother was barefoot, wearing her yoga clothes. I stared at her long, lean body for a second. It may sound strange, but I've always been struck by how attractive my mother was. She was not only pretty, she was appealing. People were drawn to her. She had an aura about her that was hard to define, but it made you stop and look at her. It's like catching a glimpse of a cardinal. No matter how many times you see one, that splash of red is always a surprise and draws you in. If you saw Emily from across the street, you'd swear she was a teenager. When you move up close, you see she's older, but she could still pass for twenty-something, not thirty-nine. Not that she ever told me her age. I figured it out from her driver's license. I was obsessed with my mother. Not in a good way. Emily was always just out of my grasp.

"Did you go to yoga this morning?" I asked her, knowing the answer. She could wake up to go to yoga, but she couldn't come to my game.

"Uh,huh."

I sat on my favorite stool next to the gigantic, granite-topped island in the center of our kitchen. My mother had the kitchen custom built and it looked like a magazine picture, which was amusing because Emily never cooked. She ate out, heated things up, brought food in--she had every restaurant with delivery service on speed dial--but she never cooked. Ever. When there was an exceptional meal on the table, Daddy would look at my mother, grin and say, "How long did this take you to order, Emily? She would roll her eyes and say, "I didn't know you married me for my kitchen talents."

My sister and I would chime in and tease her about her lack of domestic skills. At some point, Rachel would remind me

13

that she had four more years of deprivation than I did. "Once," Rachel told us, "my friends were talking about favorite dishes that their mothers made. Finally, they looked at me, waiting for my answer. Jello. That was the best I could come up with. So sad."

Of course, that was when Rachel still spoke to me.

Emily had every appliance known to exist: a restaurant refrigerator, a six-burner chef's stove, food processor, well...you get the idea. A family of four could have lived comfortably in our kitchen. Margot's kitchen was huge, but Margot's mother cooked all the time. She took classes with famous chefs in Philly and she made these incredible dishes. Like halibut in avocado and mango sauce, which I still think about sometimes. I loved to eat pretty much anything at Margot's. It was partly why she was my best friend, I think. The craziest thing was that Margot would rather be at my house. She envied the fact that my mother ordered out. I guess no one is happy with what they have. Until they don't have it any more.

"I'll have my leftovers from *Angelo's*," I replied to my mother's question about what I wanted for lunch. "Amy's mom gave me a ride. She comes to all the games," I said with a smidge of sarcasm. I thought it would sail by unnoticed, but it didn't.

"I hate football. You know that. And I hate the outdoors."

"You could come to see me cheer. It's not about football."

"It scares me to see you up on top of all those shoulders. What if you fell and I was there? I don't think I could stand it."

I stared at her. I didn't have the words to try to explain how much I wanted her to come and see me. Maybe if I got picked scholar athlete for my eighth grade class at the end of this year. Maybe then she would get excited and see how good I was.

The microwave beeped. I jumped off the stool and took my leftover shrimp scampi out. "I'm going up to my room. I have homework."

"Want to go shopping? I'm redecorating the media room and I want to check out some chairs."

"I can't. I have homework." Shopping was not as important as keeping my grades up.

"We can get those boots you want."

I tapped my foot, thinking. I had so much to do. But those boots... I shrugged. "Sure. I'll go."

"We'll go in an hour." My mother looked at me. "Ask Rachel to come." She watched me for my reaction.

"Really?" It had been a long time since I enjoyed doing anything with my sister. My mother seemed to have no idea that Rachel had never forgiven me for what I had done.

"She probably won't go. See if she's up. Ask her."

"If she says no, can I ask Margot?"

Grabbing a fork and a bottle of water, I took my food and climbed the stairs. I had no idea how to repair the damaged relationship I had with my sister. It had been nearly a year since we stopped being close. Standing outside her door, I realized I couldn't knock. My hands were full, so I gently kicked the door and called at the same time.

"Rach, you up?" I waited for one brief moment. I tried again. "Rach? Emily wants to know if you want to go shopping with us." I decided to take no answer as a no. Later, I'd feel guilty about how relieved I was she didn't answer me.

~~

"Stop it, Cordelia! I'm going to wet myself right here in the dressing room!" Margot was laughing uncontrollably and doing the pee pee dance as I struggled to get out of a dress I was stuck in.

"It's not funny! I can't get this off. The zipper's stuck." I was half in and half out of the dress and I couldn't stop laughing. My cell phone was ringing and one of my arms was stuck inside the dress. With my free hand I reached into my bag and tried to speak, but I was laughing too hard. I could hear Emily in my ear.

15

"Delia! Where are you? You were supposed to meet me outside of Abercrombie's fifteen minutes ago."

I knew that tone. I hated that tone. When my mother was displeased with me for any reason I got a knot in the pit of my stomach.

"Hurry up," she said. "I got you everything you wanted. I want to go look at those chairs."

Twenty minutes later we were prisoners in a furniture store. Margot and I were plopped in comfy chairs with shopping bags strewn at our feet. I discovered I could make my chair spin by moving my feet. That entertained me for at least two minutes. I looked around. Emily was nearby with a sales person. She was looking at swatches. We could be here a while. I turned back and looked at Margot to see if she was as bored as I was. Margot was watching Emily.

"I wish Emily was my mother," Margot said.

"I wish I had your legs," I said.

She raised her eyebrows at me.

"You have seriously got rockin' legs. Not stumps like I have."

"Please," Margot said. "I hate being tall."

"What did you mean?" I asked.

"About what?"

"About Emily."

"Oh. Your mom is good at so many things. Look at her."

"Emily is good at two things. Looking good and spending money." I looked over at Emily, trying to see her from Margot's eyes. "I'd take your mother any day. She's always there to do stuff for you. And she cooks."

"True. My mother is a great cook. But I seriously wouldn't mind some take-out every now and then."

"She won't let me have a dog." I was pulling out all the stops for the sympathy vote.

Margot's eyebrows shot up. "I did not know you wanted a dog."

"I've always wanted a dog. Or a brother."

"What did you mean, my mother's there for me? Emily doesn't work. She's home, too. Isn't she?" Margot asked.

It was hard to explain even to my best friend how your mother can be physically there, but not be really there. How I always felt invisible. Like I could vanish tomorrow and it would hardly make a difference to my parents.

Margot and I both shrugged, digesting what the other had said.

I yelled over to Emily. "Can we go soon? I still have homework."

Emily put five fingers in the air, signaling that we should be patient for five more minutes. I knew it was pointless to rush her. No shopping trip with my mother was ever quick.

Margot grinned at me.

"What?" I asked.

"Only you would worry about homework while shopping."

"I want to do well."

"You always do. When was the last time you got anything less than an A?"

"I got an A- in art."

Margot rolled her eyes. "Oooo. Did you get punished?"

No. My parents didn't notice or if they did, they didn't care.

I never should have gone shopping, even though I did get the pink Uggs@ I'd been lusting after. My mother took forever to pick out new chairs and cushions for the media room. Like anyone cared. It was late and I still had homework to do. I should have started my paper for Language Arts sooner. Can't fall off my honor roll pedestal. I don't know why I cared. Cheerleading, gymnastics, dance, honors classes...I tried so hard. Rachel used to be the same way. Until she wasn't. I didn't want to think about her anymore. I just wanted to go to sleep. I was crampy. Maybe I was getting my period.

I squinted at the clock on my nightstand. 11:30. I shut my eyes. A few seconds later, I realized why I was up. I could hear my parents arguing. Their voices were escaping from their bedroom. I wondered what they were fighting about. Was it about Rachel again? I opened the door to my bedroom so I could hear them better, and then I tiptoed back into my bed.

"Emily, stop defending yourself. You have to stop. There's no reason to keep doing this over and over!" Daddy's voice was getting louder, like he was coming closer.

"Don't walk out of the room like that, Mark. Can't we finish just one argument?" My mother sounded like she was crying, but I wasn't sure.

"Em, there's nothing left to say. I don't know how many times we've had this fight in the past year. You. Can't. Keep. Spending. Like. This." He paused. "Am I making myself clear?"

"I don't understand why not. You own five stores. You're never home because that is all you do. All you seem to care about. I'm alone all the time. Why can't I at least shop? It's the only thing I enjoy."

There was total silence for what seemed like forever. The silence scared me more than the raised voices. I couldn't believe my mother. How could she buy chairs she didn't need when my father had asked her to stop spending?

"Last week you spent $11,000. That's more than some people make in a month." I wasn't sure I had heard my father correctly. Had he said *eleven* thousand?

"I didn't want to tell you this, but I am stretched as far as I can go. It's bad, Emily. Really bad."

"At this point, shopping is the only benefit of being married to you."

"Opening these last two stores two years ago pushed me beyond my limit. I thought they'd be worthwhile in the end, but for now…with the economy in the toilet, I'm mortgaged up to my eyebrows. Take my word for it. I don't have this kind of money right now."

"Why don't you just sell the stores if it's too much?"

"What rock do you live under, Emily? Do you read the newspapers? The economy has tanked. *No one is buying anything.*" Daddy never raised his voice. He didn't have to. He was one of those people whose strength came across even when he spoke quietly. When I was little he took me to work with him sometimes. I remember how he talked to people. Even when he was clearly not happy with something at work, he spoke in quiet tones which made him seem very powerful.

"Close the stores. Take the loss."

"I didn't want to worry you with all of this. I should have told you sooner."

And then there was silence. Longer even than the last one. I didn't want to listen anymore, but I was a like a marble statue unable to move a muscle. This was like the dream you have where something is chasing you and you know there's going to be a catastrophe of some sort. You're going to fall off a cliff or a slasher is going to come at you and kill you. You want to wake yourself up, but you can't. I sat in my bed and waited, wanting to hear my mother say how sorry she was. How she'd return all the crap she bought that she didn't need.

It was Emily who finally spoke. But I didn't hear what I'd hoped she would say. "I don't understand why you work so much. I'd rather spend time with you than spend your money. If I can't shop and I can't be with you, I'm getting nothing out of this marriage."

"Oh my God, Emily. I'm doing all this for you. You and the girls."

"No you're not. I never wanted any of this. All I ever wanted was you. To be with you. I never see you unless you drag me to some function where you leave me and go work the room to drum up even more business. When was the last time you did anything with me that I wanted to do? You suck at being a husband."

"You suck at being a mother! Why the hell can't you take care of your children instead of spending your time spending? Look at Rachel…"

That was it. I put my hands over my ears and swallowed the lump in my throat that was threatening to choke me. I'd heard enough. Too much. "I will not cry. I will not cry. I will not cry," I kept repeating to myself in a whisper, like a mantra. I quietly closed my door. As I passed my desk, I could see my new pink boots sitting in their box. In the morning I'd tell my mother to take them back. Even though I loved them, I could never wear them now.

I lay in bed awake under my covers, wondering if they would divorce. Half of my friend's parents were divorced. I never wanted to be that girl. The one who says, *I've got to go to my father's this weekend.* Or worse, *my bitch stepmother is such a pain.* The next thought made me gasp out loud. What if my parents married people who already had children? I'd have step-siblings. I couldn't even stand living with my sister at this point. How would I live with steps? I wondered who I would live with. Maybe Rachel and I would split up. One per parent. Who would want her? Who would want me? I stared into the darkness with my million questions floating around me. At least now it was quiet. I couldn't hear my parents any more. I clung to the possibility that they had made up. Maybe Daddy was lying to Emily about how bad things were in order to shock her into spending less. If only that was true.

The lump in my throat was back, bigger than before. I was not going to cry.

As soon as I opened my eyes in the morning I turned on my computer. Reading my Language Arts paper one more time was better than thinking about my parents' fight. About an hour later my cell phone rang. It was Emily.

"What?"

"I never heard your sister come in last night. Can you stick your head in Rachel's door and ask her what she wants for Sunday dinner? I'm going to run some errands. I'll stop at *Falcos* to pick up some dinner. What do you want me to get?"

"Can't you call her? I'm doing my homework."

"I tried. No answer."

My stomach rolled over. I wished my parents knew how bad things were between Rachel and me. Ever since the day I betrayed her, she had shut down. She was moody and broody and sulked all the time. My sister hung by herself sketching in her room, or painting downstairs in the basement studio Daddy had set up for her. I hated to admit it, especially when we were barely speaking, but she was a wholly talented seventeen-year-old.

I crossed the hall to Rachel's room and knocked. Waiting, I started twirling my hair around my finger. I knocked again, harder this time. I was scared to open the door. I was scared not to open the door. I looked at the piece of hair wrapped around my finger. The ends were split. Maybe it was time to do something about that. Maybe it was time to tell Emily how bad things were with my sister.

I couldn't keep standing there. "Rachel? Rach, are you up?"

My hand was on her door knob. I waited a second, afraid to turn it, afraid it was locked. Relieved when the knob turned, I pushed her door open. Her bed was empty. Not only was it empty, it was made. Rachel never made her bed. Neither did I, for that matter. Marisol, our housekeeper, did. But Saturday was Marisol's day off, which meant that Rachel hadn't come home the night before. Where was she? And why, why didn't I open her door yesterday morning before we went shopping?

One time we were driving somewhere on the throughway. All four of us were in the car. Suddenly, in front of us there were ambulances and police cars blocking two of the three lanes and traffic slowed to a crawl. I heard Daddy say "damn" under his breath and then he told us not to look. I couldn't help myself. Lying right there on the road was a body on a stretcher, covered with a sheet. I wanted to look away, but I couldn't. I had to keep looking. That's how I felt when I looked at Rachel's art. Her drawings and paintings were propped up everywhere. Some were lying on the floor, neatly arranged like a show. I felt like I was seeing something I shouldn't be looking at, but it was impossible to look away. Her images were disturbing. They had elements that looked like humans, but something was always off. Way off. Body parts floating, animal parts where limbs should be, hearts and brains with tiny fantasy creatures spilling out of them. She drew pen and ink figures. Some she filled in with paint, crayons, coins, pieces of fabric, and snips of wire. Her work was fascinating. Looking at it, I felt like I was reading her diary. Like somehow, it wasn't meant to be seen. At least, not by me.

Rachel always signed each of her images in the lower right hand corner by drawing a nautilus shell into which she wove a unique *R* for Rachel. She made it look natural, like it was part of the shell. You had to look deep into the spiral to know it was there. We used to collect shells during the summer when we vacationed in Sea Isle City at the Jersey shore. Eventually the collection got to be too big and we just collected the nautilus. There's something about the shape. That perfect spiral.

I'd never seen most of these pictures before. It was a long time since I'd been in Rachel's room. I turned around to walk out. Then, hating myself for doing it, I opened her bathroom door and looked in. Not that I really expected to find her there strewn across the tiles, but I breathed out, relieved to find it empty. Where could she be?

~ ~

"Why didn't you open her door yesterday before we left?" My mother was talking in the high-pitched tone she gets when she's upset. She tried to reach Daddy. I didn't know what she expected him to do. His phone went straight to voice mail.

"I wish I paid more attention when he tells me which store he's going to be at. It's Sunday. Why can't he just come home like other men?"

"Daddy's in the store in Tredyffrin today. He told you the other day they're having a big promotion." Daddy owned stores that sold high end appliances and electronics in towns surrounding Philadelphia.

I watched as she hit her speed dial. "Where do you think Rachel is?" I asked. I so wanted her to have an answer, even though I knew she wouldn't.

"Get Mark! I don't care how busy he is. This is a family emergency." She snapped at whoever was on the other end of the phone.

What did she expect Daddy to do? *Another* family emergency, I thought, but I didn't say it. Rachel had been causing family drama for a couple of years, now. I guess it started when she went to high school and decided she wasn't going to do anything except her art. She stopped taking lessons and playing sports. Since then, she'd been in trouble a few times. Nothing big. Once she'd been caught drinking. Another time she had rolling papers in her backpack in school. The worst was when she skipped school for a week. She and some guy she was friends with went to the mall every day instead of going to school. Why would anyone want to hang at a mall all day, every day? My mother was livid with the school for not calling her. But it turned out Rachel was clever enough to put her own cell phone down as the emergency call number. Daddy punished her by not buying her art supplies for a month. She got even by shoplifting paints and brushes.

But all that was minor. The real crisis came when she got caught having sex on the Aubusson carpet in the living room. She would have gotten away with it, but I betrayed her.

One day last spring my gymnastics lesson was cancelled because my instructor had called in sick too late for a substitute to be arranged. It was one of the only times I had ever come straight home. Emily picked me up from school and dropped me at the house because she had errands to run and I didn't want to go. How many times I've wished I had not come home early that day. I let myself in and started to head toward the kitchen for a drink and something to eat. I heard a noise coming from the living room and since I didn't think anyone else was home, I tiptoed over to see what it was.

Rachel was sitting naked on top of a boy, also naked, with her back to me. I was disgusted, shocked, and I hated my sister. I don't know what I was thinking. I wasn't thinking. I backed out of the room, opened the front door, went out to the porch, and speed-dialed my mother.

"You need to come back home right now. It's an emergency." I hung up before she could say a word.

I waited for my mother on the porch, put my finger to my lips, and walked her into the living room. When Emily gasped, Rachel turned around. I left and went upstairs. I couldn't bear to see what was going to happen next.

I couldn't get the image of my sister and that boy out of my head for weeks. My mother never spoke of the incident to me after that. Not one word. I never knew what she or my father said to Rachel, but nothing was the same after that.

My parents treated Rachel like she had murdered someone, not had sex on the living room carpet. I took pleasure in watching my sister tumble out of their favor. I thought that now it was possible I would get some of the attention that had always gone to Rachel. First, for when she was the good daughter. Later, for being the bad girl. Like I said. I don't know what I was thinking.

Rachel stopped speaking to me. I thought it was because she was embarrassed I had seen her. If it had happened to me, which it would never, I couldn't have looked my sister in the eye again. I would have been so ashamed. But Rachel soon made it clear that she knew I had betrayed her and she hated me for it. Worst of all, my parents still had no time for me. It had all been for nothing.

~~

Two frantic hours after we discovered Rachel hadn't come home, my father still hadn't arrived from work, my mother was sitting downstairs drinking copious amounts of wine, and I had made myself a tuna sandwich and finished my homework. I was in my room getting ready to take a shower when I heard my mother's voice.

"Where the hell have you been? Do you have any idea how…" I walked into my bathroom and turned on the water. I didn't want to listen. I was relieved, though. At least Rachel was safe. I had ruined everything between us and I didn't know how to make it better, but I still cared about her. I told on her partly because I was angry she had stopped being close to me. She had disappeared so gradually I couldn't remember when she stopped being my adored big sister. The one who used to play dress up with me and let me crawl in her bed to sleep when our parents were out for the night and I was scared. I wished I could remember when she stopped saying, "I love you, Deal." And when I stopped knowing who my sister was. I stepped into the shower, hoping the whole drama would be over by the time I came out.

Wrapped in a towel, I came out of the bathroom. Raised voices drifted upstairs. I was drawn to the landing on the top of the stairs. I needed to hear what was happening in much the same way I needed to look at the accident on the highway. I didn't want to do it; I couldn't help myself. When I was really young, around three or four, the landing scared me. It was at the top of a long curving staircase and I used to worry that I was going to fall down the whole flight. I got over my fear as I got older. Eventually, I realized I could see and hear everything from the top of the stairs and yet, because of the curve, no one could see me. I remember sitting there when my parents had friends over. Whenever my mother entertained, the house had a special glow to it. Emily lit a million candles in candlesticks that she kept just for occasions. Sometimes, if she was hosting a party, she'd go all out and decorate with a theme. Once, she held a Venetian party and everyone wore masks. She rented a little bridge like the ones they have in Venice over the canals, and she stood it in our great room. Tiny white lights twinkled everywhere and I remember how enchanted I was. It had been a long time since Emily had thrown a party. I didn't realize how much I missed them. To me, when I was six or seven, those parties were as splendid as any ball in any fairy tale I had ever read. As I sat there it dawned on me that maybe it wasn't the parties that were dazzling. Maybe it had just been my mother.

I sat down on the top step and hugged my knees, listening. My mother sounded calmer. "Of course I was worried. Wouldn't you be upset if I didn't come home?"

Rachel didn't answer.

"Rachel, what's going on with you?"

"Aren't you ever going to trust me again?" My sister's voice was low.

"How can I?" Emily answered.

"I hate my life," Rachel said.

"What's wrong with it?"

"Everything."

"Why can't you just do what's expected of you?"

"I used to. What did that get me?"

"What…what do you want?" My mother asked.

"You don't listen. Daddy's always busy working. You're too busy pretending to be busy."

My mother sounded furious. "You have everything you ever wanted."

"Do I?"

"Are you on drugs?"

I wondered the same thing.

"You're such a cliché, Emily."

"I had to ask. It's the first thing a mother thinks about when her kid…changes."

"I don't have to be on drugs to know that I don't want to end up like you and Daddy. He works all the time. You spend money all the time."

"That's not fair. I had nothing growing up. I want you girls to have everything."

Rachel was quiet for a moment. "There's more to life than money. The only activity you and Daddy do together is argue."

Emily raised her voice again. "We fight about you."

"I had sex. I didn't rob a bank."

"What do you want?" Emily asked.

"I want you to like me. For who I am, not who you want me to be." She made a sound of disgust. "I'm going upstairs."

I jumped up and scooted to my room before Rachel caught me eavesdropping. Flopping down on my bed, I thought about what I'd heard my sister say. What did she mean? Rachel had always been the perfect daughter. Maybe a bit of an overachiever, but she was smart, athletic, and popular. And no one seemed to care. Somewhere along the way Rachel stopped being the good girl. Now she was getting the attention she'd missed. She said she hated the fighting. If she did what she was supposed to do, much of the fighting would stop. What *was* the problem with our family? Maybe no one knew. We never even admitted there was a problem. Until lately.

~~

Later, I was watching TV trying to fall asleep when I heard Daddy knocking on Rachel's door. I turned down the volume so I could hear.

"Rachel. Honey, open the door. I want to talk to you."

I heard her door open and then close again. Daddy must have gone inside. I leaped out of bed and opened my door carefully, peaking into the hallway. Empty. Years ago I had discovered that if I hid in the empty closet of the guest room I could hear everything in Rachel's room. I knew it was wrong, but she was a teenager. I thought teenagers had all these fascinating secrets so I used to spy on her. Rachel turned out to be pretty dull. All I ever heard was my sister occasionally gossiping with her friends about clothes, music, boys, and stuff like who was behaving like a diva. It didn't take long for me to get bored and give up my secret agent routine. But now that I had a reason to listen I knew where to go. I scurried across the hall into the guest room and darted into the closet. I could hear their voices. They were muffled, but clear.

"You know how much I love you and your sister, honey. I'm sorry I'm not home more."

"Of course she'd blame you. It's not your fault."

"She didn't blame me. She doesn't know what to do."

"About what?"

"About you."

"I'm fine."

"No."

"No?"

"Rach, you're not fine. You quit all your sports, you stay locked in your room with all of this…and, well you know what else happened."

"All of this? My art? I'm an artist. I quit all the other stuff because I only did it to please you and mom. It didn't make me happy. I'm sorry if that makes me a failure in your eyes."

I had to sneeze. I clamped my hand over my mouth and did a silent sneeze. The kind that you're not supposed to do. I never knew why it's supposed to be bad for you to not let your sneezes out, but I was willing to take the risk. I couldn't get caught snooping on Rachel and Daddy. Although, the truth was, I wanted to be in the room with them. To feel close to them.

"Daddy, I'm sorry Emily caught me with Axel. It was stupid. But can't you forgive me?"

"Axel." Daddy said his name as if he was saying "Satan." "Is he your boyfriend?"

"No."

"I don't know what to say to you," I heard my father say. Then it got quiet. No one said anything for a while. When Daddy spoke again his voice was quiet. "You're putting me on the defensive for wanting to give you girls everything and raise you the right way. I don't approve of the way you quit all your activities. And I certainly don't approve of your promiscuity."

Rachel didn't respond. I wished I could see her face.

Still sounding calm, I heard Daddy say, "I hate to sound like a stereotype father, but as long as you live here under my roof, you need to do what your mother and I ask you to do. And that means you cannot stay out all night. There will be *severe* consequences for your actions. Am I making myself clear?" He was quiet. He never raised his voice. I couldn't tell if he was angry or sad. I was both.

I heard Rachel's door close. I waited a few minutes and stifled two more sneezes before I dared to sneak back to my own room. I didn't know how Rachel reacted to Daddy's words, but I was terrified for her. Whatever did he mean by "severe consequences?"

CHAPTER 3
May, 2012

The day after I saw *The Godfather* for the first time, I met Denny. I also found out why Crazy Annie calls herself Crazy. And I discovered some disturbing news about Larry.

I was scheduled to use the shower at 10 a.m. Since it was only 9, I wandered over to Crazy Annie's to see if she was in. I wanted to see her art. I'd never known a real live artist before. Except for Rachel, who I didn't think of as an actual artist. I have to admit, I was nervous that I would hate Crazy Annie's work and then I wouldn't know what to say to her. I wasn't good at lying.

Her tent was easy to find. It was about ten tents down the road from ours. In front, there was a huge boulder painted blue with yellow letters that said "Crazy Annie's Place." Instead of the dot over the "I" there was a circle with a cross attached to it, which I recognized as the symbol for a woman. The boulder had dozens of little scenes sketched all over it. Each scene appeared to tell a story and I stood there a while, trying to take them all in. It was like a reading a book. Maybe it was the book of her life, I thought and I wondered what the book of my life would look like up to this point.

"Hi, Delia! You coming to visit me?" Annie was coming down the path, towel wrapped around her head. She wore a lavender caftan with tiny mirrors around the neckline and she sparkled as she walked toward me as the mirrors caught the sunlight.

"Is this a good time?" I asked.

"I just came from the showers. Give me a sec to shake out my dreads. Come inside with me."

I followed her into her tent which, oddly, had no decoration on the outside. When I walked inside I stood there frozen to the spot, utterly speechless. Her ceiling was draped in exotic fabrics in a million shades of purple and red. Her floor was painted to look like tiles and the walls of her tent were one continuous mural that were filled with symbols, birds, animals, clouds, water, trees, the sun, the moon, and the stars. I could hardly absorb it all.

"Close your mouth, Delia," Crazy Annie said, smiling. "Most people have that reaction to my place. Do you like it?"

"I love it! If I'm ever in a bad mood again, I'm coming to visit you. This is the happiest place I've ever seen. The outside of your tent is so plain, Annie. That's what adds to the surprise."

"Don't call me Annie. I'm Crazy Annie. Don't forget that again or we're not going to be friends."

She wasn't kidding. Her tone was more than a little scary. "I'm sorry. Of course. Crazy Annie. Do you…I mean…is there a reason?" I was afraid to ask, but I needed to know.

"I have no judgment when it comes to men. I'm Crazy. Capital C Crazy. I keep trusting the wrong ones. The last one stole all my money and disappeared. I lost my home, my gallery, everything. I'm forty-five years old and I've made four huge mistakes. One for each of my decades. I married three of them. I'm done. I need people to call me CRAZY Annie so I never forget. I will have no more of it. I am a man-free zone. Happy? Now you know." She looked at me.

I was relieved when she changed the subject. "I went to Morocco once. All of the homes are very plain on the outside. When you go inside, they are opulent and spacious and very welcoming. I've tried to capture that feeling here. All of the décor is inside and only to be shared with the people I invite in. When you decorate on the outside…," she paused for a long moment. I waited for the rest.

"It's all about showing off what you have in order to create envy in others." Crazy Annie looked at me. "You understand?"

I did. I thought about my house. My old house. And all my friend's houses. One outdid the other like it was a competition. If someone put in a new patio, everyone put in a new patio. Or pool. Or hot tub. Or koi pond. I did understand. Now it all seemed stupid and shallow. Crazy Annie was so *not* crazy.

31

Maybe Rachel wasn't so crazy either. Maybe that was what she had tried to tell our parents.

"My sister is an artist. I have a painting of hers in my tent. I'll show it to you sometime."

"Where is she?" Crazy Annie asked.

"She ran away before we lost everything." I didn't want to talk about Rachel any more. I regretted bringing her up. "Crazy Annie, what do you do with your art?"

"There's a warehouse that some artists I know rent. We've formed a consortium. I work there on my sculptures. There are a few galleries that come every couple of weeks and check us out. They show our pieces if they like them. I sell some. But not enough to get out of here. Yet."

"Can I come to the warehouse?"

"I'll take you if it's okay with your mom. I'll come by later and meet her."

I left Crazy Annie's to go to our tent and get my towel. It was nearly ten o'clock, and I did not want to miss my turn in the shower. I had a lot to think over. I'd never met anyone like Crazy Annie before. She didn't look or dress like anyone I'd ever known. She herself was like a piece art. I bet Rachel would love Crazy Annie. I envied how creative and free she seemed. I decided to try to be more like her and not worry so much about what people think.

I got to the shower a few minutes early. I could hear the water running. Someone was still inside. You got five minutes every other day. Water was collected in big barrels and couldn't be wasted. I was sitting on a stump thinking about Crazy Annie when I heard the water turn off. I was not prepared for happened next.

The tent flap opened and out came this shirtless guy with wet hair just below his chin and a towel slung over his shoulder. Holy guacamole, he was hot. When I say hot, I mean HOT. Chile pepper hot. Hot like the pizza just came out of the oven and the cheese is burning the roof of your mouth hot. So hot. He was skinny. I could count his ribs, he was that skinny. But in spite of that, his abs and his arms were ripped. Weights? He didn't look the type. He was wearing jeans and they hung low on his skinny hips. Very low. I tried not to look at the line above his jeans where his hipbones were. Now I knew how guys felt when they pretended they weren't looking at your boobs. I couldn't resist. I was undone.

"You next? It's all yours." He was talking to me.

My mouth went dry. I couldn't believe this was happening to me. I had more adrenaline than I'd ever had, even before a competition. He wasn't like anyone I knew in my school. I figured him to be about sixteen. He was waiting for me say something. I couldn't. I nodded, feeling ridiculous. Until this minute I had never before understood the expression tongue tied. I felt like such a *girl*. And not in a good way. A gushy, girly girl. The kind I always hated. What was it about him, exactly?

"You better hurry before the next guy shows up. Hey, you're a real cutie, you know?" He smiled, then he winked at me and left. When he smiled, I swear it was like those commercials where they make a twinkle come off the model's tooth. I turned and watched him walk away. For a skinny guy, he had an extraordinary butt. He didn't walk. He swaggered. Slightly. Not enough to be obnoxious. A little bounce. A bop. Jaunty. Cool.

A cutie. Me. What did that mean? Cute like a little kid? Or cute like a hottie? I had so much excess energy at this point, there was only one way I knew how to get rid of it; I did a cartwheel which I followed by jumping up in the air and throwing my hands up over my head. I needed to know immediately: who was this guy?

After I showered, I could hardly wait to find Larry. He must know who Mr. Hot Guy was. I figured I would play it cool and ask him if there were any other teenagers in the enclave. Sort of feel him out without being too obvious. When I got there, Larry's tent flap was closed. I wasn't sure what the procedure was. It's not as though you could knock. I sat down on the

33

grass to wait, thinking maybe he wasn't awake yet. I was only sitting there a few minutes when the flap opened and Larry rushed out. Before I could say anything, Larry stood next to his tent with his back to me. He bent over holding his stomach and he started retching, violently.

Part of me wanted to disappear and pretend I never saw him. I could have. He hadn't seen me. But I couldn't leave without making sure he was alright. I went over and stood next to him.

"Larry, what's wrong? Can I do something?"

He'd stopped throwing up, but was still bent over as though waiting for more. When it didn't come, he stood, wiping his mouth with the back of his hand.

"Water. In the tent."

I found a bottle next to his cot and brought it out to him as quickly as I could. He rinsed his mouth and spit. His forehead was wet with sweat. He sat down on the grass, his head down between his knees. He was breathing hard. I sat next to him wondering if I should go for help. I decided to wait.

After a few minutes, Larry looked up at me. "Shit damn dog. What the hell did you come here for, Delia? You don't need to see me like this."

"Like what? What's wrong with you? You're not drunk are you?" There was a strict no drinking rule in the community. I hoped he wasn't. At the same time I kind of hoped he was, because if he wasn't drunk, then he was sick and that wasn't what I wanted to hear.

But he was sick. We talked for a long time. He told me he'd been sick since he'd been at Hardscrabble Way and he was getting worse. He used to sell cars until he got laid off. He collected unemployment insurance while he looked for a new job. Around the same time his unemployment ran out he found out he was sick. Really sick. He didn't have health insurance and the free clinic could only do so much. It was just a matter of time.

"I'm sorry kid. You don't need any more drama in your life, I'm sure. Do me a favor?"

I looked at him, waiting.

"Don't tell anyone else, okay? This is between us. There's nothing anyone can do and I don't want anyone feeling sorry for me. Promise!"

"I promise." Of all people, I understood why he didn't want anyone to feel sorry for him.

He took a sip of water. "Let's seal it. You tell me a secret. Something you haven't told anyone else." He grinned.

I was relieved. He looked better.

"I don't have any secrets."

"Sure you do. Everyone has secrets."

He was right, of course. "I made my sister run away." I had never admitted that to anyone. I waited for his reaction. He had none, but sat waiting for my explanation.

"I betrayed her to my parents. My mother found her having sex with her boyfriend."

"How is that your fault?"

"I was the one who called my mother."

"What happened then?"

"Rachel ran away because she couldn't get their respect back. She never forgave me."

"That's it? That's all? She had sex and your parents flipped out?"

"They have...had...high expectations for us. I've pretty much spent my life trying to be perfect to please them."

"Why did you tell on her?" Larry asked.

"She stopped acting like a big sister."

"So these are what suburban kids call problems these days." I could tell, he didn't get it. The truth was, nothing I had just said made sense at this point.

"By the way," he said. "What were you coming to see me about?"

I smiled. "I have a crush. I was coming to see if you know who he is."

Larry nodded his head. "Ah, I'm guessing it's Denny. Around sixteen? Unless you go for older men and then it's his brother Daryl. He'd be around nineteen."

"Longish hair? Skinny. Tall?"

"That would be Denny Jaxson. There aren't any other teenagers here right now besides you, Denny, and his brother. Did you meet him?"

"Not exactly. He was in the shower right before me. I got so stupid when I saw him I couldn't even mumble. I feel like such an idiot!"

"Oh, god! To be young again. Hold on to that feeling. That awkward, inarticulate, don't think I can talk to this person feeling. Someday, you'll wish you could get it back."

"Ugh. I doubt that!"

"He'll come to the movie on Saturday night. I'll introduce you. Get your mom to come. She needs to get out and meet people."

~~

There was a spider living in a bush just outside our tent. I liked to sit and watch her spinning her web. She moved carefully and deliberately as if she had all the time in the world. I could squish her, I thought, and end her life. Or, in the blink of an eye, with a mere swipe of my hand I could wreck her beautiful web. I wasn't going to do either one, but she had no idea she was so close to disaster. She had no shelter, nothing to safeguard her. I watched her create her design, bit by bit, weaving her silky threads into an intricate pattern. The web was nearly invisible. You could see it only when the light hit just so. That was the danger for all the small bugs she was hoping to catch to turn into a meal. Once when I was watching her, a cricket lurched right into her trap. She swooped in and wrapped it so fast I couldn't see exactly was happening. She destroyed the cricket so quickly, it never knew what happened. The strength of the sticky thread was impossible to escape. The cricket was doomed from the instant it hit her web. I wondered if all webs are the same. Hers was so geometric, symmetric, mathematic. Maybe each spider is an artist. Spinning a unique pattern that satisfies her need to create something beautiful as well as feed herself. There's so much I don't know about the world.

I had way too much time on my hands. I tried filling the space until Saturday by fantasizing about Denny and what it would be like to be his girlfriend. My daydreams all took me back to a version of my old life where I was a cheerleader in high school and Denny had lettered in some sport and gave me his sweater to wear. My daydreams let me escape reality for a while. Ultimately they led me to think about how much I had looked forward to going to high school. As much as I tried to shut my mind down and not think about all that had happened, I couldn't help myself. To keep busy while I waited for Saturday, I decided to start working on a few cheerleading routines so my muscles didn't turn completely to mush. The days dragged by. Emily mostly slept. Gloria searched for work. I wished I had someone to talk to, or at least a TV to fill up the hours.

While I was working out I thought about how much I missed Daddy and Rachel. I couldn't bring my father back, but my sister was somewhere and it was up to me to figure out how to find her.

Finally it was Saturday. I counted the hours and waited for darkness to fall. I thought about asking Gloria to do my hair, but I was afraid it would look like I was trying too hard. I attempted to talk Emily into coming to watch the movie with me, but she was groggy again and decided to stay in. I put on my casual face as I left the tent and found my spot next to Larry.

"How are you feeling?" I asked him.

He gave me a look that said *shut up*. I nearly forgot. I was supposed to be keeping his secret.

"He's not here yet," he said.

It was my turn to give him a look. "Don't embarrass me," I whispered.

Larry grinned. "It's cool. Hey, have you seen *Dirty Dancing*? That's the movie tonight."

I shook my head no.

"Kid, you had a deprived life even before you came here, didn't you? Another classic you missed."

Gloria appeared and walked toward us. Even living in a tent, Gloria is one of those women who look put together and gorgeous no matter what. You want to hate her only you can't because, well…she's Gloria. She called to me on her way over. "Move over, Delia sweetie. I love this movie!"

Larry smiled. "Now, there's a girl who knows her stuff! Here we go. It's starting."

To say I was disappointed was like saying Harry Potter was a little famous. Understatement. The movie started and Denny was nowhere in sight. I almost left. After all those days of waiting for Saturday to come, I didn't feel like sitting there, disappointed. But there was nothing to do in the tent. Emily was most likely asleep, and at least here I had Gloria and Larry for company. I decided to stay.

Not leaving was the smartest thing I had done in quite a while. I thought *Dirty Dancing* was going to be cheesy, but I loved this movie. When the girl, Baby, met the dance instructor named Johnny for the first time she could hardly think straight, much less speak. All she managed to say was, "I carried a watermelon." By that time, the movie had me hooked. I was Baby! I'd had a watermelon moment with Denny the morning I met him. Mine was even worse than Baby's moment. I couldn't even talk. At least Baby got a sentence out.

Just as Johnny was teaching Baby to dance and he had his hands on her body, I spotted Denny in the flicker of light from the screen. He appeared out of the darkness wearing a tight black T-shirt and those low slung jeans. He was so skinny, yet his muscles made the sleeves of his shirt skin tight. That's when it hit me. I figured out what it was about Denny that I couldn't put my finger on the morning I met him. He was not your run of the mill hot guy. Denny was the real deal. He oozed sex without even trying. No wonder I didn't know what it was. I'd never seen this kind of sex appeal close up before. Or maybe I had, but I was too young to appreciate it. Denny wasn't just sexy, he made me think about *having* sex. Denny was Johnny to my Baby. As sappy and cliché as it sounds, looking at him took my breath away. I sat there looking at him as he stood there looking around. I watched as he nodded at Larry and pulled a chair over to where we were sitting.

There was no moon and I was grateful for the dark, since I could feel my face turning hot. I couldn't stop tapping my foot, and I had to take a few deep breaths to keep from hyperventilating. Gloria leaned over and whispered to me, "You okay? You sound like you're wheezing."

When Baby finally hooked up with Johnny, I knew this was the best movie I had ever seen. Forget *High School Musical* and all that baby crapola. I was nearly fourteen and now that I'd met Denny and had seen *Dirty Dancing,* there was no turning back.

"I wish I was young again," Gloria said when it was over. "There is no feeling in the world like your first love."

"How have I never seen that movie?" I asked no one in particular.

Larry chimed in, "A classic coming of age story." He looked at Denny. "Did you work tonight? How come you were so late?"

"We had a run out in Penn Valley. Picked up some furniture that had to be delivered to Haverford. We got started late 'cause the guy had to work and couldn't meet us."

Denny named places near where I'd grown up, not twenty miles from here. Towns that were familiar to me once, yet I felt like it had been years since they were a part of my life. Now they were just places where furniture got moved. They felt so far away.

Larry looked at me and said, "This is Denny Jaxson. He and his brother Daryl have a moving business they inherited when their dad passed. I've never seen two kids work harder. Denny, this is Delia Williams and her friend Gloria Florence."

A moving business. That explained the muscles. I tried to think of something to say. You meet a million people and it's natural, even easy to make some kind of small talk. When it mattered, when I wanted to say something, I failed. I blanked as I tried to think of something that wouldn't make me sound idiotic and impossibly young. Then, of all the possible things I might have said I blurted out, "We met in the shower."

Gloria looked at me, alarmed. "What?"

Denny laughed. "Not *in* the shower. Near the shower. So, Delia. Should you be watching this R rated stuff? You look a little young."

For a split second I thought about lying. "I'm thirteen." I was trying not to sound defensive, but I'm pretty sure I sounded snappish. I was so self-conscious, it was painful.

"Jailbait!" Denny teased.

"And what are you?" I didn't know where that came from.

He grinned at me and just like that, I knew we were going to be friends. "Touché! You got me," he said.

Gloria rolled her eyes and said to Larry, "Don't you wish you were young enough to want to lie and make yourself older than you really are? Were we ever that young?"

Larry looked away. Gloria had no way of knowing that Larry was sick, and I wasn't allowed to tell.

Then Denny said, "I'm beat. We're working tomorrow. I'm gonna get some Zs. Delia, want to go swimming my next day off? There's a creek not far from here and I know a sweet swimming hole."

Before I could say something awkward and have a watermelon moment like Baby's in the movie, Gloria saved me from having to speak. "She'll have to ask her mom. Come by soon and meet Emily, Denny. I'm sure it'll be okay."

As we all called goodnight, Larry caught my eye. He raised one eyebrow for a split second and winked.

CHAPTER 4
November, 2011

I looked up at Rachel as she walked barefoot into the kitchen, wearing a tank top and huge flannel pajama bottoms. She had a serious case of bed head. Ignoring me, she opened the refrigerator.

"Why are you up?" I had to ask. It was 7 a.m. on a Saturday. I had a competition. Preliminaries for the counties were at 9 or heaven knows I'd be sleeping in. It was unheard of for Rachel to be up before noon on weekends.

"Need OJ. I have a wicked hangover," she mumbled. She took a drink from the carton, then paused and looked at me. "Oops. Sorry. I probably shouldn't have said that. Now, go run to mom."

I wanted to say something. Words wouldn't form. I don't know why. I had rehearsed apologies in my head and visualized this conversation dozens of times. The reality of Rachel glaring at me short circuited my ability to speak.

Before I could recover she said, "Doesn't matter. I don't care anymore." She pulled a glass out of the cupboard and poured the orange juice. "Why are you up? It's Saturday. Isn't it?" She looked over at me.

"I've got a competition."

"Mmm. Course you do." She turned and started to walk out of the kitchen.

For a split second, I was going to let it go. Let her go. But I couldn't, so I blurted out, "What's that supposed to mean? You used to compete. You didn't have an issue with it then."

Rachel stopped and turned to face me. "Sorry. It's just…" She shook her head, then, for the second time, turned to leave.

"Wait! That's not good enough. Rachel, what I did to you…"

"Stop!" She put her hand up. "I can't do this now. Seriously. I feel awful. Think I'm gonna barf."

"Good." I couldn't believe I said that when all I wanted to do was apologize. "Why do you drink if it makes you sick?" I asked her.

"I don't usually. But sometimes, it's hard not to. You'll see. If you haven't already. It starts in Middle School."

"I know. BC hasn't changed. Some parents don't care. They let you drink in their house as long as you sleep over."

"Exactly." She turned to leave. "But you would never drink, would you?"

It was hard to tell if she was mocking me. "Never. But why do you?" I repeated.

Rachel shrugged. "I'm a tormented teen. You're too perfect to understand. You're the good girl. You just want to please everyone."

"What's wrong with being the good girl? I like being liked."

She looked straight at me. Her eyes filled with tears. "When did you start hating me, Delia?"

I was so confused I couldn't process what I'd heard. She turned her back and walked away from me. I called after her, "I don't hate you, Rachel. I just hate *this* you." She kept walking.

I stared after her, wondering if I should follow her upstairs. Just then, my cell phone rang. I looked at the screen. It was Claudia, my ride to the meet.

"What's up, Claudia?" I hoped she was going to tell me she was running late. I wanted to talk to Rachel.

"Don't kill me, but we're on our way. My mom forgot she has a hairdresser appointment, so she wants to get going. It's at least forty-five minutes away."

Great. Just great. "Gimme a few minutes. I'll be ready as soon as I can."

"You're the best! I should've called you sooner, but she totally forgot..."

"Claud," I interrupted her babble. "If I get off the phone, I'll be dressed that much sooner." I hung up. Crap. This was gonna be a mess of a day.

~~

If the stars align there's a moment in a cheerleading competition when you know you've nailed it. You can sense it.

You are intuitively aware that every single girl is synchronized on the floor. Every motion matches like we were one person. It doesn't happen often. The most minute mistake can ruin a routine. Someone will miss a step or an arm placement will be off. Coach made us watch tapes of our practices often enough that we knew we had each screwed up more than once. But when it all comes together, the movement is pure joy.

This was one of those times we were an organized, synthesized spectacle of maroon and gray. We rocked our county competition and we didn't need to wait for our scores to know it. That was the appeal of competing. This was the kind of day that made cheering addictive. When everything else in my life was falling apart, I could lose myself completely in my sport. I was really good at that, although I have no idea why. It's a gift, I guess. I never got anxious before I competed. Half my teammates were nervous wrecks before we went on. They paced, they tapped their feet, they chewed their nails. They were a hot mess. I thrived. I got so absorbed before I competed, I was in a zone in my own head. Nothing else mattered. Not even the fact that no one from my family came to my competitions. Ever.

More than once my coaches told me that I had an amazing ability to focus. I knew that was true, but I couldn't explain it in words. It's not as though I told myself, "Okay, Cordelia. Now you need to pay attention and stop thinking about your fekked up family." Without trying, I shut everything out. Don't get me wrong. Doing the moves took tons of conscious effort and practice. I got upset sometimes when I didn't learn how to do routines or stunts right off the bat. Then I got obsessive about practicing. But the focus part, the concentration part, came naturally. Somehow, magically, a switch went off in my head and I was in the moment. When I was competing or doing a cheer in front of an audience, nothing else mattered. There was no other feeling like it that even came close. I couldn't imagine what would happen to me if I ever had to stop.

As soon as the competition was over, I started thinking about Rachel again. I hoped she was still home. I needed to talk. We used to be so close. Even though she was four years older than me, she used to be the best big sister imaginable. We would play school or house or dress-up and she would always be the teacher, the mom, or the teenager teaching the little nerdy kid how to dress. I loved the way she would take care of me, dress me up as though I was a doll and, when Emily would let her, put make-up on me. Rachel was kind, affectionate, loving. At some point, she changed. I guess she just got too old to play with me, and I was too young to hang out with her. I had to find a way to make her understand I just wanted to be close to her again. I didn't betray her because I hated her. Just the opposite.

I needed to talk to her as soon as I could.

"Thanks for driving, Mrs. Michaels. Bye Claudia. See you Monday," I said as I climbed out of the Michaels' Escalade. As soon as I did, I shivered. The SUV was warm inside, however the air outside was freezing. It was the end of November, but it had been a mild fall. Lots of years there's been snow in Pennsylvania by this time, so it shouldn't be a surprise that it was finally feeling wintery, but I wasn't used to the cold. I ran up our long driveway, hurrying to get inside. Just as I started to tap the security code into the keypad, a car pulled into the bottom of the driveway and honked--one long, obnoxious honk. Before I could see who it was, the front door opened, and Rachel came out. She was bundled in a parka and wearing a woolen skully pulled down over her ears. Her long, honey blonde hair hung down over her shoulders out of the hat, and I was struck by how lovely she looked. Rachel never wore make-up, she was just a wholesome kind of pretty. Then I noticed the giant, pink duffle she had thrown over her shoulder.

"Where are you going?" I asked.

She looked at me for a long second. I thought she was going to say something, but she shook her head and rushed past me.

"Who's that in the driveway?" I was bulleting her with questions and I couldn't stop myself. I felt frantic, but I knew I sounded nasty. "Does Emily know you're going somewhere?" The moment I said that, I regretted it. Rachel stopped. She turned around and looked at me. I thought she looked sad. Maybe scared.

"Couldn't you have gotten here five minutes later?" She started down the driveway again.

"Where are you going?" I asked again.

She turned to stare at me. "Since when do you care where I'm going?" She put her bag down on the driveway and walked back to where I was standing on the porch. She looked at me for a minute before she spoke.

"I didn't want anyone to see me go. I can't do this anymore, Delia. Can't live here. This screwed up phony Main Line life. Mom, Dad, perfect you. It's too much. No one will ever forgive me for falling off the family perfection wagon." I heard her voice crack. She shook her head, just slightly. As though she was trying to shake off her feelings.

"I'm going away. I'm starting another life. My life. I can't live up to this family...the guilt, the expectations. I want...I want to figure out what *I* want." She stooped to pick up her duffle. She turned to look at me. For a second, she looked like she was going to say something else, but she didn't. I wanted to call after her, to say something, to say a million things, ask a million things. If I said something, anything, the right thing...maybe she would stay. Maybe. But I didn't have the words.

I stood there in the driveway, shivering. I watched my sister, my big sister, my only sister, climb into some car with some boy I didn't recognize. As I watched the car drive down the street, I realized my hands were shaking. I turned to go in the house, but the door had slammed shut. I started to punch in the security code. For a moment I couldn't remember the numbers. When the light finally clicked green, I put my hand on the metal doorknob. It felt ice cold. *I need gloves,* I thought.

As I went inside my empty house, my whole body was shaking and I realized this wasn't just the cold. It was anxiety. The kind of anxiety you develop when you're watching a movie and you know something horrible is going to happen. Dark and dramatic music begins to play in the background. Your heart starts pumping, your mouth goes dry, you want to close your eyes and hide. Dread. You dread watching the next scene unfold because you know it's going to be awful. I had no idea what would happen next, but I knew it wouldn't be good. As I ran upstairs to my room, I tried to shake off the feeling, but this was no movie.

~~

Daddy and I were in the attic over the garage pulling out the Christmas decorations. We did the same thing every year on the day after Thanksgiving. Rachel used to help us, but she hadn't done the attic thing for a couple of years. Even so, she was on my mind. After the initial shock and drama of finding out their daughter had run away, my parents didn't say much about her. No one said much about anything lately. We went out to eat Thanksgiving dinner to the same place we always went. There were so many topics to avoid it had been hard to make small talk. I was relieved when dinner was done and I could go meet my friends at the movies.

"Do you miss Rachel?" Daddy asked as he open a plastic bin marked **LIGHTS**. I had been wondering if Rachel was on his mind, too.

I wasn't sure how to answer. "I miss the old Rachel."

"Yeah," he said. We pulled boxes out in silence for a while.

"It's been two weeks. Where do you think she is?" he asked.

"I don't know, Daddy."

"None of her friends know. The police checked with them. If they do know, they're not saying. She took down her Facebook page."

"I know." I'd been checking it every day. "Are the police still looking for her?"

"They say they are. But she left on her own and she's close to turning eighteen. Your mother…we…weren't willing to go to the press. What would people say if they knew?"

"I don't know. What would they say?"

"Doesn't Emily…doesn't your mother talk to you?"

I shook my head. "We don't talk about Rachel." We don't talk about much, I thought but I didn't say it.

I looked over at Daddy. His face looked tight, old. He had lines like parentheses on either side of his lips I had never noticed before. They weren't smile lines; I hadn't seen him smile in a long time. "Where would you go? If you ran away?" he asked.

"I would never run away."

"I didn't think your sister would either." Daddy reached over to me and pulled me closer. He put his arms around me and squeezed me as if he held on tight enough I wouldn't go anywhere. I closed my eyes and hugged him back, my face buried in his brown, woolen sweater. The kind he loved because they buttoned down the front. The kind we teased him about and called his Mr. Rogers' sweaters. I breathed in his scent. He smelled like raisins. He smelled like home. I didn't want to let him go.

When he finally pulled away he said, "I thought she'd be back by now. By Thanksgiving. The holidays. I'm going to hire a private detective. This has gone on long enough."

I blurted out, "But the money…how can we afford…" As soon as I said it, I knew it was a mistake.

"I'll find it," he snapped. "That's not your problem." Then it hit him.

"How did you know? About the money? Did your mother…?"

"I heard you arguing."

"I didn't want you girls to know. I didn't want to worry you." His eyes looked down and I could see how hard this was for him. My father, who had always looked so large, so powerful to me, looked smaller. The space he filled was shrinking. I wanted to blame Rachel, but I knew that her leaving wasn't the only reason he appeared crushed.

He looked at me as if he had just thought of something. "Did Rachel know? Is that why she left?"

I shook my head, no. "She didn't know," I said. At least I hadn't told her. Maybe I should have. I thought about what she'd said to me when she was leaving. I was certain that if Rachel had known about the financial mess Daddy was in, she would have stayed.

"I'm sorry, Daddy. I didn't mean to upset you. I love you."

His voice soft again he said, "I love you, too, Deal."

~~

The holidays came and went with no sign of Rachel. Every year we hosted a huge buffet on Christmas Eve. Catered, of course. All our friends and neighbors came and Daddy invited all his employees to stop in. People dropped by from late afternoon well into the night. This year, we broke our tradition. Emily put out a few hors d'oeuvres, but it was just the three of us. I don't know what, if anything, she told all the people she used to invite. Emily didn't talk much lately. I don't know what she did with herself all day. She used to go to her yoga classes and shop. I was pretty sure she still went to yoga, but she had definitely stopped shopping.

Christmas morning was quiet. We ate breakfast first, which was our custom. Then we opened our presents. I tried to remember what it was like last year when we were all together. The house felt empty. I didn't realize that one person missing could make such a difference. All Christmas day I waited, sure that the door would open or the phone would ring and it would be Rachel. I refused to believe she could stay away for Christmas. Did she really hate us that much? I kept thinking how strange it was that sometimes you can feel a person's absence more than you felt their presence when they were around. I never noticed when Rachel was there as much as I now noticed that she was not. We played Christmas music during dinner to fill the awkward lack of conversation. I tried to think of something to say, but I couldn't.

Then Daddy made a sound almost like a laugh. Emily and I both looked at him.

"I was just remembering when Rachel used to sit in front of the Christmas tree blinking her eyes open and shut as the tree lights blinked."

Emily laughed. "Oh my god. The first time she did it, we didn't realize what she was doing. We were in a panic thinking there was something wrong with her eyesight. She must have been about three."

"More wine, Em?" my father asked. My mother held out her glass.

As he poured he cleared his throat. Then he said, "I hired a private detective. He traced Rachel to Venice, California. She'd been painting T-shirts and selling them on the board walk for a couple of weeks. But she was gone by the time he got there. He couldn't locate her."

"When was that?" I asked.

"Two weeks ago."

My mother swallowed a gulp of wine. "Is he still looking?"

My father looked down at the table. He shook his head no. In a voice I could barely hear he said, "He got five hundred a day. Plus expenses. I couldn't…"

In the background, Joni Mitchell was singing *The River*. In the song it's Christmas and Joni want to run away. I'd never really understood the words before. Now I knew exactly what she meant. I too wished I had a river I could skate away on.

I blinked hard, but it was useless. A tear escaped. And then another. I couldn't help it. It was Christmas. Silent night. Holy night. All is calm. All is bright. That was how things were supposed to be. But they weren't.

CHAPTER 5
January, 2012

I had the January blahs. Football season was over and I wasn't a big fan of basketball. School was getting intense because mid-terms were coming. Besides, I think we were all growing anxious about going to high school in the fall. Although no one actually admitted to being nervous, it was practically all we talked about. When we weren't talking about clothes, parties, or boys.

"Did you get an outfit for my birthday party yet?" Alexa wrote in the note she passed me in Language Arts class. Something I'd asked her not to do at least a hundred times. I could see from the corner of my eye she was staring at me, waiting for an answer. I shook my head a little. No. Not now. I wished I could text her **ttu ltr**, but there is a strict no cell phone rule which was always enforced and there was no way I would risk getting caught. Besides, I didn't want to upset Ms. Louis. She was my favorite teacher and Language Arts was my favorite class. I needed to stay focused. What if she called on me and I wasn't paying attention? I had a perfect straight A average in her class. Alexa and her party could wait.

"Take out your literature logs and get into your groups. Discuss last night's assignment," she was saying.

I didn't think I was going to like a book about the south that was written so long ago, but *To Kill a Mockingbird* was my favorite book I'd read so far in my entire life. I finished it the first weekend we got it. Since then, I was bored out of my brain while the rest of the class slugged through it. And to think, I had once been worried about taking 8th grade honors.

"You're such a suck up! Why didn't you answer my note?" Alexa said, as soon as we got into our group. "This is such a boring class. Ms. Louis is nice, but she is such a dork. So...*did* you get an outfit for my party?"

"Parties are overrated," I said.

"You're just being mean about parties because you're the last one to turn fourteen. Summer birthdays suck. All the good party venues will have been used up by then." Alexa babbled on and I stopped listening.

Ever since I learned that money was a problem, I'd been really careful not to ask for anything. I hadn't told any of my friends what was happening. I kept an eye on Emily to see if she was cutting back on her spending. As far as I could tell, she hadn't made any big purchases, but we still ordered food every night.

"Are you listening to me?" Alexa asked.

"No."

"I'm starving. I'm dieting," Alexa said. "I wish I had your metabolism."

"Metabolism? I work out three hours a day," I said. This was classic Alexa. The truth is, she was curvy, but in a good way. No amount of starving was going to change her shape. Funny. Alexa wanted my body. I wanted Margot's long legs. No one is happy with what they have when they're in eighth grade.

A boy in our group named Robbie said, "I have some chips you can have if you're hungry Alexa." Robbie has some special needs and speaks slowly. "But I think we should start to do what Ms. Lewis asked us to do."

"Thanks, Robbie. But I haven't had a carb since sixth grade," Alexa stated, in a tone suggesting that not eating carbs was a virtue equal to feeding the poor.

I smiled at Robbie. "You're right. We're sorry. You go first."

"Delia, one more thing. Are you still coming with me after school?" Alexa asked.

"I have practice."

"You promised me."

"I can't miss this practice."

"Why not? You promised. My sister's picking me up. We've got to get fitted for our bridesmaids' gowns for my brother's wedding."

It didn't bother me at all that I had forgotten my promise. What bothered me was the fact that Alexa's sister was the same age as my sister. They're both juniors. I didn't understand why Rachel couldn't do normal things. Like be a big sister to me. She was the only 17-year-old I knew who didn't bother to get her driver's license. Every teenager lives for that and for the day they get their first car. Except for my sister.

"Even if I blew off my practice, I've got gymnastics tonight right after," I told Alexa.

"You're not a good friend."

"I know."

Alexa made a face at me and all I could see were her pink braces. "You work hard at being perfect, Cordelia Elizabeth Williams. But you're never have time for your friends."

I shrugged. Her criticism was true, but I didn't care. I had to focus on what was important: school, grades, sports.

"Okay, guys. Two minute warning," Ms. Louis said. Just as we started moving our desks back into place, the phone on Ms. Louis's desk rang. As she picked it up, she said, "Shhh. Class, please stop moving chairs for a second. I can't hear." Everything went quiet and I heard her say, "Yes. Yes, she's right here." She stopped to listen and I glanced over at her. Her face didn't visibly transform, but something made me continue to watch her. She was looking directly back at me. My face was on fire at the same time my body went cold. I realized I was holding my breath. I also realized that I had been waiting, somehow, for something to happen. I had a sense, not only of dread, but of expectation. I'd had it for a while, just under the surface. I hadn't been completely conscious of it until this moment when I knew that the phone call was about me.

"Oh…okay," Ms. Louis said, hesitating. "Right." She turned her back and spoke very softly, but I could still hear her. "What should I say? What should I tell her?"

I was in a tunnel and everything was moving in slow motion. Someone next to me was talking, but I couldn't hear him. I was watching Ms. Louis as she turned back around and looked at me and I knew what she was going to say next even before she opened her mouth to speak.

"Cordelia, can you come up here please? I need to speak to you. You need to bring all your things with you."

My ears were pounding as I gathered my papers, books, and my backpack. I vaguely heard the talking all around me. Different voices were speaking at the same time, saying the stupid things eighth graders say, "Oooo, Delia. You're in trouble! Did you cut class? Lucky! I'd do anything to get out of this class."

Someone was pulling my sweater as I walked up to the front of the room. I looked down. Alexa said, "Delia, text me! Tell me what's going on." I kept walking.

When I got to her desk, Ms. Louis could barely look at me. She steered me to the door and walked me outside to the hall. I was queasy, like I'd eaten too many greasy onion rings. She looked at me and spoke in a voice that was so quiet I had to lean in to hear her. Clearing her throat, she said, "Go to your locker and get your coat and your other books. Then you need to go the office. Something's happened. You're going home."

With paste in my mouth nearly gluing my lips together I asked, "Did something happen to Rachel?"

"Rachel?"

"My sister. Did something happen to my sister?"

"Oh! N...no...no," she stuttered.

"What happened?"

She looked down. "You need to go to the office."

I walked away from her as fast as I could.

I sat waiting for what seemed like forever. School time often operates in slow motion. Hours can be lost watching a classroom clock stand still, refusing to move. This is a phenomenon that only affects students, evidently. Adults are immune. And when people get to be a certain age, their memory of school time stoppage gets erased. Otherwise, teachers would realize why so many kids act out. They are lost in the school time warp continuum and they don't believe they are ever getting out of that classroom.

53

When I got to the office the secretary told me to have a seat. She said Mr. Rose, our principal, would be right with me. I was confused. Ms. Louis had said I was going home, so I'd half expected to see my mother waiting for me. Had something happened to Emily? I kept looking at the clock. Naturally, it didn't budge. In between answering the phones, which never stopped ringing, and dealing with the endless traffic in and out of the office, the secretary kept glancing over at me. I could hear voices, loud voices coming from inside the principal's office. I wondered if Mr. Rose was yelling at some bad kids. No wonder I never got in trouble. I couldn't stand it if someone scolded me.

Then, oddly, the office got quiet. The phones stopped and there was no one at the counter. I could hear a woman in Mr. Rose's office saying, "And after I take her home, what then?" I couldn't hear the rest. The phone rang, the office door opened and the whole place got loud again.

I'd had enough. I couldn't imagine what was going on. If someone didn't come out soon…The hell with it! I didn't care if I got in trouble, I needed to know what happened and I needed to know immediately. I unzipped my backpack and dug deep, searching for my cell phone. Just as I found it and started to call home, the eighth grade guidance counselor, an anorexic-looking woman with unfortunate wild hair, came out of the office.

"Cordelia, we're *so sorry* to keep you waiting. Will you come in, please?" She had this artificially sweet way of speaking. Like *Splenda* in a voice. I was so upset I didn't even bother to hide my phone. I didn't care if I got suspended. I had a feeling it wasn't going to matter.

There are moments, specific moments when the world changes and nothing will ever be the same again. My parents used to talk about September 11, 2001 being one of those moments. Every time we drove to New York City and we got to that piece of the Turnpike where you used to be able to spot the Twin Towers, Daddy told the same story. He said that the minute the second plane hit he knew it was a terrorist plot and knew the world as we knew it in America was gone.

The moment my world changed forever was that morning. January 10. Daddy died. He had a heart attack at one of his stores and died before the ambulance even arrived. Daddy was dead, my mother took some kind of pills to numb herself, and my sister Rachel had been missing for weeks and didn't know any of this. I didn't need pills. I was numb without them.

Ms. Stiffano, the world's worst guidance counselor, drove me home from school. She didn't want to be alone with me. Clearly, that was the cause of the loud voices I heard coming out of the principal's office. I've never seen anyone so uncomfortable. She was not prepared for this kind of tragedy and had no clue what to say or do. I almost felt sorry for her. The ride home was horrific. It was like having the worst nightmare you've ever had. Like the one where spiders are crawling all over you and you're sure it's not a dream and you want to wake up, but you can't. Eventually you do and it's all okay. I couldn't wake up. This was no dream.

Ms. Stiffano made everything worse. Her attempts at conversation were beyond awkward. I have no idea how she got to be a guidance counselor. She chattered on about not wanting to leave me alone once she got me home. She said once they got the call about my father from a family friend, they couldn't reach Emily at home. She informed me in her sweet, artificial voice how grief counseling would be available when I was ready (from *her?*), and rattled on about how awful it was that I had no real family nearby, only a grandmother (my father's) that I didn't really know way out in Seattle. She didn't pause for a breath. I was sure she never took a class that prepared her for any crisis worse than a girl fight. All I could do was hope she would one day realize how badly she had botched the way she handled the most devastating event of my life. I could imagine her years later telling the story of how badly she'd managed the first major crisis of her career. I knew

55

I was spending too much time obsessing about Ms. Stiffano. It was easier to think about her than to process what had happened. Or what would happen next. The future was a blank chasm that had opened up in front of me.

The house was full of people when I got home. I stood in the living room like I didn't belong there. My mother looked at me and started crying. Her friends huddled around her, offering her pills; Valium, Ambien, Xanax. No one seemed to remember I was there, too. I felt lost, abandoned. I was essentially invisible. After a while, Emily left with her friend Ginger and her husband to "see about arrangements." Whatever that meant. No one seemed to remember I was there. I went upstairs to my room and shut the door.

My friends kept calling my cell, but I didn't answer. I shut my phone off, finally. I couldn't talk to anyone. I didn't know how to do this. How to be the girl whose father died. The only thing I knew for sure was there would have to be a funeral. I supposed I had to wear black. I wasn't sure I had anything black.

The day was a blur. At some point, Margot's mom came by with food. She asked me if I wanted to come home with her. I didn't want to be with anyone. I don't even know how everyone found out what had happened, but what they say is true. Bad news travels fast.

I guess I was in shock. Up in my room, I tried to block it all out. If I didn't think about it, I could pretend nothing had happened. I escaped for a long time by watching some reality shows. I couldn't shut off my mind forever though, and at some point the numbness was gone and I was filled with rage. Why was I here dealing with this by myself? Where the hell was Rachel? I was so furious I wanted to shriek at the top of my lungs, but I didn't want to upset my mother any more than she was. I took my pillow with me into the bathroom, turned on the shower so no one would hear me and screamed as loud as I could into my pillow. I cursed my sister with every ugly word I'd ever heard. I stopped when I thought of something that seemed so obvious. Too obvious, but I had to try. I had to do something.

Going back inside my room, I located my cell phone, turned it on, and dialed Rachel's number. Maybe, just maybe, she had the same number and would pick up her phone. A computer voice answered. "I'm sorry. That number is no longer in service." I must have been delusional. Daddy would have tried her cell phone a thousand times when he was trying to find her. I can't believe I was stupid enough to think she would answer.

Of course her phone was disabled. She probably didn't have any money. Or she got a new phone so my parents couldn't find her. Parent. I didn't have parents any more. Or, apparently, a sister. And to think, that morning I thought my biggest problem was not having money for an outfit.

I wanted to cry, but I had no tears.

I wished I knew more about Rachel's friends. I wished I'd paid more attention to her and her life. I should never have stopped hiding in the closet and listening for her secrets. I knew I had to stop blaming myself. It wasn't my fault she shut me out of her life. But now I needed to know who she was with. Then, maybe I could find her.

I messaged Ariana Middlebrook through Facebook. Ariana and I went to grade school together. We'd never been friends, but her sister Molly was a close friend of Rachel's. Or she used to be. I wasn't sure if they were still friends before Rachel left, but I was desperate. Ariana messaged me back on Facebook and gave me Molly's cell phone number. I texted her and asked if she would call me. A few days went by and I didn't hear from her. Then, out of the blue she called.

"Delia? It's Molly. Middlebrook. Sorry it took me so long to call you back. What's up?"

"Um...I know this is weird, but have you heard from my sister? I kinda, well, I need to talk to her and she changed her cell."

I knew how lame that sounded. I didn't know how much people knew about the whole Rachel thing.

"I'm so sorry about your dad...I didn't know what to say. That's why I didn't call you back right away." Well, that was over with. She sounded relieved to change the subject. "We've all been worried stupid about Rachel, but I don't know where she is since she left Dan's place."

"Dan? Her boyfriend?" I wanted to sound like I knew what I was talking about.

"Dan was never her boyfriend. They're just friends. Well, they were. Until the fight."

As embarrassing as it was to admit I knew nothing about any of this, I decided to stop pretending. I asked Molly to start from the beginning. The story went nothing like I expected. Dan Foley was a sponsored skateboarder. He was nineteen and graduated high school a year ago. Being sponsored meant that Dan had an income. A good income. His sponsor gave him an apartment in Venice, California and he was going out there to compete. Rachel had apparently asked him if she could go with him. It was her plan to get a job once she got out to California. Molly didn't have a clue what work Rachel thought she could do. She hadn't even graduated high school.

"She and I weren't really hanging out much this year. I was busy looking at colleges and..." Molly stopped. And Rachel wasn't, I thought. She had made it clear she wasn't going to spend my parents' money on college. A waste, she said. If anything, she would go to art school for a year or so.

"What happened when they got to California?" I asked.

"The story gets fuzzy. She and Dan had some kind of wicked fight. Rumor has it he wanted to be more than friends and got jealous 'cause she started seeing someone. All I know is, she moved out of Dan's."

"When?"

"Dan came home for a visit around Christmas, but he didn't know where she was. I don't know anyone who's heard from her. I'll ask around."

After we hung up I didn't know whether to feel better or worse. I felt better because at least I knew where she had been. But the only person she'd been with after she left home didn't know where she was. Rachel had truly gone missing.

~~

Daddy was cremated. It was the least expensive of all the options. Uncle Arthur, Daddy's friend, helped Emily take care of everything. I suspect he helped pay the costs. I never knew funerals were so expensive. It's bizarre that people can't afford to bury someone they love. A funeral can cost as much as a wedding. I'd never been to a funeral before so I didn't know what to expect.

We aren't religious and never went to church, so the whole funeral was an awkward ordeal. With no casket and no service, people didn't seem to know what to do. I was under the impression funerals were supposed to be consoling, a way of saying goodbye. I did not gain comfort from sitting in a room with my dead father in an urn with people parading past him not knowing what to do or what to say to me or my mother.

Emily was still trying, in her semi-conscious state, to keep up appearances and not let anyone know we were broke or why Rachel wasn't there. My grandmother, my father's own mother, didn't even come. I'm not sure why. She sent a huge floral arrangement and a basket filled with food. I hardly remember her. We went to Seattle to visit her once when I was little. I remember her as being old even then. I guess she must be really old now. Emily told me once that my grandmother was angry when she and Daddy got married and moved to Philadelphia. He was her only son and she didn't want him to leave Seattle.

Of course Emily was stunning in her role as the grieving widow. Black was always her color. She sat in a blue satin high-backed chair and Daddy sat next to her in his elegant white urn on a pedestal that looked like a Greek column. Emily's friend Ginger made a poster board collage with pictures of Daddy and us. People stopped and looked at the photos and talked to each other or to Emily and me. At least looking at the pictures gave people something to do since there was no casket to view. I was disturbed that our private photos were out there for everyone to see. I got the most upset when I saw one of the four of us on vacation at Sea Isle City on the Jersey shore.

I stole the photo. I guess it wasn't really stealing, since it belonged to my family, but I felt like a thief. Like I was stealing back a piece of my own life. Odd. I can't remember who snapped the picture. But I remember everything else. Staring at the photo, I got lost in a moment that at the time seemed as if it would never end. One of those long, sunny summer days.

I sit digging, carving, patting the sand into place. First thing in the morning the sand is soft and cool. No one has walked on it yet. There are symmetric lines with ridges that are made by the dragging rake attached to the truck which comes through to sweep the debris that washes up during the night. The seabirds leave their footprints as they stroll along the shore line; seagulls, sandpipers, terns. I inhale, deeply. The unmistakable aroma of beach-a concoction of ocean, salt, dead clams, suntan lotion, and wet bathing suits-surrounds me. It's early enough that the sun is still rising over the water. The light is sparkling, reflecting in the sea. The only sounds are the waves as they come and go, cresting and crashing, and the occasional gull crying out as it sails by searching for scraps to eat. I jog down to the water's edge to refill my bucket. I need more water to wet the sand. Building castles is serious, summer business here in Sea Isle City. The routine never varies and was established years before.

Daddy wanders out of the beach house, coffee mug in hand. He settles his cup in the sand, circles the project, and silently claps his hands, then raises two thumbs up. Squatting next to me, he starts to make the intricate gargoyles that will jut out from the turrets. His specialty in the family assembly line.

I get up again and trot back to the fluctuating line where foam forms and tiny bubbles burst. In a moment another wave breaks, the edge vanishes, lost forever as the process continues. I scoop another bucket—the millionth?—in the routine that is as practiced and as familiar as one of my cheerleading sequences.

Finally, Emily arrives. Late as usual. Glamorous as usual. She's wearing a pink sarong tied around her waist over her black bathing suit with her long, blonde hair blowing slightly in the breeze. She pushes her sunglasses to the top of her head and performs a detailed inspection. Then, she smiles her stunning smile. That was her only job. To give her motherly good housekeeping stamp of approval. It was all I ever needed to feel loved, complete.

I ran my finger across Daddy's face in the photo. At the beach, the days were long and time seemed to stand still. In a good way, though. Not like school. How strange, I thought. A photograph is magical. It reproduces a moment, this moment, of us. How is it possible you can capture an image and yet we can't go back to that place, that time? I wanted to crawl into the picture and do it all again. Only this time, I'd know that moments are just moments. They disappear like the waves breaking against the shoreline.

CHAPTER 6
May, 2012

Denny pulled my ear bud out, "Who are you listening to? Taylor Swift?"

"Don't insult me," I said. We were on our way to the creek to go swimming. It was a bus ride and a short walk to his swimming hole. I didn't care how long it took. Spending time with Denny was the best thing that had happened to me in a long time.

He grabbed my iPod. "Let me see that playlist." He scrolled down and then whistled. "Wow. Old school. I'm impressed. Who are your favorites?"

"Pink Floyd. Tom Petty. The iPod was my dad's. I never listened to his music when he was alive, but I took his iPod when we moved. I love this stuff." I hesitated a moment before I admitted, "I didn't spend much time with him. He worked a lot. His music makes me feel closer to him."

We got off the bus and walked for a while. Denny broke our silence. "I know how it feels. You miss him," Denny said. "You're lucky you still have your mom."

I nodded. "When did your dad pass?" I asked.

"Two years ago. Daryl was a senior in high school. He stepped up and took over my dad's moving company. And he still managed to graduate and keep up our apartment. Until business slowed. Nobody's buying houses lately so nobody's moving. But Daryl refused to give up the business our dad started. So last winter we moved to Hardscrabble Way to save money."

"Where's your mom?"

"Good question. She split when I was four."

"I can't imagine..." Emily might be a mess, but I didn't know how I'd manage if I didn't have my mother. "You must be so grateful to have your brother."

"What else do you miss?" he asked. "Besides your dad?"

"Nothing, really." I needed to change the subject. I never let myself think about what I missed.

I wasn't planning to talk about Rachel, but I guess I needed to confide in someone. I told him all about my sister and what I had done.

"You must think I'm a horrible person," I said when I finished.

"There's no point in beating yourself up."

I listened to the tone of his voice trying to determine if he was disgusted with me. I wondered if I'd made a mistake telling Denny about Rachel. We walked in silence for a while. Then I asked him, "What do you miss?"

"My band." He answered without having to think about it.

"You were in a band? Cool."

"I play guitar. Sing a little." He grinned.

Delia, you're breakin' my heart, you're shakin' my confidence daily..."

I smacked his chest. "I know that song. It's Cecelia, not Delia. Why did you quit the band?"

He told me that he quit to work with Daryl.

I smiled up at him. "How old are you?"

"Sixteen. I'm gonna be a junior this fall. What about you? Freshman?"

I nodded. Then I realized I wasn't sure that was true. "Well, maybe. I didn't finish eighth grade. I don't know what's going to happen if I try to go to high school in September. I'm kind of a fugitive."

Then I told him everything else. About Daddy losing his money, about Emily being such a mess, and about running away from Joy Pierce, the social worker. I told him how I accidently dropped out of eighth grade after we lost our house so I wasn't technically a freshman. I was relieved to tell someone the whole story.

"Man, Delia. You've had your share. You're overdue for some good karma."

"It's my mother I'm worried about."

"It's you I'm worried about." Really? Denny was worried about me?

"Me?"

"What are you gonna do in September? About school? You can't just quit."

"I don't want to quit. But I'm petrified they'd make me go back and do eighth grade again." It was a relief to admit that to someone who would understand. "And if I do register, won't that make it easy for my social worker to find us? She wants to put me in a foster home."

Denny was quiet for a while as we walked to the creek. I could tell he was thinking. He had the same look on his face my father used to have when I asked him a tough question. Then he stopped and took my hand. "We should go to school one day soon. We can see if there's a counselor. Someone you can talk to who can help."

"I don't think so," I answered, thinking about my last encounter with a guidance counselor. "It wouldn't help."

"It couldn't hurt," he grinned. He started walking again, letting go of my hand. "The worst thing that could happen is you'll find out where you stand...if you have to repeat eighth grade. But at least you'd *know*. It's better than worrying. Right?"

Coming from Denny, it made sense and didn't sound so scary. "What about social services? I can't let them find me."

"We'll use my address. My old apartment. They won't find you."

"Will you come with me? To talk to the counselor?"

"Of course."

I hadn't realized how much school had been gnawing at me until now. I had one more fear I had to confess.

"Is it bad there? My old school was pretty much a country club."

"School? Bad? That depends. I'm sure it's not what you're used to. It's pretty safe. And the classes are okay if you don't take dummy classes. You seem pretty smart."

"I took honors. I'm not all that smart, but I work hard."

"You should be fine. Besides, I'll be there. If anyone messes with you they'll answer to me."

As if I wasn't already cuckoo crazy about Denny, this sealed the deal. Maybe he was right and I was due for some good luck. At this point, he seemed like a UPS truck delivering the luck. Maybe he *was* the luck.

As soon as we got to the creek, he threw his towel on the ground, kicked off his sneakers, peeled off his T-shirt, and dove in. After agonizing for two days about which of my two bikinis to wear, I got shy. I took off my T-shirt, but I left my shorts on and dove in. The cool, clear water shocked, then refreshed me. I wiggled my feet like they were a mermaid's tail, trying to stay under as long as I could. When I couldn't hold my breath another instant, I burst through the water and came up for air. I felt like a new person.

"That water is freezing," I said. "You should have warned me."

"In the interest of full disclosure, I should tell you a couple of things about this swimming hole," Denny said, doing the breast stroke over to where I surfaced.

I threw my head back and I could feel the water drip down my neck, washing the heat away. This week the temperature had spiked even though it was only May. "I'm listening."

"This is known as Johnson's Creek, but its nickname is Creepy Creek. Rumor has it that a few people have drowned here over the years. Mysteriously."

"You're not scaring me."

"Me either, but the other rumor is more disturbing. There may be drainage that runs off into the creek and it's probably unhealthy. So don't open your eyes and whatever you do, don't swallow any water. I don't want to be responsible for you growing hair on your chest or a third eye or something."

I laughed at him as I dove deep under the water. It felt so good to be swimming. When I came up I did a few laps. I realized how out of shape I was when my lungs began to ache. I flipped over and started to do a backstroke to catch my breath.

"You're in amazing shape! Where did you get those abs?" Denny asked.

"I'm a gymnast. Well, I was. And a cheerleader. Competitive cheering."

"I'm impressed. You look like a skinny little bit of nothing in clothes, but you've got quite a body…um…I mean…this isn't coming out right."

I couldn't help it. Denny was so uncomfortable that I laughed. I couldn't stop. It felt good. I couldn't remember the last time I'd laughed.

"Are you hitting on me?" I asked when I caught my breath. I knew he wasn't, but I couldn't resist teasing him. He was dying of embarrassment.

"No. Oh my God, Delia! You're like the sister I always wished for. I'd never hit on you."

He was so sincere, I couldn't tease him anymore. Besides, I was crushed. I shouldn't have been. I knew Denny saw me as a kid. But it hurt just the same. Still, I'd take him for my big brother in a heartbeat. For now.

I swam over to him. "Pick me up and put me on your shoulders. I'll show you what I used to do."

As I balanced on his shoulders with my arms outstretched for balance, I felt my confidence return. I could still do this. It felt exciting to be on top again. My heart was pounding. Maybe I could try out for cheerleading if I somehow managed to get into high school. Maybe the new school wouldn't be so bad. I already had one friend.

I leaped, tucked, flipped, and did a perfect dive. Denny was waiting for me, beaming and clapping when I came up for air.

"I love your swimming hole," I told him. "Is it always this deserted?"

"Hardly ever," he said. "It can get really crowded sometimes."

The creek poured over a giant boulder into a natural pool about twelve feet wide and at least twelve feet deep. There were many places to jump in and I tried them all. I pretended I was standing on top of a pyramid in nationals. I did all my routines only instead of landing on two feet, I landed in the water. A part of me was showing off for Denny, but mostly I was just having fun.

"I lied before when I told you I didn't miss anything," I told him on the way home. "I miss cheering." He put his arm around my shoulder and gave me a squeeze.

That night I fell right to sleep and slept through the night for the first time in a long time.

~~

We were never religious. I envied my friends when they went to church and religious instruction, even though they usually complained about having to go. Mostly I was curious. Despite the fact religion always seemed mysterious to me, even a little scary, I had always felt like I missed out on something by not having a religion. I didn't even know how to pray. So when Reverend Willy came to do a sermon, I went.

Reverend Willy drove The Church of the Purple Bus up as close as he could get to where the tents were pitched on the path. You really had to know where we were to find us, because you couldn't see Hardscrabble Way from the road. That was deliberate. Chief Cheyenne did not want to attract anyone's attention. The community was vulnerable, he said. We could be infiltrated by what he called "the wrong sort" or we could be harassed by the government since we were technically squatters on property owned by the city.

When Reverend Willy pulled up in the purple bus, anyone who wanted to attend his service met him on the outskirts; way over on the edge where the paved road disappeared beneath the abandoned overpass. The Church of the Purple Bus looked like an old school bus that had been painted. The side windows were covered in a dark, transparent film that made it impossible to see inside the bus. There was a sign on the outside window that said "No Riders." Inside, there were posters hung with sayings like: Yesterday is history, tomorrow is a mystery, today is a gift, that's why we call it the present; Dare something worthy; Dare to dream; and my favorite, I know I'm perfect because God doesn't make junk. Although I'd never been inside a regular church like the ones my friends went to, I was fairly sure they didn't have posters with slogans. And although I didn't know any other Reverends, I was willing to bet most of them didn't have an earring and a ponytail, or wear jeans and a Ramones T-shirt like Reverend Willy.

Reverend Willy brought clothing, food, and supplies that had been donated, and I suspected that at least some of the people came for the supplies, but stayed for the service. I know I would be embarrassed just to take things and run right off.

I wanted to hear the service and I wanted to learn how to pray. I figured I needed all the help I could get. I felt greedy asking for everything I needed, so I kept my prayer list to three essentials. I prayed for my mother to get well, to get back into school, and to find my sister. I thought maybe prayers were like wishes. In folktales, wishes came in threes.

I took a seat in the back of the bus and watched from the darkened window. Reverend Willy had two bins filled with clothes he placed outside the bus for people to rummage through to see if there was anything they could use. He brought bottled water, canned foods, loaves of bread, and huge blocks of cheese. People brought their own bags to carry everything. Next time I would know what to do. Next time I wouldn't be embarrassed to take what he offered. No one else was.

The service wasn't long. It was more of a talk than a service, not that I knew exactly what a service was. It wasn't what I would call religious, either. Reverend Willy referred to "the God of your choosing" which I took to mean that you could worship anyway you wanted or any God you picked, instead of just one particular religion. He talked a lot about being grateful for what we had and told us we needed to spend time taking care of each other. Instead of feeling sorry for what we didn't have, we should think about all that we did have. I was feeling a sense of comfort from the whole experience, and I didn't expect the event to end so soon, but when the Reverend Willy asked us to bow our heads in a silent prayer I realized it was nearly over. Instead of praying for my three wishes like a princess in a fairy tale, I silently said a thank you prayer for what I still had in my life.

Then Reverend Willy said, "I'll leave you today with this message from Psalm 68:5. 'A father to the fatherless, a defender of widows, is God in his holy dwelling'." He looked at me when he said that. At least I thought he did. I felt like he was speaking directly to me. Before he stepped outside, he asked if anyone needed a ride to the clinic or to the free dentist.

When I climbed down the steps and exited the bus, Reverend Willy was standing there. He put out his hand to me and said, "Thank you for coming. You're new."

I shook his hand. It was warm and he had a good, firm handshake. "Thank you," I said. For some reason, I was getting emotional. "What you said at the end..." I choked up. Reverend Willy smoothed my hair back from my forehead, then he patted me gently on the head.

"In The Church of the Purple Bus, people hear what they need to hear. I hope you'll come back."

I nodded my head, afraid that if I said anything, I would cry. I would definitely be back. In the meanwhile, now that I knew there was no right way, I would keep praying.

The chapel tent was tiny, only three feet wide and about five feet deep. Standing around six feet tall, it came to a point at the top. It reminded me of a circus tent, only miniature. There was a painted wooden sign stuck in the ground in front of the entrance that said simply, The Chapel. Inside, there was an altar and one folding chair. There wasn't room for anything else. The altar was made of two milk crates stacked one on top of the other and covered with a red and white checkered tablecloth. The cloth wasn't very long, so you could see the bottom crate. Sitting on top, instead of a cross or a star or any other holy symbol that you might expect, someone had placed a collection of tiny porcelain figurines. The closest thing there was to a religious figure were some cherubs. Maybe they were angels. I wasn't sure I knew the difference. Mostly there were animals. My favorite was a brown hedgehog about two inches big. For a while, I tried to figure out if the entire scene was supposed to be symbolic. Then I decided it didn't matter. It made me feel good to be in the chapel, so I went every morning for a few minutes and, after I spent time being thankful for my mother, Gloria and our new friends, and for having to place to live I prayed for my three wishes to come true. Secretly, I prayed to the hedgehog. I thought I'd have a better chance of being heard if I prayed to one character instead of the whole menagerie. I didn't mind people knowing I prayed. Telling someone I prayed to a hedgehog was a whole other matter. I wasn't even sure if the hedgehog existed in the world, or if it was a fictional creature like cherubs and angels. If I was ever on a computer again, I'd look it up.

Just as I was going to leave, I noticed a small carved box on the floor. There was a zip lock bag next to it. I bent over and picked up the bag, which had a pad and a pen inside. There was also an index card with hand-printed instructions. "THIS IS A GOD BOX. PRINT YOUR PRAYER ON A PIECE OF PAPER AND SLIP IT INTO THE BOX. GOD WILL TAKE CARE OF THE REST."

I opened the wooden box. Inside were tiny pieces of paper. Feeling as if I were reading someone's diary, I picked up one of the pieces and read "praying for propane." I put it back. Was it a sin to read these? I wasn't God. I wasn't able to help anyone with their prayers. Yet, it was irresistible. I read another. "God is propane. God is everywhere. Propane is not." I decided not to read any more prayers. Not only was I invading private thoughts, the prayers scared me. I didn't want to be living in Hardscrabble Way when winter came. I printed my sister's name on the paper, carefully folded it, and placed it with the others in the God box. I needed a plan to find my sister. It couldn't hurt to ask God to help me figure out how to find Rachel.

CHAPTER 7
March, 2012

After Daddy died things unraveled quicker than school emptied out on a Friday afternoon. The house and all Daddy's businesses were in foreclosure. He hadn't paid his bills for over a year. I didn't even know what foreclosure meant before this happened. Daddy didn't own anything anymore. The bank owned everything. I was, at the very least, confused. I couldn't process how you could go from having money to not having money so rapidly.

Uncle Arthur tried to help us. He's not really my uncle. He was daddy's accountant and one of his best friends. One night Uncle Arthur came over and started to try to explain everything to Emily. She was pretty out of it most of the time. I think the word is inconsolable. I decided I needed to sit with them at the kitchen counter and understand what was happening in case Emily couldn't focus. At first, he didn't want me to be there.

"You poor kid. You don't need to hear this."

I told him I did. I said I needed to know the truth about what was going to happen to us. What I didn't tell him was how I wasn't sure Emily was capable of listening to what he was going to say. Uncle Arthur stared at me for a minute, then he cleared his throat a few times. I got up and got him a water bottle. He took a long gulp before he started to talk again.

"Sorry. This is rough...Mark was my friend and I..."

Emily interrupted him, her voice cold," Spare us your sorrow, Arthur. Get to the point."

He looked as if she had smacked him across the face. Emily didn't look at him, she just stared into her wine glass.

"How much do you know? I mean, did you and Mark talk about finances?"

"No. He handled everything. We talked about making a will, but we never got around to it." She raised her eyebrows. "Wait. Is there a life insurance policy?"

He shook his head slowly. "If there is, you must have it. Or his attorney. He never gave me a copy." He sipped his water again.

"There's no easy way to say this. The mortgage on the house hasn't been paid in sixteen months. The bank started foreclosure proceedings about six months ago. Mark didn't tell me any of this until a few months back. He kept hoping he'd find a way to make it right. We started exploring options: investors, bankruptcy, refis…Anyway, I've reached out to the banks. His businesses are gone. Dissolved." I could see he was struggling.

He shook off his grief and put his business face on. "Look, Em. There's a slim chance I could tap dance around the bank and we could save the house *if* we could show income." He stopped and took a deep breath in. Then, he spoke very slowly. "Emily, that means you have to get a job. It still may not be enough to satisfy the bank. But if I can show them you're working…"

Until then, I wasn't sure how much of this my mother was taking in. But it soon became clear Emily had heard every word. She wasn't having it. In a voice that was as crisp as the first cold day in winter she said, "My husband deceived me about our finances. He screwed everything up and then he had the nerve to die. Now I'm supposed to find work? What do you think I'm going to be able to do? I haven't worked since Rachel was born."

Uncle Arthur tried. He really did. "Emily, I know all that. I know how hard this all is. Just the shock of losing Mark…But weren't you…didn't you work as a decorator?"

"Didn't Mark have life insurance?" she shot back. Uncle Arthur raised his hands in a gesture that said he had no idea.

Emily stared at him and I immediately thought of one of Ms. Louis's vocabulary words. Withering. She gave him a look that was withering. She didn't say another word. She got up off the stool, poured more wine into her glass, and left the kitchen.

Uncle Arthur put his head in his hand and I was afraid he was going to cry. He sat there so long I thought he'd forgotten about me. After a while he looked up and said, "Delia, honey. Isn't there anyone who can help? Any family at all that you know of?"

There was no one.

The next morning, when my mother came downstairs she told me everything was going to be fine. She told me she knew there must be an insurance policy that would take care of things. Then Emily trashed everything in the house looking for it. I mean everything. The house looked like those pictures of what homes look like after a tornado strikes. The only difference was our house still had four walls and a roof. Her search turned up nothing at all. Neither did a phone call to my father's attorney who said he had no paperwork regarding either a will or a life insurance policy.

Emily had become scary. Sometimes she ranted random things that make no sense. Other times she sat and cried. Ginger stopped coming over to keep her company. I'm not at all sure what happened. Weird as it felt, I stopped staying after school for practice. The first time I came home straight from school I didn't even know where my regular bus was in the parking lot because I had always taken the late bus. There was no choice. I couldn't stay after. I couldn't leave Emily for more hours than I already was leaving her when I went to school. When I came home from school, I tried to get her out of bed and I'd make her something to eat. Every day I hoped I'd find her feeling better. I tried to help her snap out of it. I told her over and over that it was just a matter of time and she would start to feel better. She needed time to grieve. After, she could find a job and everything would get better. Not the same as it used to be, obviously. But better. I said these things to her so often, that I convinced myself they were true.

I thought I would miss cheering more than I did. I didn't miss anything. I didn't feel anything. Coach Alicia came to find me and took me out of class one day. She was so nice I ended up feeling bad about not feeling bad.

"Cordelia, I know this is an awful time for you. I've tried calling your mom to see if there's anything I can do to help...You know. Give you rides to your lessons, or practice, or..." She looked straight at me. "She doesn't return my calls. Is she...how is she doing?"

"She's fine," I lied. "We're fine."

"Why don't you come back to practice? You might feel better. Get back into a routine. Exercise. You know. They say it helps. With depression."

Strange how that was the first time it hit me. Depression. That's what this was. We were depressed. Of course. My mom was drinking wine and she was hiding under her covers. And I had gone numb. At some point I realized Coach Alicia had just asked me a question and was waiting for an answer.

"What?"

"I'm sorry this has happened to you, Delia. I want to help. Do you need a ride to your lessons? You're so talented. I don't want you to give up your cheering or your gymnastics."

I didn't know what to say to her. I couldn't afford my lessons. There was no reason she would know my father's death was not my only concern.

"I know you'll never get over the loss of your dad, but someday you will feel better. I promise. And I don't want you to regret giving up something you love and are so good at."

I should have dissolved in tears by now, but I didn't. I couldn't explain my life to her, the ways things were right now. There was no way I could ever focus on cheerleading while my mother was grieving like this. I had no words, no way of telling Coach the truth. Losing my dad wasn't the only problem I had. I was losing everything. My sister was gone, my mother was basically gone, we were losing our house, and we had no money for food, never mind lessons. Coach was watching me, waiting for me to say something.

"I'll think about it, Coach. Thank you for thinking about me. I'll be fine. Really. Can I go back to class now?"

Coach looked at me for a long time. For a minute, I was afraid she knew I was lying. I never lied much because I was really bad at it. You could look at my face and know in a heartbeat I was lying. She put her arm around me and gave me a hug.

"Go back to class. When you're ready, just come back to practice. You don't have to ask. Just come."

I forced a smile. "Don't worry, Coach. Everything's fine." And I went back to my class.

Alexa whispered to me, "Is everything ok?"

I wanted to scream on the top of my lungs "When is everyone going to stop asking me that and leave me alone?"

But I didn't. "Fine." I said again, I smiled just to show that I meant it.

~~

My mother was definitely not fine. Nothing else was either. I started cutting school because I was afraid to leave her alone. Emily rarely got out of bed. We had run out of alcohol, so she wasn't drinking anymore. There wasn't any money in the house for food, wine, or anything else we needed. I was afraid to charge anything because I doubted the cards still worked. I did the only thing I could think of at that point. I asked Uncle Arthur to sell my mother's jewelry. I asked her permission first, but she was in bed and her room was dark when I asked her. She mumbled back at me she didn't care what I sold. Then she told me where the key to the safe was.

I didn't sell everything. I kept her first engagement ring, the one that Daddy gave her when he proposed. For their tenth anniversary he bought her a diamond the size of a doorknob, but she'd held onto the original. I'm not sure why she kept the ring, but it had sentimental value to me, if not to her. I'm not sure why, but I promised myself I would never sell it, no matter how poor we got. I kept a few other pieces she wore often, and I kept a pair of her diamond earrings, too. The little ones, as we called them. Rachel loved to borrow them and they looked perfect on her. She joked about them being the Goldilocks earrings; they were just right. There were two other pairs; one medium and one supersize. Rachel wore her favorite pair to Sweet Sixteen parties and to her junior prom. She'd looked so beautiful for prom, not at all slutty like so many of other girls in their boob displaying mini-dresses.

"We're going to a prom. Not a night club," I remember Rachel saying when she put on the dress. She was ranting about the choices some of her friends had posted on Facebook. At first I didn't understand why they wanted anyone to see their dress before the prom.

"They post to avoid repeats and the *who wore it best* conversation," she laughed as she explained to me.

Rachel looked like a princess. The dress was the color of a robin's egg; simple and elegant. She wore glittering silver sandals with her hair pushed behind her ears and the diamond earrings sparkled like firecrackers when she moved her head even slightly. I thought she was the prettiest girl I had ever seen.

The junior prom was less than a year ago. That seemed unreal. So much had happened. I didn't know what was worse. Not knowing where Rachel was or her not knowing our father died. I stopped myself. I couldn't think about what had happened. Later, I would make a plan to find Rachel. Right now I had other worries. I put the little diamond earrings away to save for Rachel. The big ones, the ones we laughed about and called the ice cubes, went in the velvet pouch I was giving to Uncle Arthur to sell. At the last minute I decided to keep the mid-sized ones for now, too. I could always sell them later. I hovered over the doorknob ring, deciding if it should stay or go. I slipped it on my finger, remembering when my mother used to wear it every day. I wondered when she had taken it off and put it in the safe. I stared at the giant stone on my finger, riveted by the colors it shot off when I moved my hand, its facets catching the light. A miniature display exploded inside the stone. Shimmering, sparkling, shooting off sharp hues of yellow, red, blue, purple. No wonder women love diamonds. How ironic, I thought, remembering the slogan I'd seen in magazines: *diamonds are forever*. That might be true, but nothing else lasts forever. I imagined myself grown and I wondered if anyone would ever give me something as precious as a diamond. I took the ring off my finger and dropped it into the pouch. We needed the money.

Uncle Arthur resisted selling Emily's jewelry, at first. He was afraid Emily would regret it later. At some point, he accepted the fact there was no other choice. He gave me some cash in advance, and then he seemed to take his time selling the jewelry. He said he wanted to be sure we were getting top dollar, but I think he just kept hoping for a miracle. Once I had some cash, I discovered a nearby **Stop and Shop** that delivered groceries which was a lot less expensive than ordering take-out and delivery every night. Emily's car was still in the garage, but she didn't leave the house and I didn't want to ask her to go grocery shopping. Daddy's car had been financed, and Uncle Arthur arranged for it to go back to the dealer.

I brought the mail inside every day and put it on the sideboard. Emily never looked at it even though she did seem better. She was getting up in the morning, sometimes even taking a shower and getting dressed. Mostly, she watched TV all day. At least she was getting out of bed. At some point there was so much mail I had to find a shopping bag to put it all in. I took my biggest Abercrombie & Fitch shopping bag out of my closet where I kept all my favorite shopping bags neatly folded and stashed. I dumped all the mail into my Abercrombie bag, feeling sorry for myself because it seemed unlikely I would ever shop there again. That was a low moment. But not nearly as low as the day my cell phone stopped working. The lowest moment of all came when I realized I had no internet connection and I couldn't do my homework. The landline didn't work either. There didn't seem to be much else that could go wrong.

The day the internet stopped, I dumped all the mail out of the Abercrombie bag and I began to tear open bills. I organized them into three piles. One pile was for bills related to the house like the mortgage, gas, water, and electric. A second pile was for credit cards, and the third was for other odd bills that didn't fit anywhere else. At first, it made me sick when I saw how much we owed. No wonder Daddy was upset. But then I got angry. Furious. With both of my parents. What was wrong with them? Why didn't Daddy just tell us what was going on? I would have understood. I didn't need to have all the things I had. I didn't need to have extravagant parties, or every new style that rolled off the racks. My mother certainly didn't need everything she had. I couldn't even begin to understand why she spent so much. I stared at the credit card bills. There were eleven different bills. Eleven. I couldn't comprehend why anyone would need eleven credit cards. I was so angry I wanted punch something. Maybe…just maybe…if Daddy had told us the truth about his businesses Emily would have stopped spending and he wouldn't have had a heart attack. But I didn't blame Emily. Not entirely. It was Daddy's fault, too. He bought more stores when he shouldn't have. He let her spend when he shouldn't have. Even if the economy was in some part to blame, there was no sense to the way they had both been living.

Nothing would change what had happened. After I sorted the bills, I read them one by one. There were old warning letters from the phone, gas, cable, and electric companies going back a few months. A feeling of dread took over my whole body as I tore into all the bills. There were letters stating different utilities were being turned off. One letter at a time, I faced the pile that my mother wouldn't. Then I found the bombshell. Eviction. On April 22 we were going to be evicted. The bank was going to lock our house and they expected us to be out.

We were three weeks away from losing our house. And I thought things couldn't get worse.

I tiptoed into the guest room where my mother was sleeping. She hadn't slept in her own bed since the first night Daddy didn't come home.

"Emily. Mom." I spoke softly at first, shaking her a bit.

"Mmm." It was more of a moan than an answer. She moved her arm, and put the back of her hand to her forehead.

I got louder. "Mom, you need to get up. We need to talk."

"Uh, uh. Later. I need to sleep. Go 'way. We'll talk after school." She pulled a pillow over her head, shutting me out.

"This can't wait. I didn't go to school. You need to get up." This couldn't go on. She needed to get herself together. I couldn't face this by myself. I had no idea how to keep the electric from being turned off. Or how to keep from being evicted.

The pillow came off and she looked at me. "No school? Is it Saturday?"

I was starting to lose it. "No, it's not Saturday. I stayed home to take care of you. I'm worried about you. You've got to get up and make some decisions. There's no one else who's going to fix this." It was tough love time.

My mother sat up in bed. Her face had sheet wrinkles, she wore no make-up, her eyes had circles under them, and her hair was a blonde bird's nest. She reached for the bottle of water on her nightstand. She drank from the bottle and water dribbled down her chin falling onto her stained T-shirt. A shirt she would have thrown out just weeks ago. Emily didn't seem to notice that her shirt was wet. Why would she? She didn't even know what day it was.

"Okay. I'm up. What do you need me to do Delia, honey?"

What did I need her to do? *Be my mother,* I wanted to scream. Be in charge. Fix things.

I looked at the sad, scary, confused woman who was waiting for me to answer.

"Never mind. It can wait. I'm going to go get you something to eat. I'll be right back."

I went down the stairs two at a time. As I hurried into the kitchen I knew my mother wasn't capable of fixing anything. It was all up to me. At least for now. But I had no clue what to do. I even thought about getting a job, but no one would hire a thirteen year old.

~~

I sat alone in the kitchen eating some too salty frozen dinner I'd microwaved. I wondered how hard it could be to learn how to cook. Out of habit, I stared at my dead cell phone. Outside of school I was avoiding my friends. I could pretend to be normal during the day, at school. It was easy enough to make small talk in the cafeteria. I could talk about homework or tests or pretend to care about who was wearing what. When someone asked me why my phone was off I shrugged it off and didn't answer. I'm sure my friends think I'm still grieving and they don't press me for answers. They don't know the rest of the story. They don't know we have no money and that I am living like an orphan. I didn't only lose my father, but my mother has disappeared as well.

Margot invited me over for Sunday dinner. She said her mother missed me and wanted to see me. I considered going. I could certainly use some real food and some normalcy. Even for a few hours.

Emily was sleeping when I left the house and walked to Margot's. It wasn't far, and only took me about fifteen minutes, but I'd never walked there before. I guess that seems peculiar, but we never walked anywhere. Even if my mother was awake I couldn't have asked her to drive me. Her car was gone now, too. After Uncle Arthur filed the papers dissolving the business, the court seized my father's assets. Evidently Emily's car was owned by the business. I felt less guilty about selling the jewelry after I heard that. They might have asked for her jewelry, too.

Margot was cool about everything. She didn't act uncomfortable around me or like she didn't know what to say. Her mom, Loretta, hugged me and told me how happy she was I came. She put us to work in the kitchen as soon as I got there. She was slow cooking pot roast and the aroma drifted throughout the house. It shocked me to realize that my house never had food smells. Loretta handed me carrots to peel and dice and gave Margot potatoes with the same directions.

"Do you want a peeler or a paring knife?" Loretta asked me. I stared at her. It was like she was speaking a foreign language. She laughed. "I forgot. Emily doesn't cook, does she?"

She grabbed a peeler and showed me what to do. It was easy and fun. I wished I could stay in Loretta's kitchen forever. Margot's little sister Amy was sitting at the kitchen table writing a report on her laptop.

"What are you working on, Amy?" I asked. Amy was nine. I had always wondered why my mother didn't have any more kids after me. I had asked her once. She laughed and said, "I have two perfect girls. Why tempt fate?" I didn't know what she meant. Margot had two younger sisters and a brother a year older than us. Frank was a freshman. Big families were alien to me and therefore very desirable. There was always someone around, someone to bicker with, or talk to, or tease.

Amy looked up. "I'm doing a PowerPoint@ on penguins. Third grade studies penguins. Second grade gets to study butterflies. They're so much sweeter than penguins."

"I remember doing that report," I said. "The most interesting thing I learned about penguins is they're a bird that doesn't fly."

Amy nodded and went back to typing. Loretta cleared her throat. She looked at me and said, "Margot told me you're not cheering any more. Or doing gymnastics. I don't want to be intrusive, but is that a good idea for you?"

I didn't see that coming. I thought I could escape the reality of my life for a little while, which was the only reason I decided to come to dinner. And, of course, the home made food. "I don't want to talk about it," I said, feeling badly. I didn't want to be rude.

"Are you talking to anyone?" Loretta asked. "I mean, like a grief counselor or…"

"Mom. Enough. If Delia wants to talk, she'll talk," Margot interrupted her mother.

"I just want to be sure…Delia, it's important not to keep things inside. Stuff has a way of building up. You can talk here. You don't have to be strong, you know."

I didn't? The thought hadn't occurred to me. The kitchen was so quiet I could hear the roast simmering on the stove in the blue Dutch oven. If I ever have a kitchen of my own, I thought, it was going to be blue. Like wildflowers. Like the color of Daddy's eyes. No. Blue wouldn't work. Blue would remind me of Daddy and make me sad. I wanted my kitchen to be a happy place. I would have a yellow kitchen. The cheerful color of butter and sunshine. I would grow yellow roses in a garden I could see from my kitchen window. Yellow would make me happy.

I realized that Loretta, Margot, and Amy were looking at me, waiting for me to say something. I couldn't remember what we were talking about. Then it came back to me. Maybe Loretta was right. Maybe I should tell them what was going on. Tell them we had no money and were going to be thrown out of our home. The only home I'd ever known.

I didn't know how to make the words come out. These were sentences I had never spoken before. "My father…he, um…he didn't leave us anything. He never expected this to happen. Dying, I mean. Of course everyone dies, but not now. Not yet. So we have nothing…" I was having a hard time saying exactly what I meant, but I thought they understood what I was trying to say.

Loretta came over and put her arm around my shoulder. I felt very small. "Of course he didn't leave you ready for this. He had no idea his time was so short. I'm sure he would have left things in better shape. But you and your mother have the businesses, your house. Emily is a bright woman and she'll get things sorted out as soon as she feels a little better. You shouldn't worry." The timer on the stove went off.

"Oh good," Loretta said. "Time to add the vegies. We'll eat in an hour. Why don't you girls go watch a movie or something 'til then? I'm going to make an apple crumble for dessert."

She had no idea what I was talking about. It was unimaginable to anyone we knew that my father had left literally nothing, so she couldn't comprehend what I had said. I made a choice then and there. That was the last time I would attempt to tell anyone what I was living through.

Twice a week Ms. Louis let us write anything we wanted during Language Arts class. Now more than ever I was grateful for that time. My journal was the only place I felt safe enough to tell the truth. It was the only place I didn't have to pretend or be strong. After my pathetic attempt to confide in Margot and her mother, I refused to say another word to anyone about my circumstances.

Sometimes, though, Ms. Louis collected our journals. She said we could fold down any pages we didn't want her to see, but I wondered if I could trust her. All my pages were turned down. If she collected our journals, I decided I wouldn't hand it in. I'd take a zero rather than run the risk she might read even one of my pages.

March 15

No one knows how hard this is. They think they know, but they don't. Everyone knows about Daddy, of course, and I suppose they imagine how they'd feel if they lost their father. But they don't know the rest. They don't know that my sister is a runaway and no one can find her. My mother made up an elaborate story about sending her to a boarding school in Switzerland. Why anyone believes it, I don't know, but Emily refuses to have people know the truth. Maybe they don't believe it, but no one talks to me or asks about Rachel. Sometimes,

83

I feel like she's not real. Like I invented her. An imaginary sister, like some little kids have imaginary friends. I want to talk about Rachel to my mother, but I'm afraid. I'm afraid to talk to Emily about anything. She's so fragile. I'm doing the best I can to take care of her, but I'm not sure what I should be doing. My mother has fallen apart. Daddy dying was bad enough, but now to find out we've lost everything...She's barely holding it together. I'm the only one she has. I'm scared that she won't hold on, that she'll do something bad to herself. I remind her sometimes how much I need her. If I tell her that often enough, maybe she'll remember that it's true. Maybe that will give her enough of a reason not to give up. I want to be mad at her for all the awful things she said to Daddy. But every time I look at her, I know that my anger can't compare to whatever she is going through right now. I need her more than ever.

I wish this was a nightmare. Only I know it's not because I can't make myself wake up. I want my old life back. I want to wake up and have things be like they used to be. I want to turn the clock backwards like they did in A Wrinkle in Time. Then my Daddy would be here and I could ride on his shoulders like I used to when I was little and Rachel would be by our side shouting, "Me too, Daddy. Me too!" In some naïve part of my brain, I expected my parents to be there for me for my whole life. To watch me get ready for prom, to see me graduate, get married...

I don't understanding death. How can someone be here in the morning and be gone that night and you are never going to see them again. Never. With all the human beings on the planet, this one person is missing. The one I want to see the most. Even though Rachel disappeared, there's a chance that I will find her and that we'll be together again. But Daddy...

I feel sick inside and out. I feel like I fell from the highest pyramid I ever stood on top of when I was cheering. I've face-planted on the ground and I want someone to pick me up and hold me and tell me everything's going to be alright.

But there's no one. So I have to be that someone and take care of Emily.

The bell just rang. I have to go to Social Studies.

CHAPTER 8
April, 2012

A few days after I found the eviction notice, I borrowed Margot's phone and called Uncle Arthur. I told him my mom wanted to see him. I hoped he would know what to do. I thought if anyone could fix this, he could. He was an accountant. He understood money. Maybe he could stop the eviction. Now I can't believe I was so foolish, but I was desperate.

When Uncle Arthur came over, Emily refused to come downstairs and talk to him. I showed him everything. All my neatly organized piles of exorbitant debt my parents had accumulated. When he read the eviction notice he heaved a big sigh and slammed his hand down on the counter making a loud smack that made me jump. He took off his glasses and rubbed his eyes. When he stopped, his eyes were red. He sighed again, his head shaking slightly from side to side. "Delia," he said at last. "At this point, there's nothing I can do. I had power of attorney for your father which allowed me to file for bankruptcy for the businesses, and I have papers here that will absolve your mother of the personal debt. If Emily will sign the papers. Maybe you can talk to her. I've tried. If she signs, the bankruptcy trustee will relieve her of all responsibility for these." He waved his hand over the piles. "Do you understand what that means?"

I nodded my head yes. "I think so." I paused before I said, "It's not right."

"No. It's terrible that you have to go through this," he said.

"That's not what I mean."

He looked at me, not understanding.

I was angry. "It's awful that my parents spent all this money that they didn't really have and all these people will not get paid."

Uncle Arthur stared at me. He looked even more uncomfortable, if that was possible.

"You're...you're right in a way, Delia. But you don't understand. Credit is...well, it's the American way. No one pays cash for things..."

I interrupted him. "Maybe they should."

He cleared his throat. "There's more we have to talk about."

I looked at him, waiting. My father was dead. My mother was useless. My sister was missing. We had no money. What else could there be?

"You can't stay here anymore. I've thought about...well, you know I'm alone. I've been divorced a long, long time and my only daughter is married and lives in New Jersey."

I didn't understand what he was talking about.

"I'm going to ask your mother if the two of you want to stay with me. At least until she can figure out what to do next. It's not ideal, but...what do you think?"

I went upstairs to get Emily. She needed to face this with me. I couldn't make these kinds of decisions on my own. I shouldn't have to.

Emily sat staring into her coffee mug, while Arthur repeated what he'd told me. I couldn't tell her reaction to what he was saying.

"I'm sorry, Em. I wish there was better news. If Mark had told me sooner...I can't sleep thinking about..." Uncle Arthur looked lost. "Will you consider my offer?"

"Is that all?" Emily asked.

"Do you want me to reach out to someone else? Mark's mother?" he asked.

My mother's laugh was shrill. She hadn't brushed her hair, and her face looked thin and colorless. "I'm going upstairs," she said.

"Emily, wait. You need to...will you sign these papers? It's the only way you won't be held responsible."

I'd never seen that look on anyone's face before. She looked deflated, defeated, and more depressed than anyone deserved to be. Emily stared directly into Uncle Arthur's eyes as she took his pen and scribbled on the paper he was holding out.

"Go file your papers and leave us alone."

"Emily, it's not my fault. I didn't..."

She cut him off. "No you didn't. You didn't protect him or my family. You expect me to believe you didn't know what was going on?"

"I know you need to blame someone, but...I'll file the papers in the morning." Shaking his head, he said, "I'll contact social services to help you find a place to live."

"Save your grand gestures, Arthur. I don't want your help. I never want to see or hear from you again. You know where the door is."

Uncle Arthur looked sadder than the abandoned dogs they show on commercials when they're trying to get you to donate money. "I'm so sorry," he said, his voice cracking. "Delia, if you need anything..."

"She will not need you. Go."

He left. With him went my last hope for anything to go right.

The next few weeks were a blur of unreal events. Emily pulled herself together enough to hire someone who helped us empty the house. We sold what we could of our furniture, clothes, TVs, and most of what we still owned. I didn't want to, but Emily kept bugging me to go her and Daddy's old room and take anything I wanted before they removed Daddy's things. I could hardly bear to go inside. As soon as I saw their bed I remembered snuggling in between my parents and watching TV on Sunday mornings when I was little. Rachel usually wandered in some time after me and plopped herself across the foot of their king-sized bed. These recollections were too much for me. I turned around to walk out of the room. As I did I passed Daddy's dresser. I grabbed a bottle of his cologne and Daddy's iPod. I didn't need anything to remind me of him. I had Daddy locked in my heart, stored away with all my memories. Someday, when I could bear it, I'd take them out and reminisce. Someday, maybe I'd spray the scent and pretend he was there.

The doorbell rang. I was up in my room doing homework and I didn't want to answer it. Hardly anyone ever rang our doorbell. It rang again. I knew Emily wouldn't get up to answer the door. Whoever was there seemed pretty determined. With a jolt, my heart started racing as I thought maybe it was someone with news about Rachel. As I flew down the stairs, I dared to fantasize that it could even be her. I could hardly open the door, I was so excited.

Disappointment is not a state of mind you ever get used to. A tall woman stood on the porch. She was bundled in boots, a coat, hat, scarf, gloves, and she still looked frozen. It wasn't *that* cold, I thought.

"Yes?" I said, making it sound like a question.

"Are you Cordelia Williams?" the woman asked. She was fumbling to take off a glove.

I wasn't sure I should talk to her alone. She was a stranger and that loop had certainly been drummed into my head all my life. I watched as she reached into her pocket with her ungloved hand.

"Mom! There's someone here. I think you should come down," I yelled, hoping Emily would hear me.

"Good. I need to talk to your mother, too. Here's my card." She'd found what she was groping for in her pocket, and handed me a slightly crumbled business card. Before I could read it she said, "I'm Joy. Joy Pierce, your case manager. I'm here to help."

I didn't know what she meant. Then I looked at the card and it all became clear. She was from The Division of Family Services. I had no idea what she could do to help, but at this point I felt grateful she was there.

"Call me Joy", she said in a flat voice. She was least joyful person I think I'd ever met. "Can I come in? I'm so cold."

She was as skinny as she was tall. Even bundled up, you could tell how thin she was. As soon as I let her in, she turned to me and leaned down so her face was right at my eye level. "Cordelia, I am so sorry for your loss," she said. She was so close to me I could see spit in the corners of her mouth.

I backed away and went upstairs to find Emily, hoping she was together enough to deal with Joy. I knew I wasn't.

We kept some of our furniture and a few other things. A van and two men came and moved what was left of our possessions to a small storage unit. Emily used some of the money we got from selling her jewelry to rent the unit for six months. That seemed like a long time from now. So much could happen in six months, as I well knew.

Before we moved, I had to pack and decide what I would bring and what I would put into boxes labeled **STORE**. Everything else went into green garbage bags to be donated. By this time, I didn't much care what I kept and what I got rid of. I looked at my possessions in a completely different way than I did a short while ago. As I was packing, I counted thirty-two pairs of boots. It was clear to me now that no one on earth needed thirty-two pairs of boots. The only thing that got to me, the only objects that mattered to me, were my awards and my trophies. I knew they were just worthless dust collectors, but they meant something to me. I was someone when I won them. Actually, I never thought of it as winning them as much as I felt as though I'd *earned* them. All the hours of lessons, practices, drills, early mornings, late nights, soreness, and pulled muscles...I had loved every second, but it was work. I decided to keep my trophies because nothing in my future seemed certain. I didn't know if I would ever get another chance to compete. I wrapped my trophies in tissue paper, one at a time, and placed them in the **STORE** box.

If I thought my heart broke when I packed my prizes, that was nothing compared to how I felt when I packed Rachel's things. I pretended to *be* Rachel. I needed to make ruthless decisions about what to keep and what to give away. If I was Rachel, what would I want? I sat on her floor for a long time, closed my eyes, and breathed deeply. I was breathing the same air she'd breathed when she lived here. I felt her presence. After a long while, I knew what to do. Possessions hadn't mattered to my sister. Whatever mattered the most to her, she'd taken with her when she left. I packed up her art and her supplies to put into storage. I put aside one small painting to keep with me. A dreamlike watercolor of a mystical figure that was part spider, part hummingbird, and part angel with the face of a girl. I thought she looked a little like me. Down in the lower right-hand corner was the small nautilus shell with Rachel's signature *R* sunk deep into the spiral.

I was going to take the painting with me wherever I was going. The only other thing I kept was Rachel's blue prom dress and her silver sandals. It seemed like a frivolous thing to do under the circumstances, but I had a vivid picture in my head of Rachel wearing the dress. I couldn't bear to leave it behind. I told myself it wouldn't take up much space since the dress was so light it floated.

We were evicted at the end of April. We knew it was coming, of course, but knowing didn't lessen the shock. I went from having it all to having nothing. I wasn't even fourteen and I was homeless. Joy Pierce, the case worker, was going to find us a place to live. She was helping us with other "social services" as she put it. Whatever that meant. I stopped listening when it sank in that I'd become a case. When we first met Joy, I'd held out a glimmer of hope that maybe she would prove helpful to us. I even said that to Emily, who shrugged her shoulders and said, "Maybe. But I wouldn't count on it."

Joy told us she would pick us up in her car and help us move. We had no idea when she was coming since we no longer had a phone. Nor did we know where we were going. When she did show up, she was in a hurry, leaving us no time to get upset or become sentimental. Which was not a bad thing. The house was already empty. Things that hadn't been sold were in storage. We were taking some clothes and a few personal items as we left the only home I had ever known.

I refused to turn and look out the window of the back seat as we drove off down my street. If I did that, the memories of my entire life would have swallowed me. If I had expected Joy to be chirpy and chatty like my awkward guidance counselor had been, I couldn't have been more wrong. She was a lot older than Ms. Stiffano, and I guess this was routine for her. Joy drove for miles in silence, lost somewhere in her own head. She still hadn't told us where we were going.

At a stoplight, Joy seemed to snap back into the present. She glanced over at Emily, who was next to her in the front seat. "I'm sorry. I'm not very communicative." She looked at Emily again. She seemed to expect my mother to say something. Emily had been beyond small talk for a long time.

"I'm not going to tell you anything you don't already know," Joy said. "This is happening more and more. Homelessness is the elephant in the living room no one is talking about. Take it from me." She shook her head. "Twenty-two years I've been doing this. It's bad."

Then she got quiet again and we rode along in silence. I don't know how long we had been driving when she pulled the car into a parking lot and stopped. Turning around in her seat, she looked at me. "I tried to find you a place to live that was close to Bala Cynwyd, so you didn't have to change schools. I know that would have been preferable."

I thought she was insane. As if I could continue to show my face at BC as though nothing had changed. It didn't matter to me where I went to school. In fact, it was better for me if I transferred. At least in a new school no one would know me or anything about me. Most of all, no one would feel sorry for me. I know I hadn't done anything wrong, but I felt so ashamed.

"There was no affordable housing near where you lived," she said with a deep sigh. "This was the best I could do. I'm sorry." Then she turned to face Emily. "I'm going to have to let you out and run. I'm on overload with cases. The manager here is expecting you. She handles a lot of welfare cases and lucky for you, she has a vacant efficiency. You've got my card if there's a problem."

It was then I realized we were in the parking lot of a motel. After we got out of the car and got our bags out of the trunk, Joy rolled down the window. She called out to me and said she was going to register me in the local middle school. She would call in a day or two on the motel phone and let me know when the bus would pick me up. Then, she held up her hand in a sort of wave, only her fingers were spread apart and it looked more like she was holding her hand up to say "stop." The car was already moving away from us. She'd dropped us off as casually as Emily used to leave laundry at the dry cleaners. Or so it felt.

Efficiency was a senseless name. There was nothing efficient about the place. Essentially, it was a bedroom with a tiny stove, a mini-fridge, and a microwave. "A kitchenette," the motel manager said when she showed it to us. Where do they come up with these euphemisms? Until I saw where we were, I had imagined we were at least going to get an apartment. Always the optimist. Shame on me for being a fool, but in my own defense I knew nothing about how any of this worked. We had one motel room for my mother and me. A room. We went from living in a four bedroom stone house in Lower Merion to a single room in a welfare motel and we were supposed to feel grateful to get a room. My mother's walk-in closet was as big as the room we were going to have to live in. Maybe bigger.

When the manager showed us the place, I was horrified. I watched Emily's face to see her reaction. She didn't appear to have one, and I could only dream what was going through her head. At first she didn't say a word. When we checked out the bathroom, there was a filthy, paper thin plastic shower curtain. Emily looked at it and spoke for the first time. "We're going to have to do something about that," she said in a voice with no expression. I stared at her. The place was a hell hole and that was all she could say. We needed to do something about the shower curtain.

~~

By the middle of May we had been in Motel Hell for three weeks. I had never registered for school. Joy never called or came back, which was fine with me since I wasn't going to leave Emily alone anyway. So on top of everything else, now I was an eighth grade drop out. Since I wasn't going to finish eighth grade, there wasn't going to be an eighth grade graduation. I wasn't going to my dance, either. The eighth grade dance is the big thing in middle school. Finding the perfect dress, getting a group together to get a limo, the after party…those things that were so important to me just a few months ago. I was not the same me anymore and it was hard to remember that girl. The girl whose biggest worries were about straight As, cheerleading, new boots, and a new dress for a dance or a party.

That life seemed irrelevant. Now I was worried, really worried, that Joy would turn up and make me go to school. No one could really expect me to transfer schools in the last six weeks of eighth grade. All I could hope was that her case load was so overwhelming, she'd forgotten about me. For good.

Even if she hadn't forgotten me, I still couldn't go to school. I knew I could never leave my mother alone in Motel Hell all day. The room was worse than anything I could have conceived. We lived on the ground floor and you could see daylight under our door. Bugs crawled in through the space. Ugly, black, beetle-like bugs. I stuffed newspaper in the crack to keep them out. There were mystery stains in the carpet, if you could call it a carpet. The walls were dirty and seemed as though they were made of cardboard. You could hear right through them without trying. Believe me when I say, I didn't try. There was an old man living next door to us. He woke me every morning coughing up what sounded like buckets of phlegm. Worse, his bathroom sounded like it was in the middle of our room. You heard plenty of things you didn't want to hear. I hated all of the noises. You could hear the TV in the room upstairs over our heads as well as the TVs on either side of us. It was as if everyone who lived there was trying to drown out the sound of their own lives. Or, they were just hard of hearing. And not that it's important, but our TV was so old it wasn't even a flat screen. In Motel Hell there were no good sounds. Even our mini-fridge made a racket in the middle of the night. It clattered, the motor revved up, then it shuddered, made some sort of ultimate death rattle before it finally stopped. As awful as the noises were, the smells were worse. The entire place had an odor like the inside of an old sock. The worst was when someone in another apartment was nuking something in their micro-wave. I don't know what people cooked, but their food smells made me gag.

It rained every day for two weeks which meant we were stuck in our room. Since I had dropped out, there was nothing to do except watch TV and try not to think. Which wasn't hard because I was busy obsessing about my mother. She slept almost constantly. Sometimes I reminded her to take a shower and change her clothes. There was a tiny closet and one dresser so most of our clothes were still in our suitcases. I don't know what we were thinking about. We each brought two giant suitcases of clothes and shoes. Where did we think we were going?

The motel was across the street from a strip mall, so at least we could do laundry and eat. There was a pizza and hoagie place, a cafe that served breakfast, and a convenience store that sold milk, chips, and other junk food. I was existing on Oreos and milk. Thanks to our disappearing social worker, we were getting food stamps. I don't know why they're called stamps. It's a plastic card that you spend like money. We soon discovered there are some items you're not allowed to buy, like wine. Emily found that out when she tried to use the card at the liquor store.

She rarely came with me when I went out, but she wanted to get some wine so we went together. She picked out a bottle at the liquor store and I had selected a bag of salty peanuts. The trouble started when she swiped the food stamp card. It didn't register. The man behind the counter said, "Lady, what are you trying to pull? You know you can't use that here."

Emily looked back at him, not comprehending. She was foggy all the time anyway and this was not registering with her at all. I was no help either. "What's the problem?" I asked.

He looked me over and said, "Is she buying this for you? How old are you?"

"I'm thirteen."

"Really? Why aren't you in school?"

I didn't know what to say. "What's wrong with the card? My mother just wants a bottle of wine."

He grabbed the card from Emily's hand, looked at it and copied something down on a piece of paper. "Did you just get this?" he asked Emily.

She nodded her head.

"Okay. I guess they didn't explain. You can't buy certain things. Wine, junk food. It's for basics. You see?"

Emily nodded again. I wished she didn't look so dazed. The man looked at me again. "I'm going to watch you. I've seen you outside the store. Don't be trying to get anyone else to buy you liquor, you understand me?"

"I...uh...I..." I was stunned. I couldn't speak.

"If I was you, I'd get myself back to school before you're arrested for truancy."

Arrested? I couldn't tell if he was serious. Could that happen? This shopping trip had turned into a major ordeal. Emily took my hand and we left as quickly as we could.

With nothing else to do, I discovered the world of daytime television. I had no idea what mindless yet addictive shows were on during the day, even without cable. I guess a lot of people don't have jobs or go to school and spend their days watching TV. There was an endless array of talk shows all morning long. The guests were people I'd never heard of.

Mostly doctors, a few people who had written books to give other people advice, mostly about eating right and losing weight. Different authors contradicted one another's advice. In the middle of the day, I watched soap operas. On those, everyone hooks up with everyone else's boyfriend, girlfriend, husband, or wife. The actors all gorgeous and they all sneak around and hope not to get caught. But they do. Or, even more incredibly, they grow a conscience and tell the truth. One time, this smoking hot guy slept with his girlfriend's sister. He was so guilt-stricken he decided to confess to his girlfriend. Now, I'd never had a boyfriend, but I could clearly see where this was going. I mean, really? Did this guy think his girlfriend was going to forgive him?

After the soaps, there were more talk shows, usually featuring people or houses in need of a make-over. I was stunned to discover that there were, apparently, dozens of ways to beat belly fat. If that was true, then I was confused as to why obesity was such a problem in America. See what I mean about contradictions? Then I began to worry that people became obese because everyone sat around eating Oreos and watching daytime TV like I was doing.

Later in the day, there were uber-depressing news shows. The world was in a terrible state. And Philadelphia must be the crime capital of the entire eastern seaboard. I always thought New Jersey was scary, but crime in Philly was through the ceiling. We didn't live that far outside the city, but I never knew any of this. Talk about being sheltered. I was learning way more from these shows than I ever learned in social studies.

That wasn't all I saw on the news. My mother and I were not the only the only ones who were homeless. I discovered there were thousands of people who lost their homes in the past year. The shape of the economy was as unhealthy as...well, as living on Oreo cookies. I was beginning to understand how Daddy's businesses crumbled. I found myself wondering why we didn't learn more about economics and money in school. Maybe I wouldn't have been so astonished when my family's economy came tumbling down. I always thought homeless people were drunks or crazy people who babbled to themselves as they sat on cardboard on the sidewalk. That is, if I thought about them at all. And never, ever did I think there was even a remote possibility that I, Cordelia Elizabeth Williams cheerleader and gymnast, would be one of them.

After two straight weeks of being indoors, when it finally stopped raining I made Emily get up and start sitting outside with me by the motel pool. I figured being outside in the sun would cheer her up. It definitely cheered me up. The weather was perfect. Warm, but not hot, and the humidity that would come later hadn't kicked in yet. I guess it shouldn't have been surprising, but we weren't the only welfare cases at the motel. Strangely enough, my mother made a friend who didn't look like she belonged on welfare any more than we did. When I first saw her, I couldn't help staring at her gorgeous complexion and her crimson hair. She reminded me of Christmas. Her skin was pure white like the linens my mother put on the dining room table at holidays and her hair reminded me of the red napkins we used to have. The contrast of her face against her dramatic red hair was striking.

Gloria was sitting by the pool one day when we came outside. She didn't notice us at first. She was wearing a straw hat that kept the sun off her face, a salmon-colored floating shirt, and white capris. She was looking down at a newspaper. Every once in a while she wrote in a little notebook. I stared at her for a while intrigued, and trying to figure out what someone so stylish was doing in a welfare motel, then I buried my nose in an **US Weekly** I'd found. Stupid Brad, Angelina, and their litter of children were on the cover. By the time I became engrossed reading about how celebrities fight cellulite, I realized she was staring at my mom. I looked over at Emily. Her eyes were shut.

"What's the matter?" I blurted out.

97

"Sorry. I didn't mean to stare. Shouldn't you be in school?"

"I'm sick."

"You seem to be sick a lot. I see you all the time." She looked at my mother. Emily opened her eyes. "Sorry. I was staring. You're a truly beautiful woman. But your roots! You really need a touch up."

My mother laughed. I was shocked. That was the first time I'd heard my mother laugh in months. It was a genuine laugh, too. Like she was really tickled.

"That's not all I need. Do I look that bad?"

"I'm a hair stylist. I notice these things. I'm Gloria Florence. I can do your hair for you, if you want."

"I was going to do it myself. Turns out you are not allowed to buy hair dye products with food stamps. Who knew? If the people who give out food stamps understood how important it is for a woman to look good when she's depressed and homeless, they might change their minds."

I was stunned. My mother was being so honest about everything.

But Gloria didn't raise even one of her perfectly arched eyebrows. "You are absolutely right! They're probably men."

My mother nodded. Gloria added, "And how could a woman with three inch roots ever hope to find a job?"

Little did Gloria know that my mother wasn't looking for work. She couldn't work. She was still such a mess. Besides, what would she do?

"I'm Emily Williams," my mother said. "I would love to have you do my hair, but I can't afford it. We barely have enough to get by."

I loved Gloria from the minute she said, "No problem! I need the practice. I don't want to get rusty." And she smiled this toothpaste commercial kind of smile (I was definitely watching too much television). She looked like an angel who'd flown straight from heaven down here to Motel Hell. I could tell she was lying. There was no way she was doing mom's hair for the practice. She was being kind.

~~

A couple of days later we were hanging out by the pool again. Emily had goop all over her head and we were waiting for it to do its magic. Gloria looked at Emily and asked, "What are you going to do next?"

My mother stared at her. "You mean today?"

"Don't you have a plan? For you and Delia?"

My mother shook her head. "I've never had to plan anything by myself."

"Never?" Gloria looked amazed.

"I had my parents, then I had my husband."

They sat for a while in silence. Then my mother looked at Gloria. "Do you have a plan?"

"I'm working on it. I'm trying to find a job at a salon. It's hard without a car. I lost that when I lost my business."

"You had your own business?" Now it was my mother's turn to be amazed. Gloria was around my mother's age, I guessed.

"I owned a salon and a day spa. *Elegante* in Narbeth. You know it?"

"I've been there. One of my friends gave me a gift certificate. I can't believe you owned that. You're homeless."

Gloria snapped back, "Well, I can't believe you were in my shop. *You're* homeless!"

"Sorry. I didn't mean it to sound like that. I just meant…What happened to you? To your business?" I hadn't seen my mother this engaged in anything for weeks.

Gloria looked away. I could tell this was hard for her to talk about. After a moment, she told us her story. "From the time I started doing hair I always knew I wanted my own shop. I had a vision. I knew exactly what I wanted to do and what my shop would be like. I even knew where it was going to be." She stopped. She cleared her throat.

My mother's voice was soft. "You don't have to tell me this."

"No. It's okay." Gloria breathed deeply and started again. "I worked for ten years and I saved as much as I could every month. Meanwhile, I took business classes at the community college. I learned how to write a business plan to show to the bank. Finally, when I thought I had saved enough, I took my plan and went to the bank for a small business loan." She put her hands on her cheeks and shook her head. "I don't know what I was thinking. I had no equity. No house. No co-signer. All I had was a fabulous plan. They turned me down. Told me I needed another fifty thousand. Or someone to co-sign the loan in case I defaulted."

"That would have sent me under the covers," Emily said.

Gloria smiled. "Not me. I had a dream. I saved for another *three* years. But it still wasn't enough." She pushed a piece of her beautiful red hair behind her ear. "It was like I was running to catch a bus, but the bus kept going faster and faster. I was never going to catch it at the rate I was going."

"But you didn't give up."

"I revised my tactics. One of my clients had some money to invest. She financed the rest of the money I needed to start *Elegante*. It was the only way I was going to be able to get my business going before I was fifty."

Emily shook her head. "Sounds too good to be true."

Gloria continued, "That was six years ago. It took a while, but I built up the business. It was thriving. I had figured I would pay back my investor in five years, tops. Then, the one thing I couldn't control happened. The economy came undone and so did my business. My clients were pretty upscale. Like you." She smiled. "As their discretionary funds dwindled, they began to cut back on luxuries. Like spa treatments. For a while, I thought the salon would hold me up. Everyone needs a haircut and a dye job, right Emily?" She looked at my mom and they both smiled.

Emily said. "It was all so easy. Until it wasn't."

"I couldn't make full payments. My investor was not happy. She threatened to sue me for my share of the business. I sold everything I had including my car to pay her. I kept hoping things were going to turn around any minute and I'd be alright. I was an idiot in denial."

Gloria went quiet. I knew how she felt. I hadn't wanted to accept we were losing everything until we did. I kept thinking there would be a happy ending. Someone would rescue us.

When Gloria spoke again, her voice was so soft I could barely hear her. "Nothing got better, of course. She took the business. My business. She hired someone to run *Elegante*. Everything I'd worked for all those years was gone."

I felt like I'd been struck by a train. The jolt was so hard it forced me to see everything clearly. I'd been struggling to understand my father for months. Gloria's story made me realize what my dad went through. He went from owning multiple businesses, to being in overwhelming debt. No wonder he didn't tell anyone. He must have felt like Gloria. Somehow, some way, he would turn it all around. How awful he must have felt. How scared and ashamed. I realized now why he didn't tell his family. I looked over at my mother. Did she get it?

"I'm so jealous of you," Emily said to Gloria.

Gloria stared at her with an expression showing her confusion.

"I'm serious," Emily said. "I've never wanted for anything. Never had to do anything for myself. I don't even know how to take care of my own daughter." She covered her eyes with her hand.

"I thought I was better than women like you," Emily said. "Working women. What an idiot I was. You are so much smarter than me. You had something. You knew what you wanted and you went after it. I thought I had everything because I had money. My husband's money. I wasted so much of it trying to feel good about myself."

And just when I thought I couldn't take any more, my mother looked at me. She said, "Can you ever forgive me? I put so many things before you. I drove your sister away and

101

your father is…Delia, I'm so sorry." And she broke down and sobbed as though her heart was breaking again.

Gloria looked rattled. "I never should have started this. Emily! Come on inside. We've got to get this stuff out of your hair. Delia, wait here for the big reveal."

When they went inside, I sat by the pool and thought about the future. About my future. Until this minute I thought the future was something that happened to you. I didn't realize you could actually plan your own destiny. Maybe things didn't work out the way you intended them, but Gloria had known what she wanted and went after her dream. That gave me a lot to think about.

I hoped that letting out her emotions would make Emily feel better. That and a new hairdo. I was happy my mother had found someone to talk to. But I was also envious. I missed having friends my own age. I decided that in September if Emily felt better, I'd go back to school. But until then it was going to be a long, lonely summer. The sun was shining overhead and it was a perfect spring day. I closed my eyes and tried to imagine what my future would look like.

Sometime later Gloria came outside, beaming.

"Hide your eyes," she ordered.

I did as I was told.

"Okay. Now open them!" Gloria said.

And there she was. Emily looked like she used to look. Her hair, which is naturally dark blonde, was back to being light with pieces of gold streaked through it. She wore full make-up which she didn't need, but it made her look like a movie star. Her smile radiated light and she was stunning. Best of all, she looked happy.

"Well, what do you think? Am I gorgeous?"

I hugged her. "Beautiful! I'm so glad you're my mother."

"Delia, that's the nicest thing you've ever said to me. You're going to make me cry and my mascara's going to drip all over my new face!"

I looked at Gloria. "Thank you," I said. I wished I could explain to her what it meant to see my mother look like this again. Beautiful, smiling, self-assured Emily.

Gloria brushed off the thanks. "Next time I'll give you a make-over, Delia. Are you in, sweetie?"

"Only if you make me look like that!" I smiled at her. "I know. You can only work with what you've got."

"Baby, you've got plenty," she said, ensuring I was her friend for life. "But we'll make you more age-appropriate."

~~

Later that night Gloria sat outside with me. Mom was sleeping. She had gone all weepy again for no real reason and Gloria had given her a pill of some kind to help her sleep.

"How old is your sister?" Gloria asked.

"She'll be eighteen in two months. July."

"Do you know where she is?"

I shook my head, no.

"Can you try to find her?"

"We've tried. Why?"

"You need her. I'm no shrink, but being a hair stylist kind of qualifies me to know certain things. It's like being a bartender. You hear it all and you see it all."

"I don't understand."

"Delia sweetie, I'm worried about you. I'm pretty sure your mom is clinically depressed. Or worse. She told me what happened to your dad and about losing the house. Sometimes an event, a traumatic event, can trigger a kind of mental illness. In other words, she's not getting over this without help. Serious help."

"I'll make her go to the doctor. We've got that card, now. Medicaid. I'll get her treatment. She'll be okay." I needed to believe that. She might not have been a model mom, but she was the only mother I had. The only person I had.

"Not so fast," Gloria was saying. "It's not that simple. If they diagnose your mom with anything serious and they find out she's all you've got, family services could step in and take you."

I pictured joyless Joy Pierce as I stared at Gloria. "What does that mean? Exactly?" I couldn't take one more thing. I just couldn't.

"I don't mean to upset you. You've been through so much already. But it could mean they'd put you in a foster home."

The first time I jumped off the high dive at our swim club, I was terrified. I jumped feet first, too afraid to dive. Which was weird because I was never afraid of heights when I was on top of the pyramid, cheering. I remember when I hit the water in the pool, my body pushed down, down, down. At some point I had to hit the bottom, I thought. Everything progressed in slow motion as I traveled through the water. Eventually, I became certain I was going to run out of air and drown. A strange calm took over me as I prepared myself to die.

Hearing these words from Gloria made me feel exactly the same way I felt in the pool. Would I ever hit the bottom and start to come up? Or was I going to drown?

In the book *Tuck Everlasting*, the main character Winnie has to choose between immortality with a boy she loves or staying in the real world; the world she's familiar with. These were your basic rock and hard place choices. I felt like Winnie. I was torn between two unbearable possibilities. I had to choose between my mother's mental health or possibly going off to foster care. I had no idea how to make that kind of decision.

My optimism knows no limits. Either that or I am the stupidest person on the planet. My mother needed help and I decided to take my chances. I gambled that nothing bad would happen to me because I was trying to get her help. My experience so far with social services added to my optimism. Joy, the social worker, had never returned. As far as I knew, I had no case worker. I totally dropped out of eighth grade and no one had come looking for me.

At first, Emily refused to go to the doctor. I promised her I'd go back to school if she went, so she agreed. I was lying.

There was no way I was going back now. We'd see what happened in September. First things first.

With Gloria's help, we found a clinic that accepted the Medicaid card Joy had given us when she gave us our food stamp card. We made an appointment, using the phone in the motel office. When it was the day of the appointment, my mother and I took the bus to the doctor. It took us a while to figure out the whole bus thing. People take busses every day and we felt ridiculous because we had no idea what to do. All we ever did was jump in our car. One more luxury I'd taken for granted. I never thought of our car as a privilege. I'd never considered what people did for rides if they didn't have a car.

Eventually we got to the doctor's office. After sitting in the waiting room of the free clinic for nearly two hours we finally went inside. The doctor, a woman named Dr. Roslyn, asked Emily a bunch of questions and then told my mother she was depressed. As if we didn't know that. Dr. Roslyn was concerned that my mother might be bipolar. The doctor explained that sometimes a life-changing event can trigger this disorder. When Dr. Roslyn described the symptoms, one of them was out of control spending! When she said that, I almost fell out of my chair. Maybe my mother had this all along.

Dr. Roslyn also said that people who are bipolar have dramatic mood swings and their energy levels change drastically. They can go from being hyper-energetic to complete lethargy. Couch potatoes. I thought of the way my mother used to exercise like a maniac. I didn't remember any of the couch potato symptoms before Daddy died. But I was never home. I was either in school or at practice. Maybe she'd had those periods and I didn't see them. So many things the doctor said were true of my mom long before Daddy died. Somewhere along in the conversation, my mother seemed to tune out. Dr. Roslyn talked directly to me and explained everything slowly and clearly. I felt comfortable enough to ask her some questions. Her kindness tricked me. I thought I was safe.

When she had answered all my questions, she looked directly at me and said, "I need to tell you something, Cordelia. And then I need to ask you something." And then she paused.

My heart was standing still. I had no idea what was going to happen next. Was she going to call the authorities and have me taken away? Would I have to grab my mother's hand, yank her out of the office and run like hell to escape? Could I do that? Could my mother?

"Cordelia. Are you listening? This is important." Dr. Roslyn's voice forced me back. I had to stop freaking out.

"Yes."

"This kind of depression can run in families. As can bipolar disorder. I'm not saying this to frighten you. I just want you to be aware throughout your lifetime that you may be susceptible to depression. You need to remember that in the future. If there is ever a time that you feel depressed for what seems like a long time, you need to seek treatment. Do you understand?"

I nodded.

"You've had a lot to deal with, but you seem to be handling everything remarkably well. I need to ask you, who's there to help you? Delia, who's taking care of *you*?"

I didn't miss a beat. "My grandma. My dad's mom." Emily had already told Dr. Roslyn her parents were dead.

"Good." Dr. Roslyn appeared relieved. "I was worried. Your mother is not capable right now of taking care of herself, or you. You both need help. If your grandmother is overwhelmed, I can contact family services. They can help, too." She was so nice it make me a little sick to lie to her.

"We're alright. But I'll mention it to Grandma."

"Maybe she can come next time. I'd like to talk to her." She'd been talking to me as though my mother wasn't in the room. Now, she turned to Emily. "Mrs. Williams. Emily. I want to see you back here in two weeks. Do you have any questions?"

We left with some samples of medications for anxiety and depression. Dr. Roslyn explained how important it was for Emily to take the drugs every single day. Dr. Roslyn also wanted Emily to see a therapist, but the clinic where we were didn't have one. She gave us a phone number of a shrink at another clinic some distance away. I had no idea how we'd get there. Before we tackled that problem, there was the fact that we didn't have a phone which made it challenging to make appointments. Nothing about being poor was simple.

My mother was silent on the bus ride home. I wondered if she was upset or relieved at her diagnosis. I didn't ask.

~~

Someone was banging on the door. I sat up and looked at the clock radio. 8:30. Who would be knocking at this hour of the morning? I waited, hoping they would go away. More banging, then I heard someone call my name. I wanted to hide and pretend I wasn't there.

"Mrs. Williams? Cordelia? Open the door or I'll have to get the manager." I wanted to hide in the closet or climb out of the bathroom window and run away. I looked over at my mother in the other bed. She'd put a pillow over her head to block out the noise. The knocking continued. I got out of bed and opened the door.

"There you are. I was starting to worry," Joy Pierce said in a tone that sounded anything but worried. I waited for what came next. I knew it wasn't going to be good, but I could never have predicted how bad her presence was going to be.

Joy brushed past me and came in the room. Emily was sitting up in bed by now and looked disoriented. She had been this way for days. The anti-depressant drugs weren't working. In fact, they seemed to make her worse. She looked stoned. Dr. Roslyn had said that might happen. Everyone had unique body chemistry so people had different reactions to drugs. To me, the whole thing sounded like a human science experiment. Joy Pierce stared at Emily for what seemed like an hour.

Finally she asked Emily, "What's the matter with you?"

Emily shook her head. "Nothing. Just not awake yet." She slurred her words and sounded like she had swallowed cloth.

"Hmm." Then she turned to me. Joy tilted her head and said quietly, "Cordelia, you haven't been to school. Have you, dear?"

"You never called. I had no idea where to go. Or how to get there." She was going to make this my fault.

"Someone reported you. My office got a call that a girl from this motel was not going to school."

Who could have called? I mentally went through the list of possibilities. Gloria? She'd never...

"It was reported that you were trying to get alcohol and that your mother seemed, well...disoriented."

"That's a lie!" Emily was on her feet now and she looked like she wanted to scratch Joy Pierce's face off. I prayed she didn't. I couldn't imagine Emily in jail.

"Which part?" Joy asked, calmly. "Is she going to school?"

I answered before Emily could. "No. I can't leave my mother. She's not..." I stopped, realizing I was making this worse, not better.

"Just as I thought," Joy said. "I have to make some calls. I'll be back in a few minutes. Stay here!" she ordered as she left the room. Emily started to cry uncontrollably. I wanted to go get Gloria, but I was afraid to go outside. I sat on the bed hugging my mother, trying to comfort her. I wanted her to get herself together before Joy came back and saw her like this.

Before I could figure out what to do, the door opened and Joy's tall frame filled the entrance to our room. "Pack your things. I'll be back in an hour. Emily, I'm going to take you somewhere to get help. I know you won't think so right now, but this is for own good." I felt Emily go limp in my arms, like she had given up.

"NO! You can't do that," I yelled at Joy.

"I know this seems harsh, but you see, I can't pretend I don't see what's happening here. I got chewed out, Cordelia, for not following up and getting you into school. It's on me, now. I have to dot my Is and cross my Ts where you and your mother are concerned or I may lose my job. Do you understand?" Her tone was soothing, like warm water in a bubble bath. But her words were like razor blades, thin and sharp, waiting to slice you open.

I shook my head. No. I didn't understand anything.

"You should have gone to school, dear. Even if I didn't come back. Now it's my problem. So I'm going to hospitalize your mother and you will be placed in temporary foster care. Where you *will* go to school. Now am I making myself clear?"

All the air left the room and I could no longer breathe.

Joy Pierce smiled a small smile, showing no teeth. "You'll see. It's for your own good. Now pack and get ready. I'll be back soon."

~ ~

Gloria didn't say a word as I told her what had just happened. When I finished, she asked, "Are you packed?"

"No."

"Get to it. There's no time to waste."

I stared at her. She was my final hope and here she was, telling me to pack. She was going to send me off to a foster home.

"What are you waiting for? We've got to get out of here," she said. "Come back to my room in ten minutes. No longer!"

"We? We've got to get out of here?"

"Yes. Move it!"

Fifteen minutes later we were at a bus stop. Gloria, my stoned mother, me, and three suitcases; one for each of us. We left half of what little we had. I don't think I took a breath until we climbed on the bus. I was sure Joy would pull up any second and cart me off to a foster home and put Emily away somewhere horrible.

"Do you know where we're going?" I asked Gloria when we were safely seated.

Gloria looked nervous as she explained. "I went into Philly last week to look at a tent city someone told me about. It's called Hardscrabble Way. I talked to Chief Cheyenne and after

109

he interviewed me, he gave me permission to move in. I was going to wait until the first of next month but..." She pulled a folded sheet of paper out of her pocket. "We have to get a few supplies first, though. And we have to read the rules and make sure we can live by them. Once we sign off we're in."

"Are you sure you want to do this?" I looked at her. "You're not the one in trouble."

"I was going tell you both about it when I made my final decision. Invite you to come with me. This just hurried the process along."

"What's a tent city?" I asked.

"Just what it sounds like. A bunch of homeless people form a group and live in tents. Most of them are off in the woods. This one happens to be in the middle of the city. Under an abandoned overpass. It's set apart, so it seems remote, but it's in the heart of Philly."

"Is it safe?" I asked.

"The Chief runs a tight community. Once you're in, you have to live within the rules or you're out."

"But you have a place to live. And the motel is indoors." I didn't get this tent city concept at all.

"Look, talking to you about my old shop has made me more determined than ever to get back on my feet. We'll be closer to Septa busses and trains, which will improve my chances of finding work. Plus, no rent. I can save my rent allocation and put it towards a deposit on an apartment." She paused a second. "Well, if I don't get caught and arrested for welfare fraud."

Emily looked up. "Hardscrabble Way? What does that mean?"

"Everything runs on propane. Hot water for the shower, small heaters. Fortunately, we won't need to worry about heat for a few months." She shook her head. "I'm not saying this will be easy, but it will give us time to save and keep Delia out of a foster home. What do you want to do, Emily?"

Emily was snapping out of her stupor. "Let me see if I'm getting this. We're going to live in a tent under a bridge with a community of homeless people?"

"Yeah. That's it."

"That's it? You say that like your telling me you just bought a cute condo in Ardmore. You make it sound perfectly ordinary."

"This is my new normal. I run with homeless people now and I'm trying to make the best of it. You'll see. What they've done is pretty impressive." Gloria wasn't faking this good mood. She appeared genuinely enthusiastic. I wondered if she was trying to keep Emily's spirits up.

"I hate being outdoors. It's too hot or too cold or there's bugs." That was the truth. Emily had always hated being outside. Unless we were at the beach house.

Gloria raised her eyebrows. "But you were always outside, at the motel."

"I hated that room more than I hated being outdoors," my mother said, her voice hushed. "I couldn't even stand to go in there to sleep."

She'd never told me that. Remarkably, my mother had never complained about anything.

"Do you think I should be in a hospital?" she asked, looking at Gloria. Her voice was a whisper.

Gloria took my mother's hands in hers, looked her straight in the eyes and said, "No, honey. You need rest and you need to grieve. You need to keep taking the meds and give them a chance to work. You don't need to be in a hospital away from this child in order to do that."

Emily nodded her head. "One more thing. *Who is Chief Cheyenne*? Is this a Native American thing?"

Gloria laughed. "I'll tell you all about him. Quite the character."

Gloria had become our lifeline. She was the only person who cared about us. She was, in fact, the only person who even knew where we were. We had told no one where we were going when we moved. I hadn't said goodbye to anyone. I wanted to. Especially to Margot and her family. But I couldn't. I couldn't bear to see how they would have looked at me. That look that all my friends had at Daddy's funeral. Pity. Combined with sorrow. Combined with relief. Relief that this was happening to me and not them. No. Saying "goodbye, I'm moving to a welfare motel" was not an option.

But it worried me that no one knew where we were. At night when I couldn't sleep, which was most of the time, I thought about Rachel. What would happen if Rachel came back? She would find us gone from our home. The neighbors would tell her what happened to Daddy, but they had no idea how to find us. I had mom and now we both had Gloria. Rachel had no one, as far as we knew. I stopped myself. I couldn't think too much about Rachel. The possibilities were terrifying, and for now there wasn't a thing I could do about finding her.

PART 2

CHAPTER 1
June, 2012

"What are you thinking about, Delia?" my mother asked.

My mother's eyes were clear. She looked good. Maybe the drugs were working.

I waited a moment before I decided to tell her the truth.

"I was wondering...do you have a plan? Are you thinking about looking for a job?" I was terrified my questions would upset my mother, but I needed to know what kind of future we were looking at. Gloria already had a job as a stylist on Walnut Street in Center City working for an upscale salon and day spa. They loved her resume and after her interview they gave her a try out. After she did a cut, color, and foils they hired her on the spot.

Emily let out a long breath. "I've been thinking about work. I didn't realize you were...well, I'm sorry I didn't say anything to you. I'm still trying to figure out what to do. I have to find work. I can't risk losing you."

"No. It's...it's fine. Really. I shouldn't have..." I stopped.

"I don't have any clothes," my mother said.

"What?"

"I keep thinking I'll go into the city and look for work in a high end decorator's shop. Or something. But then I realize I have nothing to wear."

I didn't know whether to laugh or cry. Leave it to Emily to make lack of an outfit her biggest issue. I made my face completely neutral before I spoke.

"There's that place in Philly Gloria told us about. The gently used shop where she got a bunch of clothes. We could go."

"Right. She also mentioned the consignment place where people get rid of the designer clothes they're sick of wearing. Or wore once." She smiled. "Like I used to."

I shrugged. I didn't want to upset her. I remembered the conversation. Gloria had also said the consignment clothes were overpriced and she couldn't afford them.

"Yeah. We could look there, too," I said.

"That would be great! All I'd need is one good outfit. You know. To make the right impression."

I heard Denny yelling from outside the tent.

"Delia. I'm outside. Let's go. I don't have all day."

"Plans with Denny? You going swimming?" she asked.

"No. No. We're going…he just wants to show me something. We'll be back around lunchtime. He has to work at 1."

I hated lying. Especially to my mother.

"Is it okay if I go with him?" I asked.

She smiled. "I'm glad you have someone to hang out with. He's a really nice kid. So is Daryl."

I hated leaving her alone, especially since Gloria was working. But today it couldn't be helped. I hugged her and hurried outside. I called over my shoulder as I left. "Let's make a plan. We'll find you something nice to wear."

I didn't want to tell my mother where we were going. Denny had called and made an appointment for me with a guidance counselor at Center High School. If things didn't go well, if I was going to have to repeat eighth grade, I didn't want to upset Emily just when she was starting to feel better.

On the way there I looked over at Denny. "Thank you. I would never have done this alone."

"Don't worry. I'm here for you, Deal."

I didn't want him to know how terrified I was. I was scared of going high school, especially since it was in the middle of the city, but most of all I was scared of not going to high school. What if they didn't let me in?

In order to avoid talking about my fear, I talked about Emily instead.

"Sometimes…" I stopped. I wasn't sure I could say what I was thinking.

"Sometimes?" he egged me on.

"Sometimes I think I screwed up. What if Joy Pierce was right and Emily would be better off in a hospital getting help?"

"No way! There's no possible way she'd be able to get better thinking she was responsible for you going to a foster home. She'd never get better. Besides, state hospitals are a nightmare."

"Really?"

"You don't know the kind of care she'd get in a state hospital. She could get worse."

Everything Denny was saying made sense.

"She needs time to heal," Denny continued. "She'll rest, take her meds, and you'll be there for her. You'll see. Emily will get better, stronger."

"I guess."

"You should go back to the clinic. See what they say."

I sighed. I wasn't sure I could talk my mother into going back. She was ready to go shopping.

~ ~

We were in an office across from a tall African American man named Mr. St. Clair. Denny did most of the talking, occasionally looking over at me and saying, "Right, Delia?"

He told Mr. St. Clair more of my story than I would have. Way more. Mr. St. Clair nodded and took notes while Denny rattled on. The only significant thing Denny left out was where we were living. We had agreed it wasn't a good idea to be truthful, with Joy Pierce hanging over my head. Social services probably wouldn't approve of under-aged kids living in a tent city. We used the same address Denny used when he registered. It was, in fact, his old apartment. Gloria had a post office box and we used that as my mailing address. We put down Denny's cell as my phone. As we had rehearsed, we told Mr. St. Clair Denny was my cousin and that Emily and I moved in with the Jaxsons when we lost our house. A few tiny lies, but most of the story was true. Denny even went so far as to tell Mr. St. Clair how depressed Emily was and that's why she didn't come with us.

I sat tapping my foot, dry-mouthed, and sweating. When Denny stopped talking, Mr. St. Clair continued to take notes. When he finished, he looked up at me.

"You've been through quite a lot for a very young lady. I'm truly sorry." He had an accent that sounded French, but I wasn't sure. It was elegant though, and made him sound very smart. I was starting to feel better about guidance counselors.

"I can certainly assist you in getting back into school. But…"

"But" was never a good word. In my experience, when people said "but" the words following the b word were never what you wanted to hear. I panicked and was sorry I had let Denny talk me into this. I didn't want to listen to what he was going to say next. I wished I could put my hands over my ears.

"But," he repeated, "You're too late to apply for Central. You missed the deadline for this year. I can however, help you to get into another school in the city."

"No," Denny interrupted.

Mr. St. Clair raised his eyebrows.

"She lives here. With me. My family. You can't split us up. After all she's been through, she needs me. Please, Mr. St. Clair, can't you bend the rules?"

Mr. St. Clair explained the entire procedure to us in his lovely accent. Basically, all the applications were processed through a director on Broad Street who reviewed the transcripts of each applicant and each spring decided who got in and who didn't. Some Philadelphia schools, like Central, were more desirable because they had better records overall. There were a ton of applicants and getting accepted was competitive. When the counselor was done talking, Denny looked at me. My face must have shown how defeated I felt. Denny looked back at Mr. St. Clair.

"Isn't there any other way? Can't you…just…skip some of those steps? She's been through enough."

The pause seemed to last an hour. I just wanted to get out of his office, at that point. Finally Mr. St. Clair asked, "Delia, is it alright with you if I call your old school? I want to ask them to fax over your transcripts so I can take a look at them."

He asked us to wait outside while he called.

"We should go," I said as soon as we were back in the outer office.

"Don't be ridiculous. He didn't say no. Sit down," Denny ordered and so I sat.

Denny and I sat watching the clock, not saying a word for forty-five minutes. I was afraid to get my hopes up. The secretary must have felt sorry for us because after a while she offered us some cookies. Denny took two. "Thanks. I'm starving," he said. She urged him to take more. I couldn't think about eating anything. I was ready to give up. I thought Mr. St. Clair had forgotten us and I was about to tell Denny we should leave, when the door opened and he asked us to come back inside. After apologizing for taking so long, Mr. St. Clair tapped his finger on his desk for a long moment. I braced myself. I was prepared for the worst. I was going to have to repeat eighth grade. Or go to a different high school, away from the only friend I had.

"Delia, I had a long talk with your former principal, Mr. Rose. He had wonderful things to say about you. You had impressive grades. He was quite disconcerted to hear that you had not been going to school. We put our heads together and came up with what I believe is a viable solution for your...situation."

Whenever adults used fancy words when regular ones would do, I got nervous. I couldn't imagine what they had come up with. At least he hadn't said "but." So far.

"I'm going to give you your final exams for your eighth grade courses. If you pass them, Mr. Rose will issue your eighth grade diploma and you will have graduated with full credit. Then, I can register you here for September."

Denny jumped up out of his seat. "That's amazing news, Delia."

"Really?" Stunned, I thought about my prayers, the God box, and the hedgehog.

I didn't know what to say. It had been a long time since I'd heard good news. "All I have to do is pass my finals? When?"

Mr. St. Clair tapped his finger again and I realized he was tapping on a manila folder. "Mr. Rose faxed them over. You can take them whenever you like."

"Do it now, Deal." Denny looked at me.

I reminded him he had to go to work. Besides, I wasn't confident I could pass the algebra test. I missed about eight weeks of school at the end.

Denny called Daryl to explain where we were. Daryl told him to stay with me. He said he would pick Denny up later. So I decided to stay and take the English and social studies finals. We made a plan to come back on Thursday to take science and algebra. Mr. St. Clair lent me an algebra book to study from and told me not to worry.

By the time we went back on Thursday, he had graded my two exams and I passed them both. But those weren't the exams I was worried about. They were both essay exams and I was a good writer. Science and math were a whole other story. I took the science test first and it was pretty easy. I struggled with the algebra, but I felt like I might have passed. We waited while Mr. St. Clair graded the exams.

I ended up passing the Algebra exam with a C. I was pretty sure Mr. St. Clair cut me some slack. A lot of slack. It was shocking how much math I'd forgotten in such a short time. After he gave me my grades Mr. St. Clair helped me choose my courses and I registered for classes. I didn't know if my prayers were working or if I was just due for some good luck. Either way I was over the moon with relief. Before I left, Mr. St. Clair said, "Mr. Rose told me what a good athlete you are, Cordelia.

I expect you to try out for our teams in September." I thanked him a million times.

As soon as we got outside Denny picked me up and spun me around. "Stop! You're making me dizzy," I laughed. But I wasn't dizzy and I didn't want him to stop. When he finally stood still, I hugged him tightly, holding on a little bit longer than I should have. I don't know what came over me, but while he had me up in the air, I leaned in and kissed him. A full-on mouth kiss, not a peck on your cheek thank-you kiss. It was my first kiss so I had nothing to compare it to, but even I could tell, he didn't resist. Denny kissed me back. When the kiss broke we looked each other straight in the eyes. "I don't know how to thank you," I said and he lowered my feet back to the ground. The whole event was over in a swift second. And then we both acted as if nothing had happened.

I couldn't wait to go home and tell my mother and Gloria. As excited as Denny was, Emily was even more thrilled. "Why didn't you tell me where you were going? I would have gone with you," she said. Her face was glowing and she was shining from her inside out. I never thought I'd ever see her look that happy again.

"I wouldn't have had the courage to go to register without Denny," I said. He and I took turns telling her the story, interrupting each other and finishing each other's sentences. When I told her how Denny had stuck up for me and gotten Mr. St. Clair to bend the rules, her eyes filled and she hugged him so long he started to squirm. Then, Emily being Emily, she grinned at me and said, "We're going to have to get you some new school clothes!" It felt familiar. Some things hadn't changed.

"What about cheerleading?" she asked. "Did you ask about tryouts?"

"I completely forgot. I'll ask as soon as school starts."

I had eight weeks before I'd be in high school. Thoughts of Joy Pierce faded to the background of my worries. She still loomed as a danger, but as time passed, she had become a more distant threat.

Images of my father were drifting away. He was becoming more faded around the edges. I could see his face, but I had to look at a photo to be sure that the image I had in my mind was him. I couldn't hear his voice any more. I thought we'd packed some family DVDs and put them in storage when we moved, but I wasn't sure and I didn't want to ask my mother. If I didn't remember, it was doubtful she did. I didn't want to risk upsetting her.

As time passed, Rachel was growing fainter, too. I recalled events, of course. The pain and guilt over what I had done to her was still sharp. The whole idea that there *was* a Rachel became unreal. It was as though I had invented her like a make-believe friend. I plotted ways to find her, but they all seemed unrealistic. I had no starting point and so Rachel, like my father was fading further away from me.

If it was troubling not to be able to recapture the essence of my sister and my father, that was nothing compared to the struggle I had trying to remember who my mother used to be. A few months earlier my mother was self-assured, poised, and always knew what to say in every situation. That seemed like a long time ago. Emily had changed.

~~

I wished we had never taken the bus into Center City to go shopping. We were going to look for school clothes for me and an interview outfit for my mother. Her sheer terror at taking the bus into Philadelphia disturbed me more than witnessing her crawl under her covers when Daddy died. The formerly classy, gorgeous Emily came unraveled on the bus. She clutched my hand until it hurt. She was visibly frightened. So much so, I was afraid her silent melt-down would be noticed and someone would call the police or an ambulance. I feared that this simple trip would lead me straight to Joy Pierce and into the grip of the social services system.

After what seemed like the longest ride ever, I was relieved to be finally off the bus. I had hoped that Emily's anxiety would fade, but as we walked from the bus stop to the consignment shop, her head moved in jerky motions as she scrutinized the crowds. She moved along the city street as though she had never been out in public before. Her arm was hooked through mine and she held on as if for dear life.

"We're not far," I tried to assure her. "Gloria's directions are easy to follow."

She nodded. I felt her arm tighten through mine. "I'm sorry I freaked on the bus. I've never…I don't know how to do this," she whispered.

I wanted to suggest we turn around and head back to Hardscrabble Way, but I knew I couldn't manage to take her on my own. Our plan was to meet Gloria after we finished shopping and the three of us were going to go back together. I needed Gloria. Now, I just had to get Emily into a store. Maybe, I wished, Emily's old shopping instincts would return and she'd snap out of this fearful state she was in.

Consignments by Crystal had beautiful things. Emily did brighten up when we walked through the door. There were Louis Vuitton handbags on a shelf near the front and she touched one lightly, as though greeting an old friend she hadn't seen for a while. Glancing around, the store was filled with racks of clothing and there were a few people shopping. Toward the back of the store I saw shelves filled with boots and shoes. My mother saw where I was looking and said, "Go. Look. I'm okay."

She did look better. I had packed a pair of boots when we left our house, but I left them when we fled the hotel and escaped from Joy Pierce. I headed back toward a pair of boots that were calling me. The first thing I did was look at the price. Gloria had been right. Although the boots were used and cheaper than new ones, there were no bargains here. I put the boot down and as I did, I heard a bell jingle as the front door

121

opened. Three girls around my age entered the store talking and laughing just like I used to do with Margot and Alexa. A woman in a yellow sundress wearing white sandals was with them. She pushed her sunglasses to the top of her head and said something to one of the girls who rolled her eyes and nodded. This was all so familiar. I knew that look. That was the look I used to give my mother.

The girls were each lugging several shopping bags and headed right to the cashier where they dumped out what was in the bags. At first I thought they were returning things, but after a moment I realized they were here to get rid of items they didn't want anymore. Then it hit me. I used to be them. Now, I was here to buy their cast-offs and, what was worse, I couldn't even afford those.

"Let's go." Emily was standing next to me. She had tears in her eyes.

"What's wrong?"

"I found a perfect suit. Chanel. Anyone would hire me if I wore it."

I couldn't help myself. Like a bee instinctively drawn to suck nectar from a flower, involuntarily I turned away from Emily to watch as the girls left the store, all talking at once. They didn't have a care in the world. The mom shifted her sunglasses back from the top of her head to her face with one hand, as she held the door for the girls with the other. One of them, a pretty blonde with long legs like Margot, said something to her and she tossed back her head and laughed. The door closed causing the bell to ring once more. And, like my old life, they were gone.

"It cost $1500 new. Maybe more," Emily was saying. "It's a steal at $400.

"So…" I knew without asking.

"$400 might as well be $4000. We don't have that kind of money."

"Show me the suit," I said.

When she held it up I knew she was right. The suit, off-white with black piping, screamed Emily. It was elegant, expensive-looking, and no one seeing her in that suit would ever be able to say no to her. This was the perfect get-a-job outfit.

"Let's go," she said. "Maybe I can find something at the thrift store. Gloria said it's just a few blocks away, right?"

"I kept your earrings," I said.

"What?"

"Not the big diamonds. The middle-sized ones. I didn't sell them with the other jewelry. I kept them in case of an emergency."

"Losing our house wasn't an emergency?"

"They weren't going to save the house. And this is an emergency."

"How?"

"You need to get a job if we're ever going to stop being homeless. This is an investment in your future. Our future."

She was quiet for a while. Then she asked, "Where are they?"

"Are you mad I kept them?"

"No."

"They're in my bra. I keep them with me all the time."

We asked the woman behind the register in the consignment store where we could sell the earrings. I knew, even as we walked to the jewelry exchange, that this was insane. Buying a $400 suit for my mother when we were living in a tent made little sense. And yet, it was easy to convince myself it was a sensible thing to do. If it gave my mother her confidence back, if it gave her the courage to go out and look for a job… if it made her feel like Emily again, well, it was worth every penny.

On the way back to *Consignments by Crystal*, I confessed to my mother that I still had the small diamond earrings, too. The ones Rachel loved. "I couldn't bear to sell them," I told her. "I'm sorry."

Her eyes filled for the second time that day and she hugged me as we stood there in the middle of the sidewalk.

"It was the right thing to do. She's coming back to us. She has to."

Talking about Rachel had made her real again. I could see her walking away from me, down the driveway that cold November day. I was overcome with remorse. I had to make things right. I had to find my sister.

CHAPTER 2
July, 2012

I tried to keep to a schedule. I spent the early part of my mornings working on routines to keep in shape for cheerleading. After I worked out, I concentrated on my summer reading for Honors English. Then lunch. After lunch I worked on my plan to find Rachel. I was struggling with both reading and making a plan. I needed an ideal spot in order to read. To locate my sister, I needed the internet.

I missed my favorite spot in our sunroom on the side of the house. There were windows on three sides and sunlight followed the room all day long. Even in winter, it was the brightest room in the house. There was a stone fireplace that you lit by flicking a switch. It was the best place to curl up and read. My spot was an over-stuffed velvet chair opposite the fireplace. Draped over the back of the chair was a cashmere throw that was as soft as a cloud. I'd wrapped myself in the blanket and disappear into the pages of my book. It was the only place I was ever able to read.

I tried to read in our tent, but I couldn't. One morning, after I worked out I took a walk. I brought my book along in case I found an inviting spot. I hadn't gone too far away from the tents, when I found an alcove just off the path. Small and grassy, it looked promising, so I sat and leaned against a narrow tree trunk and settled into my book. I had to read three books before school started. I thought I'd start with *A Separate Peace* because I find it hard to read books with boy characters.

I stopped when I became hungry. Forty pages was a good start. I decided to finish the chapter and head back for lunch, when I heard leaves crunching. It sounded like footsteps, but I wasn't sure. I hadn't told anyone where I was going and now I thought maybe it was foolish of me to come here by myself. I was positive someone was coming down the path. I didn't know whether to hide or just stay put. While I was deciding, the light was blocked by a shadow and a man was on the path standing right in front of me. He stood there, looking down at me. I felt vulnerable and stupid for being there, when I realized I knew him. I wasn't sure I should feel relieved, though. It was Sarge, the veteran who served in Iraq. The one the Chief said didn't talk to anyone. He had never spoken to me before.

"You shouldn't be here alone," he said. "It's not safe."

I nodded. "Okay," I said.

He stood there not speaking for a long while. I wasn't afraid of him, although I probably should have been. He didn't seem scary as much as he seemed sad and lost. Ultimately, I realized he wasn't going to speak again.

"I'm Delia. Do you want to walk back with me?" I asked.

He nodded. I got up and we started back towards Hardscrabble Way. Neither of us said a word. I had never met anyone who had been in a war. I tried to imagine what he had seen or done when he was in Iraq. I wanted to ask him, but I knew I couldn't. Until Sarge, I don't think I ever thought wars were real. If I thought about them at all, I thought of them more like science fiction stories. You know, made-up worlds like the Matrix. For some reason, Sarge and his silence shocked me into understanding that there was a place, many places, in the world where war was real. My life here didn't seem so terrible by comparison.

"Thank you for walking me, Sarge," I said when we got back to the tent city.

He nodded. I started to walk away.

"I'll go with you tomorrow," he said. "If you want."

"I'd like that," I said. I waved goodbye as I turned and walked back to my tent.

~~

"Do you want something to drink?" I asked Emily as we sat outside our tent one night hoping for a breeze to spring up and cool us off. It was so still, the sound of my voice startled her. She was barefoot, wearing shorts and a tank top. She was thinner than ever, but somehow still looked muscular and fit. And beautiful. To me, my mother's beauty was like a fairy tale. The kind where the queen was magnificent and you were drawn to her even though she had some fatal flaw that would be her undoing.

The night was silent with heat. Leaves didn't move, birds didn't sing, critters didn't stir, and there was no hum of voices in the background. The air hung heavy with humidity, though it hadn't rained for a long while. Not that I wished it would rain. The tent got damp and cold when it rained and sometimes it took days for the mud outside to dry up. Every day seemed to get hotter. Summer had always been my favorite season. But that was when I had air conditioning. I had never before spent any time, anywhere without air conditioning. Except for the beach. There, we had the sea breezes and the chilly ocean to cool us down. Remembering the beach made me think about Rachel and our summers in Sea Isle City. Back then, we dreaded fall and the return to school. It wasn't even that we minded school so much as the routine. Summers meant sleeping in, staying up late, not having to be anywhere at a certain time. And of course, no homework. Now, experiencing the true heat and humidity of a summer night I found myself wishing for fall for the first time in my life, even though I was anxious about starting a new school. Once I was in school I could go to the library and have regular access to the internet, which would make it easier to find my sister. I wondered if Rachel was somewhere safe, if she ever longed for our beach summers. If she ever thought about me. My head throbbed. The night, the heat, and my own thoughts enveloped me until I felt as though I would suffocate.

"Did you ever notice the blackbirds?" Emily asked, her question disturbing the silence.

I shook my head.

"There are three of them," she pointed up to a branch on her right. "They sit right there."

"No," I said. "I haven't seen them."

"Blackbirds are ominous."

"What?"

"Nothing," she said.

127

"You're feeling better, aren't you?" I asked her.

Her attempt to find work had been a setback. She had researched the top interior design studios in the city and, dressed in her $400 off-white Chanel suit, she had gone to each one and applied to work as a designer. She had never anticipated rejection. Each asked her for her resume. She had none. Each asked her about her previous experience. None. They all wanted to know where she had interned. I suppose she should have known how this all worked. One place was blunt enough to tell her that for a forty-year-old she was incredibly naïve to think she could walk in unannounced and expect to be hired in a high-end design studio. Two places offered to let her intern for no pay.

Emily had returned defeated and furious. She felt demeaned and insulted that she had been offered a job for no salary. I was relieved that she was angry, not depressed. But I was becoming more hopeless as weeks went on. I couldn't envision how we would survive if Emily couldn't find work. I feared I might end up in foster care.

"I feel worse and worse to tell you the truth," she said.

I stared at her. "Maybe we should go back to the clinic. Maybe the drugs aren't working."

She pushed her hair behind her ears. "I don't know."

"We've been through a lot," I said. For some reason, I had an urge to sit in her lap. I couldn't remember if I had ever sat in her lap.

"It's hard to look back, to face what I did to you girls. To your father." She gazed over to where she had seen the blackbirds. I had the sense she was thinking out loud, not talking to me. "I was so poor growing up. I never had enough of anything. When I married your father, I thought buying things would make me happy...I want to start over, but I can't. I never even started."

I felt as though I was eavesdropping. I wished I understood what she meant.

"I never had a career. I aborted my interior design fantasy as soon as I got pregnant with Rachel. I told myself I was going to devote my life to being a good mother to you girls while you were young. Give you the love I never had." She reached under her chair, fumbling for the water bottle that she'd placed there. Her grasp missed it by several inches. I wanted to get up and grab it for her, but the heat held me immobile, stuck to my seat. I watched as she gave up reaching for it.

"None of it was real to me. I went through motions of what I thought I should do. I thought there would be plenty of time to have a career after you girls got big. I failed at both. No career. Terrible mother."

"Mom…" I started, but then I stopped. I searched for something to say, but she'd know if I strayed from the truth.

"I never had a plan. I can't defend any of it."

"Did you love Daddy?" I didn't realize until I asked how much I wanted to hear her answer.

She looked at me. "I don't think I knew what love was. I know I didn't understand what marriage was. I had a notion of what a perfect family should be. But it was my own invention. I never knew my own parents. You know that."

I did know that her parents had been killed in an accident when she was three. An only child, she'd been raised by her grandmother. I'd never before stopped to consider what all that had meant, really. What it must do to a person to grow up an orphan.

"I'm worried about Rachel," I said. "What if she comes back? She'll never find us."

Emily looked away. "I think about her all the time. She came to me in a dream one night. She'd cut her hair off and at first I didn't recognize her. She started to cry. 'Mommy, Mommy it's me. It's Rachel.' When I realized it was her, I asked her where she was." A tear slid down Emily's cheek.

"What did she say?" I whispered.

"She said, 'I'm right here Mommy. I'm so close. You can find me. You just have to know where to look.'"

I felt goose bumps rise on my arms and legs. Good, I thought. It's cooling off. There's finally a breeze. But a moment later I realized there was no breeze. It was just as hot as it had been all night long.

We went back to the clinic after that and the doctor changed Emily's medications. The Lithium for her bipolar disorder made her speech slurry and the Prozac, for the depression, kept her sluggish. Again the doctor explained how hard it is to find the right balance since everyone's body chemistry is different. She reminded us it could take a few tries before she got on the right meds. Even then, it was upsetting to learn that these doses might need to change again after a while since the body sometimes becomes immune to medications. Even more disturbing was the fact that bipolar disorder is not curable and my mother will need lifelong treatment. Once again, the doctor stressed that Emily needed to go for therapy and told us that drugs alone were not the answer.

We explained to her that making appointments was difficult, since making phone calls was a problem. She told us there was a program that would help us to get a cell phone. Then we'd be able to make appointments. When she was feeling better a phone would make it easier for Emily to find a job. We talked about it on the way home and Emily agreed to go for therapy when we got the phone.

We were both worried that somehow, by using our Medicaid card, Joy Pierce would be able to find us. We decided to use a different pharmacy every time we filled my mother's prescriptions. We couldn't do anything about changing doctors though, and that was something we would just have to chance. Maybe Joy had so many cases, she had forgotten about us. Maybe she had gotten fired. I felt badly about that possibility, but it wasn't my fault she had forgotten to come back to put me in school. I couldn't have been the only case she screwed up or her job wouldn't be in danger.

We were careful not to use our food stamp card in the same place every week. We had no idea if it could be traced, like a credit card. We didn't want to run the risk of getting caught buying food. We spent a great deal of time thinking of ways to avoid Joy Pierce. Maybe we were making too much of the whole thing. Maybe she didn't think about us at all.

I wondered about Joy almost as much as I wondered if Emily would ever get to a point where she could work and get us out of this mess. If Emily got well and could prove she could take care of me, Joy would no longer be a threat. When I wasn't obsessing about Joy and Emily, I was plotting ways to find Rachel. My plans were far-fetched, bordering on absurd. I used the same brainstorming technique Ms. Louis had taught us in Language Arts. List everything. No idea is too silly when you're brainstorming, she had told us. "A gem may come out of the garbage." I could still hear her voice encouraging us. But nothing I was able to conjure up had even a remote chance of leading me to Rachel.

CHAPTER 3
July, 2012

I took the long way over to Crazy Annie's tent. She was going to take me to the warehouse where she sculpts. I liked taking the long way because I could walk past Cher and John's place. In the two months since they had moved in, John had built what looked like a small house. When I looked at it, I could pretend we were all living in a suburban development.

Of course it wasn't an actual house. It was made of plywood, but still. It had a roof and a door and it was painted white. A plaque painted a bright, grassy green with white letters said *HOME SWEET HOME*. Sitting in the "yard" was a picnic table covered with a green plastic tablecloth. Cher had put candlesticks on the table and a vase filled with greens and wild flowers. Next to their door sat two painted wooden chairs. Out in front, John had placed a mailbox on a stake. The kind with a flag that you put up when there's mail. The box was painted the same green as the plaque and someone, I guessed Cher, had stuck decorative decals of birds, flowers, and designs like swirling curlicues. The thing that really got me was the address. *22 Paradise Lane* was painted on the mailbox. As if Cher and John had an actual address. As if they actually got mail. Or had an actual home.

Looking at their place didn't make me homesick. In a strange way it made me happy. Happy that people could find a little bit of their own paradise in the middle of a tent city. I loved how homey their house appeared. I also loved imagining how inside, two young people were in love in spite of their money problems. Although, I had to admit it was odd that as inviting as Cher and John's place looked to me, we were never invited. Nobody was. They kept completely to themselves. Some called them snobs and said they thought they were too good for the rest of us. Others just said we should cut them some slack. They were like honeymooners, after all.

As I walked toward Crazy Annie's tent I thought about how much my life had changed and how many experiences I'd had this summer that would never have happened if we hadn't become homeless. There had been a ton of horrible events, but meeting Crazy Annie was one encounter I wouldn't trade.

The first time I had gone to the warehouse with Crazy Annie, she was afraid I was going to be bored. I had to swear I wouldn't disturb her in any way. To tell the truth, I was worried it could turn out to be a long, tedious day. I didn't know what I was getting myself into, so I brought a book with me just in case.

I never opened my book. The warehouse was a huge space. From the outside, it looked like nothing more than...well, a warehouse. Inside, it was divided into at least fifty spaces. The dividers were more imaginary than real, but you could certainly see where one artist's space ended and another began. The day I went with her, there were about fifteen artists working. Crazy Annie told me it was fine to wander around and watch them work as long as I didn't speak unless I was spoken to.

"Artists all work differently," she said. "Some need complete concentration and don't want their flow interrupted when they're creating a piece."

I totally understood. I needed complete concentration when I was working on a routine, especially when I was learning a new one. If anyone or anything disturbed me, I lost my ability to focus. When I was performing and in the thick of it, it was different. I could shut out the world no matter what was going on around me.

I stayed as quiet as I'd ever been, observing astonishing art developing right in front of my eyes. I was awestruck by a woman named Kate who was making an enormous quilt. There were words and phrases that had been stitched into the fabric; other sections were painted. At first I thought her words were random, but then I began to see a pattern. They could be read in several different ways, each with different meanings. The entire piece was a feast for my eyes and I didn't know where to look first. The threads were shiny and metallic; silver, bronze, red, and yellow. I wasn't quite sure what it all meant, but I decided it didn't matter. Everyone who looked at it would probably see something else. All I knew for sure was I loved the way it dazzled me.

Every time I thought I had found my favorite artist, I moved to another space and I found someone I liked even better. Until it dawned on me I didn't have to choose.

I was excited to be going back to the warehouse. "What are you working on today? Your sculpture?" I asked Crazy Annie, as we waited for the bus. Last time, she was working on a free form metal sculpture that moved in the air. There was no motor, it just floated whenever a breeze moved it. She called it kinetic art.

"No. I'm working on a series of five paintings in multi-media. There's a juried show at PAFA at the beginning of December and I want to be in it."

"What's PAFA?" I asked. "And what's a juried show?"

"Philadelphia Academy of Fine Arts. My alma mater. They have a juried show every year. There are separate prizes given for alumni and another category for anyone who is a current art student. I have to submit by October 1. A jury is a panel who judges and selects the pieces that will be exhibited. It's great exposure for artists and I might even sell something."

"Why don't you enter the kinetic piece?" I said, trying on my new art vocabulary.

"It doesn't sell. No one knows quite what to do with it. I'm not all about the money, but I need to earn at this point."

After we boarded the bus and found seats Crazy Annie said, "I'm surprised you wanted to come back to the studio. I thought you'd be bored silly."

"It's the least boring place I've ever been. I had no idea there were so many types of art. And to watch it forming…"

"Artists work in different media. Unless you go to museums or *avant garde* galleries most people don't get to experience a wide variety of modes. Typically, the public wants pretty pictures to hang over their sofas."

"Isn't the money important?" I asked. I should have known the answer.

She shrugged. "Art is a passion." Then she looked at me and asked, "Why do you like it?"

I wasn't sure I could put it into words. "When I was watching the artists at work, it was like I was looking into their hearts. They…they weren't thinking. They were just *doing*. Like I do when I'm performing a routine. It doesn't come from my brain. It comes from inside."

"Mmm. But in the end, with art it's the product that matters," she said.

"Me too," I said. "My performance is judged by others. It's not just how I feel about it that counts." I thought about what I had just said. "I learned a lot at the warehouse."

Crazy Annie nodded in agreement. "What did you learn?"

"I realized that I didn't have to understand the pieces. I could just experience them. I didn't like everything. But seeing the artists create the pieces made me appreciate art in a whole new way. I'll never look at any art work again without thinking about the artist. I'll be wondering 'who created this?'"

We rode for a while in silence. "There's something else," I said.

"What's that?"

"Being around you and the art makes my sister come back to me, in a way."

"You miss her," Crazy Annie said.

"Somehow, I have to find her. I need a chance to get to know her again."

"There's got to be a way. Maybe we can run some ads. I'll talk to Emily and Gloria." Crazy Annie looked at me for a long moment, like she could see something I couldn't. "We'll figure it out. I have a good feeling about this. Right here." She put her hand over her heart.

I did too. I didn't know how it was going to happen, but for the first time I felt as though everything was going to work out.

CHAPTER 4
August, 2012

Sleeping outside with nothing but a canvas tent for walls made me become conscious of noise. I don't remember hearing outside noises when we lived in our house. At most I recall hearing a car door slam. My mother didn't see the need for fresh air, so we didn't open windows. We went straight from air conditioning to heat.

You hear plenty when you live in a tent. Birds woke me in the morning. That's not as charming as it sounds. They're loud. Some sing specific notes over and over. It's as if they're talking to each other. The blue jays are by far the loudest. They make a racket that is not a song, but sounds more like a warning. Caw, caw, caw. I dare you to come near me. Some people could be loud, too, although not as loud as the jays. They'd stand outside and talk as though the whole world was awake.

For the most part, I got used to the different sounds. In the middle of the night when it was quiet, I could hear the freeway traffic in the distance. It was a whirring, steady hum I found soothing. I'd lie in the dark and listen to it when I couldn't sleep, which was often. I never had a problem sleeping when I was home in my room.

One of those nights when I couldn't sleep I heard a peculiar sound. The noise was a cross between a puppy yelping like his tail had been stepped on and a parrot screaming in the jungle. Even though I had never before heard anything that resembled this screech, I sensed the noise was coming from a living being. I was fairly sure it was not a bird. And I was positive the creature, whatever it was, was nearby.

The only other thing I was sure about was that I was not going outside to see what it was. I sat up. My hand reached under the pillow for my mace. After a while I could still hear the beast, but the squeals were moving further away. Then I couldn't hear anything, and at some point I fell back to sleep.

The next morning I was waiting for my turn in the shower when Haysoos arrived.

137

"Delia, can I ask you a big favor? I have to go work the early shift and I stink. Can I trade shower spots with you? Just this once."

"No problem." He sat down next to me to wait for the shower. "Haysoos, did you hear anything strange last night?" I asked.

"Like what? No. No. No. I didn't hear anything," he answered. He looked away. As a poor liar myself, I easily spotted another one.

"You know what it was, don't you?"

"Nothing. It's nothing. Don't worry. Forget about it."

"I'd rather know what it is than not know. Tell me what's out there."

Haysoos stared at me. Then he put his hand out and spit in it. He held it up. "Swear you will not tell a soul." I didn't answer him immediately. I needed to think about it for a second.

"Forget it. I'm not telling you," he said.

"If it's dangerous everyone should know," I reasoned.

"It's not. Not at all. Spit on your hand and hold it up to God. Swear!"

"Why do I have to spit? That's kind of disgusting."

"Don't ask me. My grandmother always did it."

I spit on my hand and held it up. "Tell me."

"It's Roberta," he said. "She's harmless. I rescued her. I'm trying to find her a home."

"You have a dog? Here? You know the rules. Cheyenne will kick you out." There was a strict no pet policy. Not even fish were allowed.

"No dog. Roberta's a pig."

"Haysoos," I gasped.

"Don't tell anyone, Delia. You swore."

"Can I see her? Where is she?"

Haysoos promised to meet me at his teepee right after his shower. I had to spit again and swear that if anyone saw me near his teepee I would keep on going. I agreed. It would look totally suspicious if anyone saw me hanging around Haysoos's place.

The second I met her I knew I was going to become an accomplice. I fell in love with Roberta. She was the size of a beagle and was as sweet and good natured as any dog I've ever met. She looked at me with dreamy eyes, put her snout in my armpit, and started to snuggle. She was the pet I'd always wanted and Emily never let me have. Haysoos found her abandoned in the alley outside the restaurant where he works. She was digging through a torn plastic garbage bag that was sitting next to a dumpster. He took her to the animal rescue where they told him she's a potbellied pig. She was only around three and still growing. The shelter wouldn't keep her. They were over their limit for strays and were going to put her down if he left her.

"I couldn't let them do that to Roberta," he said. "She's homeless, Delia. Like us."

"Why do you call her Roberta?" I asked.

"She looks like my aunt Roberta," he said. "I miss her." He looked sad.

"I'm sorry. Did she…is your aunt dead?"

"No. No. No. She's in Texas with my uncle Dante."

"What if you get caught keeping a pig? Where will you go?" I was trying to be practical, but I could see his dilemma.

"I won't get caught. She's quiet and she listens to me. She's even housebroken."

"*I* heard her."

"That wasn't her fault. We went out for her midnight walk and a raccoon scared her." Haysoos jumped up. "Listen, I gotta go. I can't be late to work."

Not only did I agree to keep Roberta a secret, I volunteered to feed and walk her as soon as it got dark whenever Haysoos was doing a double shift at the restaurant. I didn't like the idea of conspiring to keep secrets from Cheyenne and the others, but this was a worthy cause. It made me sick to think that sweet Roberta could be put down because she didn't have a home.

That wasn't going to happen on my watch. I'd do my best to help Haysoos protect her.

About a week later, Cheyenne called a rare group meeting. Everyone was expected to be there. Haysoos, Gloria, Denny, Daryl, and some others were at work; the rest of us showed up.

Clipboard in one hand, megaphone in the other, the Chief stood on a milk crate. He held the megaphone up to his face and spoke through it, even though there were only about twenty-five people and he could have been heard easily without it. "I don't want to alarm anyone unnecessarily," he started. He looked down at the clipboard and flipped a few pages. "I have two announcements. First, I had a visit yesterday from a city councilman. Long story short, they've turned a blind eye to us for the past two years, but that's over. There's a group of do-gooders who want us out of here and into what they refer to as 'proper housing.'"

He went on to explain that a story had run recently in the Philadelphia *Times* about Hardscrabble Way and the tent city that had "sprung up", as they said. The do-gooder group, as Cheyenne called them, had seen the story and shown up at the Mayor's office demanding that he find housing for us. They were going to keep showing up until the Mayor helped us get out of the tent city.

When Cheyenne stopped talking no one said a word. All you could hear was a bird chirping. Then there was a hub bub of commotion with everyone talking and asking questions all at once.

Cheyenne stuffed the clipboard under his arm and held up his hand. Putting the megaphone to his mouth he said, "Hold on." He waited until he had everyone's attention. "I asked all the same questions as you. I don't know who wrote the story. Some reporter trying to make a name for herself. For damn sure, no one interviewed me. The councilman didn't know much. He said there's a lot of rigmarole that has to happen before they kick us of out of here. You know how government works. It could be years. He was giving us a heads up and I'm doing the same. If anything happens I don't want it to come as a shock."

Too late for that. The meeting deteriorated into loud conversations and general uproar. Just as people were starting to wander off, still grumbling, Cheyenne put his whistle in his mouth and blew hard. The megaphone squealed as he yelled into it. "Wait!   Come   back.   I   forgot   the   second announcement."

"Oh my God. There's more?" someone called out.

"Again, I don't want to alarm anyone, but there have been sightings of scat nearby. Be alert. Don't leave food around. Make sure garbage is disposed of properly and dumped only at The Pile. Okay. That's it. Meeting over."

The Pile was a huge mound of garbage on the far end of tent city.

"What's scat?" somebody asked.

"Poo. In my patrolling around the enclave, I've seen piles of poo. Steamy, green poo. Could be a bear. Just be careful."

That news scared people more than the councilman. Everyone was petrified. Except for me.

Steamy, green piles of poo was Roberta. Haysoos had given her leftover guacamole from the restaurant and it didn't agree with her. She pooed green for two straight days. We were going to have to be more careful and walk her further away from the camp.

That night my mother and I sat outside waiting for Gloria to come home from work to fill her in on the meeting.

"What are we going to do if we have to leave here?" Emily asked Gloria, after she reported what Cheyenne told us.

"We were never going to stay here forever, Em."

My mother's fingers were tapping as if she was playing a small piano in her lap. "I can't go back to that motel. I can't risk

141

losing Delia. Would we…do you think they'd put us in a shelter?"

I couldn't grasp what they were even talking about. In my mind I visualized an animal shelter. The kind they show in commercials with sad-eyed dogs who have been abused or abandoned. Were there human shelters?

"No shelters. Too dangerous." Gloria's voice was calm. "It's too soon to look for a place, though. We need two months deposit and the first month's rent. We'll have enough for an apartment before it gets cold. We'll be out of here by October."

"We?" Emily asked.

"Unless you're planning to winter here. Or wherever else the Mayor puts you."

"No. Course not. But…"

"But?"

"All I have is my welfare money. It's not nearly what you're making. I'm not ready…I don't think I can work. Yet."

Gloria smiled. "Please. The new meds seem to be much less debilitating. Let's get you back to being healthy. You'll figure out the rest when you're able. We'll be fine. Right, Delia?"

She reached over and hugged me. I hugged her back as hard as I've ever hugged anyone. I had no words for the kind of gratitude I felt for Gloria Florence.

CHAPTER 5
August, 2012

I was squished between Daryl and Denny on the crowded bus. We were going swimming and I was so excited I couldn't think straight. Spending time with Denny was a thrill that hadn't faded, but to get to hang with both Daryl and Denny had me floating. Daryl never hung out. He was quiet and kept to himself a lot. Mostly he worked.

"I'm glad you came with us today, Daryl," I said. "You work all the time. Do you ever get sick of it?"

"I was just thinking the same thing," Denny said. "Great minds think alike, Delia."

"Sick of working?" Daryl asked. "No. When I'm not at work, I'm thinking about how to build the business. Promote it. Create more work. I like having my own business."

"You don't get out enough," Denny said. "When was the last time you had a date?"

"With a girl?"

"With a girl. Or a guy. Whatever you prefer. When was the last time you went out?"

Daryl shrugged. "High school."

"Really? That was years ago," I burst out. I covered my mouth with my hand. "Sorry. I didn't mean…"

Daryl laughed. It was a great laugh, I thought, realizing that I'd rarely heard it.

"Not *that* long. Two years." He stopped smiling. "Huh, maybe it has been too long."

"She's right. You need to get out more, bro," Denny said.

"I know. I don't meet anyone. Besides, no one decent wants to date a homeless moving man."

I stared at him in disbelief. "You really don't believe that, do you?"

Daryl shrugged again.

"You're so much more than that. You work hard, you're not a jerk like most guys, and you're gorgeous to top it off." Funny how I could say anything to Daryl, but still got fumble mouthed when I tried to speak to Denny.

"Now you're embarrassing me," Daryl said. "But if you know anyone who's interested…" He put his arm around my shoulder and squeezed. Then he kissed me on my head. Daryl could treat me like a big brother all he wanted. This was the kind of relationship I wished I had with my sister. I was thinking often about Rachel and missing her like crazy. All the memories we could be sharing filled me with longing. In my whole life, I'd never known what it was like to want something and not be able to get it.

As we hiked along approaching the Creek, I could hear shouts and laughter. I glanced at Denny.

"Sounds like we're not alone," I said.

He shrugged, not seeming to mind. I realized if I was this anxious about swimming with strangers, I didn't how I'd manage to start a new school. I grew up with all the kids I went to middle school with. If I didn't know them since kindergarten, I'd played on soccer teams or been on cheerleading squads with them. I'd never been in a situation where I was the new girl getting checked out.

I heard a shrill shriek as soon as we became visible.

"EEYOW! Look who's here. Where you been all summer? Take off that shirt and let me see those hot abs."

The shriek came from a voice in the water. She swam to the edge and climbed out, wearing--well, barely wearing--the teeniest white bikini. She made straight for Denny. Putting her arms around his neck, she hugged him as close as she could.

"Sheba, stop. You're wet," Denny said. But he hugged back, then he kissed her on the cheek.

Sheba? The only Sheba I'd ever known was a dog. I hated this girl and everything about her. Instantly. She was by far the prettiest girl I'd ever seen. Her skin was the color of maple syrup and the white bikini against that gorgeous shade was a magnet for even my eyes. Sheba had long golden hair and giant black eyes topped with what looked like false eye lashes. But they couldn't be. No one wore false lashes swimming.

"Who's this white chick?" She'd gotten around to noticing me in spite of my attempt to become invisible.

"Who you calling white?" I blurted out, as if I wasn't white. I had no idea what came over me. Denny shot me a look. He must have thought I was insane,

"Sheba, this is Delia. She's gonna be at Central with us."

"Nice. C'mon, Denny. Get your buns in the water."

He grinned like a fool. "Race you to the end."

"You're *so* on."

And they were gone. I stood there not knowing what to do. When hundreds of eyes were watching me perform in a stadium I was calm, cool, unrattled. Here I was, alone with everyone ignoring me, and I felt more self-conscious than I ever had in my life. I looked around as I pretended to be busy removing my shirt and sneakers. Daryl had already jumped in and was swimming by himself. There were at least a dozen others in the water, yelling and having a good time.

I stood frozen to that spot for I don't know how long. I knew I had to do something. I moved around to the other side where I'd practiced my routines the last time we were here. I dove in, doing a mid-air flip. I swear I was just trying to get my confidence back, but when I surfaced Sheba yelled at me.

"Ur *so* showing off, girl. You too good for us, over there?"

Mortified, I dove down deep to escape her teasing. I wished I had never come. Now I had something new to worry about. What if all the girls at Central were like Sheba? I was never going to fit in. Maybe I should just become a drop out. When I came up for air, I wasn't alone.

"Don't pay attention to Sheba. She's a diva. Can't stand to share the spotlight," a male voice said. Only it was not the male voice I wanted it to be.

"I'm Matteo. And before you dis her, you should know that Sheba's my little sister."

"I wasn't gonna...I'm, um, I'm Delia. Are you...What grade is she in?"

"Junior. A year behind me. Ha! Didn't think I'd make it this far. You?"

I rolled my eyes. "Freshman."

Matteo grinned. He had a really nice smile. I searched for a family resemblance. He was not nearly as good-looking as his sister, his skin was darker, and he wasn't loud or obnoxious like her. Maybe he was adopted.

"Don't feel bad," he said. "We all started out as freshman. I was terrified to go to high school. Now I can't believe I'm at the top of heap. Almost done. Goes fast."

"You were scared?"

"Totally."

The water exploded and we were surrounded by noisy, splashing boys. "Matteo! Man, you're it. Start the game," one of them yelled as he swam away.

Matteo closed his eyes and called, "Marco!"

"Polo!" yelled another.

I'd never know if Matteo said he was afraid of school to make me feel better, or if he was telling me the truth. Either way, I stopped feeling like a complete social outcast and joined the others. At first, it was just me and the guys, but soon a couple of girls swam over. It was so funny to me. No matter where you went swimming, someone always started Marco Polo. I guess some things are not so different from once place to another, after all.

By the time the game ended, we'd all had at least one turn being *it* and I was wiped out. Matteo introduced me to the boys. There were also two girls, Aleeza and Jinaya. Both were juniors like Sheba. They weren't mean to me, but they weren't friendly either. I found my towel and went to lay out next to Daryl. He was reading a magazine with his head propped up on his backpack. Denny and Sheba were still in the water, play fighting and making a racket that was hard to ignore. Matteo wandered over. "This spot taken?" he asked and dropped down next to me.

Eventually, just about everyone was out of the water and hanging on the bank. Sheba and Denny were the last to join the group. I watched Sheba's face as she noted where her brother was. Someone had brought beers and passed them around. Someone else passed a blunt. I watched to see what Denny did. Not that I would have done either one, but it made it easier for me to say no when I saw that he turned both down. Even better, no one seemed to care. Just when I thought I was safe, and was feeling comfortable, Sheba knocked my knees out from under me. In front of everyone.

"You comin' on to my brother, girl? What's your name again?"

"Shut up, Sheba," Matteo said. "Leave her be. Not everyone gets you."

"No? Does she *get* to fool with my brother?"

As fast as ants appear when we drop food in the tent, my comfort level disappeared and I went back to wishing I hadn't come. Sheba had the nerve to smile at me.

"I'm just messin' with you. Why don't you friend me on Facebook? I'll hook you up with some of my friends' little sisters." Her tone made it sound like I was eight.

"I'm not on Facebook." I could hardly hear my own voice.

"What?"

"She said she's not on Facebook. Let it go," Matteo said.

Sheba stared at me as if she couldn't comprehend how anyone could not be on Facebook.

"I'm...we don't have internet." I don't know why I felt like I had to explain.

"That sucks," she said.

Sheba stood up and looked at Denny. "Who's ready to go back in?"

Relieved to have the attention away from me, I stood up along with everyone else. We all went back in the water and played Marco Polo again for a while. At some point, I found myself treading water next to Denny.

"You having fun?" he asked.

Clueless boy. This had been the worst day. I had done my best to avoid girls like Sheba all my life. Sheba was the girl who thrived on making other girls uncomfortable. Denny had ignored me completely and seemed hot for Sheba. Not that I blamed him entirely. Boys were boys, after all and their hormones ruled. But there was no excuse for him not standing up for me. I wished I could push rewind and erase this entire day.

"Matteo's too old for you," Denny said when I ignored him.

"Maybe he doesn't see me as a kid sister."

"Do you like him?"

"Do you like her?"

"I asked you first."

I stared him down, waiting for an answer.

"Maybe. A little. In a way."

I shook my head, disgusted, not wanting to believe what I'd just heard. "Maybe you're not the guy I thought you were."

Sheba's head surfaced through the water and she broke in between us. "C'mon Denny. Get back in the game. Sorry...am I interrupting something?" She was as transparent as the top of her wet bikini. Sheba was many things, but she was not sorry for interrupting.

When neither Denny nor I said anything, she filled in the blanks. "Delia, honey. Denny is *so* not into you the way you want him to be. No worries. You'll meet a cute freshman when school starts and you'll get over this little crush. You'll see." See, that's the other reason I hated Sheba-types. They can see right through other girls and they aren't afraid to call you out.

Instead of sticking up for me, Denny swam away. My throat burned and I felt my eyes water. I hadn't cried when my father died. I hadn't cried when we lost our house and I had to move. There was no way I was going to let this girl get to me.

Matteo left early with some of his friends. When he left, I swam over to the rocks and wore myself out diving and doing routines. I couldn't wait for this day to end.

I didn't say a word on the way home. The bus was nearly empty and Daryl stretched out across two seats, closed his eyes, and appeared to nap. Denny and I rode in silence until the next to the last stop.

"I don't understand what you're upset about," he said, shaking his head. His hair was still wet and was hanging loose around his face. I resisted the urge to push it behind his ear.

"You're an idiot," I said.

"What is your problem?"

"You're my problem."

"How am I your problem?"

"Because I like *you*. Not Matteo. Matteo treated me like an equal. Not like a little kid. And he stood up for me when his evil sister put me down and humiliated me."

Denny's eyes widened. "Delia, I didn't...I don't...ugh. Never mind." And he turned away from me and looked out the window.

I wanted to take it back. I couldn't believe I'd just admitted to Denny that I liked him. We rode the rest of the way in uncomfortable silence. When we got off the bus, on the walk back to Hardscrabble Way Daryl was the only one who said anything.

"Such a good day. I needed to mellow out. You two seemed to be having a great time. We'll do it again."

Another oblivious guy. The tension was as thick as the traffic on the Schuylkill Parkway at rush hour and he didn't notice anything. Maybe it was a Jaxson family characteristic. I kept waiting for Denny to say something. Anything. I wanted him to apologize for letting Sheba make me feel awful. As upset as I was with him, I was more upset with myself. If I had wanted him to see me as mature, I'd blown it. I'd blown our friendship as well. I wished I'd kept my mouth shut and hadn't made a world class fool of myself. It was impossible to understand what

149

he saw in Sheba. If she was the kind of girl he liked I didn't stand a chance.

~~

It was hot. So hot the air felt stiff. The temperature had hit 100 degrees during the day and it hadn't cooled down much after the sun set. I couldn't sleep. No one could. I was lying on my cot trying to figure out if it was hotter outside or inside the tent. I wanted to read, but I couldn't concentrate. I still had a long way to go to finish my summer reading. I was struggling with *Lord of the Flies*, another boy book. I had tied a flashlight over my head in the tent. It dangled down so I could read. I knew it wasn't the light or the heat which was preventing me from finishing my summer reading. I love books, but there's something about the words *mandatory reading* that had this perverted effect on me. As soon as I knew I had to read something, my desire to read disappeared like ice cubes in lemonade. Speaking of which, I would have given anything for some ice cold lemonade. Or some ice.

Mom and Gloria were sitting outside our tent talking. I was overcome with the urge to listen in. I don't why. I knew they didn't have any secrets. I could just as easily have gone outside and sat with them. They wouldn't care. But I felt like I used to feel when I sat on the top of the stairs in my house, or when I hid in the closet in the spare room and snooped on Rachel. I used to wait for some jewel, some nugget of wisdom. Like a hawk circling overhead with endless patience, watching for some small movement below that would signal a delicious prize, I sat listening for something to fill me up. A piece of the puzzle to satisfy my curiosity about what it was like to be older.

"I miss air conditioning," my mother said. "Is it bad for me to say that?"

"No. Pointless, but not bad. At least I can go to work and cool off there," Gloria said. Then she asked, "What else do you miss?"

"Jell-O. And sex," Emily answered. Then she quickly added, "Not together."

Gloria, my mother, and I all laughed. I covered my mouth. I didn't want to get caught.

"I get the sex part, but why Jell-O?" Gloria asked.

"I was always watching my weight so I ate tons of Jell-O. Sugar free. I love Jell-O. It's cold and delicious and comes in a zillion flavors. Lime, lemon, mango, cherry, raspberry, orange, strawberry, banana, grape…Achh. You can add anything to Jell-O. Bananas, pineapple, blueberries, strawberries, even almonds. And you can top it with lo-cal Cool Whip and it still doesn't have any calories worth mentioning. It fills me up, satisfies my sweet tooth, and I could eat it every single day without guilt. It is utterly sinless. Not too many things you can say that about."

My mother sighed deeply and I sensed her craving.

"Wow," Gloria said. "Who knew?"

Mystery solved. I never knew why my mother made Jell-O all the time. I always thought it was because Jell-O was the only thing she knew how to make.

"What do you miss?" Emily asked.

"I'm pining for my own bathroom. My own bathtub. I used to come home after a long day at work, pour myself a glass of wine, and run a bubble bath. I'd sit, soak, sip my wine, and think about my day. I'm not embarrassed to say I'd celebrate every day. Pat myself on the back for how far I'd come." Now it was Gloria's turn to sigh.

"Have you ever been in love?" Emily asked.

"Like you with Jell-O?"

"No. Really in love?"

"Yea. I was crazy, wildly in love. It was a mess. A hot mess."

Gloria met Cooper at a bar in Philly. She was twenty-two and had stopped for drinks with friends after work. Cooper was older. Maybe thirty. He flirted with her and they talked for a while, she said.

"I knew I had to go to work the next day, but I stayed talking to him at the bar until almost closing. There was something about him right from the beginning. I wrote my number on the back of a napkin and gave it to him. He walked me to my bus and when I was about to get on it he touched my cheek and said he'd call me soon. No kiss. Just that touch. I was vibrating."

"And he called," my mother said, continuing the story.

"The next morning. And asked me out for the next night. We did dinner and a movie and he had his hand on my knee during the movie and I sizzled. That was all. Just his touch on my leg made me wild with desire. We went out three times before we had sex. By that time, I wanted him so much I couldn't think about anything else."

"Was it great?" Emily asked.

Gloria must have nodded her head, because I didn't hear anything.

"The most amazing thing to me was that when the white heat died down, we still had things to talk about. I never got tired of talking to him. But then a week would go by and I wouldn't hear from him. I should have been suspicious because months went by, we never went to his place, and I never met any of his friends."

"Oh no," Emily said. She must have guessed what was coming next. I did not see it coming.

"By the time I found out he was married, I was hopelessly in love with him. I wanted to hate him, but I couldn't. He told me they were separated, but living together. I wanted to believe him, but…I broke it off."

"That was hard."

"No. It was a strategy. At the time I was convinced if I broke it off he would take the next step. I kept waiting for him to turn up with a ring. Tell me he couldn't live without me. He turned up. I took him back. No ring. Just vague promises. It dragged on for two more years. I was addicted to him."

"And you never met anyone after Cooper?" My mother asked the question I was thinking.

"Sure. I've dated. But I've never…well, it's not the same. Nobody since Cooper has ever made me vibrate. What about you? Could you see yourself loving someone else?"

"I've never vibrated."

"Never?"

"Mark and I weren't what you'd call passionate. We were good friends in college. We went from that to dating and before you knew it, we were getting married. It was...comfortable."

It was one thing to eavesdrop on Gloria discussing her sex life. If my mother was going to start to talk about hers, I was done.

"I longed for something, but it wasn't Mark. I have always had this yearning I never understood. Like a hole inside of myself that I couldn't fill. Maybe because I never grew up in a family. I shopped all the time...that was my passion. The only thing that made me feel loved. When I spent money, it gave me a kind of happiness. But that feeling didn't last. I wanted to care about Mark, but I didn't know how. Maybe because I never felt loved or even secure growing up. After my parents died... that made me...well, I never felt good about myself. I never let anyone get too close to me. I wasn't there for my husband or for my daughters."

I moved over and lay back down on my cot. I felt worse than if I'd heard my mother talk about sex. I had no idea she was so insecure. I didn't want to know this about Emily. I'd always been intimidated by my beautiful mother. The mother that always looked gorgeous and put together. Confident. This wasn't the secret I wanted to discover. This wasn't that prized gem of information that would let me in on the hidden mystery of adulthood I craved. Or was it? At least now I understood there was no age limit to lacking confidence. Or to being vulnerable and making a fool of yourself over a guy like Gloria did with Cooper and I had done with Denny. Maybe the secret was simply that adults are just old kids, and that growing up and being mature meant somehow just surviving it all.

But something my mother said scared me. I never let anyone get too close to me, either. My mother used money and shopping to make herself feel good. I used my cheerleading and

153

grades to please everyone else, to get their approval. I didn't want to end up like Emily. She'd pushed my father away just like I'd pushed my sister away when I betrayed her. I didn't like that person. I had to do better.

~~

It rained all day Saturday so movie night was cancelled. The rain was welcome, but the cancellation was disappointing. The big screen and the equipment were kept in Cheyenne's tent when they were not being used. By six p.m. the rain stopped and a bunch of us went over to try to talk Cheyenne into changing his mind. He said there was still a chance of more rain and he wasn't going to risk damaging the electronics. There was no appeal process to his decisions, so that was that.

It turned dark early. I wanted to believe it was just because of the weather, but I knew the truth. It was halfway through August and the days were getting shorter. Around 7:30 I went out to the meeting area to hang out. The tiki torches were lit to keep the mosquitos away and there was a small campfire. When I got there, a few people were sitting in chairs circling the fire. Cheyenne was telling a story about the time he'd decided to chuck everything and give up Wall Street. He'd gone to New Orleans to a business conference. He woke early and went for a walk before he had to sit indoors all day.

"I was miserable. The last thing I wanted to do was head back to the convention center for a day of meetings. There I was in the middle of the French Quarter and a guy with a banjo was strummin' and singin' and had a baseball cap on the ground in front of him to collect whatever money anyone wanted to throw at him. I sat down on the curb with a cup of coffee to listen to him play. I'll never forget the look on his face. He was the happiest looking bastard I've ever seen." At this point in the story, the Chief's face looked like the banjo player's face must have looked. If I live to be 100, I doubt I'll ever see anyone who looks as content.

The Chief seemed lost in his memories for a while. Then he continued. "I sat there with the sun on my face, sipping my coffee, listening to banjo guy and I had an epiphany. I was never going back to Wall Street. I was done."

We'd all heard him tell the story before, but it still made everyone go silent. Most people here had lost everything. Or so it seemed. Cheyenne gave everything up to find…what? A better life?

Irish Jimmy broke the quiet. "Did I ever tell you about the time I hitch-hiked across the country by freeloading on railroad cars?"

"At least thirteen times," the Chief said. Everyone laughed.

Ignoring him, Irish Jimmy continued. "I'd been living in San Francisco. In my drinking days. Lost my job; my wife left me. I decided to go east, get a fresh start. I had almost no money, so I'd get on a train without a ticket. I still had teeth then and I cleaned up pretty well. At least at the beginning of the trip, I did. So when the conductor would come up and ask me for my ticket, I'd fumble around in my pockets and act horrified when I discovered my wallet was missing."

"And they believed you?" I heard Denny's voice. I didn't notice when he'd joined the group.

"You'd be surprised. Many a train conductor handed me a voucher and let me ride free of charge. The ones that didn't, put me off at the next stop. Either way, I was a little closer to where I was going."

"Good thing you weren't in a hurry."

"Things were going well. Until Cincinnati."

"Cincinnati, Ohio?" I asked. I hadn't heard the story before. Everyone who had heard it, groaned.

"No. Cincinnati, the blonde." Irish Jimmy got this blissful look on his face. He seemed to be drifting off into his memories.

The Chief put his megaphone to his lips and said, "Are you going to finish the story?"

"Sorry. I went away for a minute, but I'm back. She was a beauty. She told me she was Miss Cincinnati in 2006. Maybe it was a line. I didn't care. Peachy skin, gorgeous body. Hair like Marilyn."

"Manson?" Chief Cheyenne teased.

"Monroe," Jimmy said, unphased. "Her lips were as tempting as a bottle of Jamesons. And I would know. As Irish luck would have it, that particular train had a bar car. Somehow, we ended up there. Somehow, I ended up kissing those luscious lips. One thing led to another and, let's just say…" Here, he started to sing "*I hear the train a comin', it's rollin' 'round the bend, And I ain't seen the sunshine, since, mmm mmm mmm mmm.*" He trailed off into a hum.

"Is that Johnny Cash?" Denny asked when Jimmy stopped singing.

"We found our way to a place between the cars and she had her way with me." Irish Jimmy said, and he grinned his toothless grin. "I've never heard a train whistle again without thinking 'bout Cincinnati."

"You're full of it," the Chief said. "You couldn't get away with that."

"You're right. The conductor passed through the cars just as we were wrapping up, so to speak. I was weak in the knees by that time, between the alcohol and Miss Cincinnati. The train stopped and he flung me off. I fell on my face. That's how I lost my teeth."

"You told us you lost them in a fight," Denny said.

"That *was* the fight." There were groans of disbelief at the story. "Tough crowd here tonight!" Irish Jimmy said.

I stole a look over at Denny. We hadn't spoken since the fight about Sheba. To my delight, I saw my mother and Gloria wandering over. We made the circle a little bigger and they squeezed their chairs in next to me. Emily looked good. She didn't seem the least bit groggy from the drugs any more.

She said, "No movie tonight?"

"No. It might rain."

"I was looking forward to seeing *Pirates of the Caribbean.*"

"Really?"

"You know I love Johnny Depp. I'll watch anything he's in."
She grinned.

"I hear that, girlfriend," Gloria chimed in.

"Cheyenne said he might show it tomorrow if the weather's good," I reported.

"It's not going to rain any more tonight. Look. Over there."
My mother pointed.

Floating over the trees was a full moon surrounded by an orange glow. I'd never seen a bigger, more flawless moon. It was so clear, you could see cracks on the surface; craters, maybe. A few others noticed the moon at almost the same moment. Soon, everyone was inspecting the sky, staring up at the moon as if we were seeing it for the first time.

Then Cheyenne said, "Reminds me of my favorite song." He started to hum. I recognized the song *Blue Moon*. My mother used to sing it to Rachel and me when we were little.

Then a voice said, "I know the words. Anyone have a guitar? I'll sing it, but I need a little accompaniment."

My mouth fell open. My face must have looked like Johnny Depp himself had walked into the circle. The voice was Emily's.

"I'll get my guitar," Denny said. "Back in a sec."

He came back with his guitar and with Daryl. Denny handed the guitar to my mother.

"Can't you play?" she asked. "I'm really rusty. It's been years."

"Don't know the song," Denny said, throwing his hands up as he walked back to his chair.

Emily took the guitar, strummed a few chords, tuned it a little, and started to play.

"I never learned more than a few chords. Here goes."

"Blue Moon...You saw me standing alone..."

Her voice was smooth and true. I hadn't heard her sing in such a long time. I looked around at everyone watching her and there it was. Her charisma, magnetism, whatever it was about Emily that drew people to her was there. When she stopped

157

singing, she got cheers. She seemed surprised at the reaction, but her face glowed with pleasure.

Cheyenne said, "Sing another, Em."

"I don't want this to become too kumbayah." She looked self-conscious. "Denny should sing something. Something young." She lifted the guitar from her shoulder and walked it over to him.

Denny grinned. "I don't know about young, but I learned this recently. I'm dedicating it to one of my best friends. She's a little mad at me at the moment." He shot me a look, then he started to play. Immediately, I recognized the chords to Pink Floyd's *Wish You Were Here*.

"*So you think you can tell, Heaven from Hell…*"

His voice was a mash-up; a little Bob Dylan seasoned with a touch of John Lennon. Rough, a bit nasal. But it worked. He could carry a tune for sure, and he played as though he loved it. Of course, it didn't matter to me if he played like he had three thumbs and sang like Roberta the pig squealing.

"*…We're just two lost souls…*"

Denny played a song I loved, by a band I loved, and he'd played it just for me. Maybe he didn't think of me as girlfriend material. But he was my best friend and, in a way, that was so much better. No one was perfect. I was tired of pushing people away.

Daryl reached for the guitar. "I don't want to start a battle of the bands, here, but there's only one group that matters. Gimme that guitar. Ladies and gentlemen…the Beatles."

"*Blackbird singing in the dead of night…*"

"Sing with me," Daryl cued.

And everyone sang along. At some point, a million stars came out and shimmered in the glow of the moon which had moved fully overhead. Emily was right. It wasn't going to rain anymore. Not tonight. The sky looked like a painting by van Gogh I once saw. The moon threw down a magical, yellow light that seemed to shine only on us, sitting there in a circle. I dared to look over at Denny and he was looking straight at me.

"Forgive me?" he mouthed. "Friends?"

I made my hand into a fist and placed it on my heart. "Always," I said.

I looked around the circle at my mother, Gloria, Denny, Daryl, Larry, Crazy Annie, and the others, and I felt something I hadn't experienced in a really long time. I was content. Maybe that is what Cheyenne had been missing in his other life. This was, for now, my family. This was the family time I used to long for without even realizing what I was missing. There we were in the moonlight singing, spending time together. I knew we weren't really a family, but that didn't matter. Once upon a time families and neighbors must have gathered around and done this sort of thing in the evenings. Before television, computers, the internet, and cellphones distracted us and made us forget what was important. Before fathers had to work a million hours to buy their families things they only thought they needed. Tonight no one's problems had disappeared. They'd all still be there tomorrow. There would always be problems. Some bigger than others. Some, like losing my father, could never be fixed. Tonight what mattered was that we were all there together, sharing this moment. My mother looked at me, grabbed my hand, and squeezed it hers. She smiled her stunning smile. And that was all I had ever needed.

CHAPTER 6
August, 2012

Every morning when I woke up, right after I checked for ants I looked at Rachel's painting. I looked at every aspect of the picture; the colors, the images, the spiral nautilus with her initial embedded inside. It was as though I was searching for a clue about where she might be and how I could find her. I tried to send brain waves through the painting to let her know where we were and that we were safe. It wasn't as though I believed in psychic abilities, but it couldn't hurt to try. Stranger things have happened.

I was frustrated. I'd been staring into the painting for so many mornings and I was no closer to a plan for finding my sister. And then I woke up in the middle of the night and I knew what I needed to do. The answer hadn't been hiding in the painting at all. The answer was the painting.

I spent every day the following week taking the bus with Crazy Annie to her studio. I used the computer in the main office and researched "Rachel Williams+artist" on every search engine I could find. By Friday, I was ready to quit. I had run out of ideas. Then, for some reason, I opened my old Facebook page. I hadn't posted anything since Daddy died in January and I have no idea what made me go there. Psychic vibes maybe.

There were at least a dozen messages from my old Bala friends. I scrolled through them, not really reading because I didn't want to get upset. But the last message made my heart fly with hope. Molly Middlebrook's name was staring at me. Crazy with anticipation, I clicked on her message.

> Delia, I don't know how to find you. I got this and thought you'd want to see it. I emailed her back as soon as I got it, but she hasn't answered. I soooo hope you get this and that everything is cool! I'm leaving for college in a few weeks (Penn State! OMG!) but

> message me if you hear anything more. xoxo
> Molly

Molly had attached this:

> Molls,   Yeah, it's me, Rach. Sorry for the
> disappearing act but I really needed space to
> get my life together. I'm good. Got accepted
> at CUNY in NYC and I've got an apt in
> Harlem of all places. I'm here now taking
> summer classes. Patched together scholarships
> & work study & it's all good. If you see my
> family please tell them I'm alive &
> well…that's it. Don't tell them where I am.
> Hope you're good. Love Rachel

Her email address was attached and I forced myself to stay calm as I tried to figure out what to do. She hadn't mentioned Daddy or us losing the house. I didn't have a clue what to say to her. I only knew I didn't want to make things worse.

> Rachel,   It's me. Delia. Don't be mad at
> Molly for giving me your address. We've been
> worried sick about you. We tried to find you
> but lost track of you after you left California.
> Please, Rachel. Message me back. Mom needs
> you. A lot has happened. Too much to put in
> an email. Love, Delia

I hit send and breathed out. I wanted nothing more than to sit there for the rest of the day and wait for her to reply. I knew that was unrealistic, so I went to find Crazy Annie to tell her what happened.

Every day for the next week I either checked my email at the public library or I had Crazy Annie check it when she went to the studio. By the end of the week it became clear Rachel wasn't going to answer me. I was going to have to go and find her.

It took me a few days to form a plan. Once I knew what I was going to do, the only question left was who I could trust. One by one I eliminated Crazy Annie, Gloria, Larry, and my mother. All for different reasons, but mostly because I was sure they would stop me. The dilemma was whether or not I should tell Denny. I wanted to trust him. I wanted him to come with me to find Rachel in New York. I was terrified to go alone, but I was more terrified he would stop me from going. I wrestled with this decision for days while I made my plans. I decided to go alone. I couldn't take the risk that Denny would try to stop me. He might even tell Emily.

I had $213 left from selling the diamond earrings. I was saving the money to buy school clothes, but it was more important to me to buy a train ticket. I looked up what it cost for a round-trip ticket from Philly to New York. It was more than I expected. Once I got to Penn Station in New York, I still had to take a subway to Harlem. Taking the subway scared me senseless, but a taxi was out of the question. I'd never be able to afford a taxi.

I clung to the subway map the woman in the information booth at Penn Station had given me. I knew how many stops I needed to ride and I was counting them off. It was astonishing I'd made it this far. I thought people would look at me and wonder why someone my age was traveling alone, but no one looked at me at all. I was just another face on the subway on my way to CUNY in Harlem. The train ride from Philly to New York gave me time to rehearse what I would say to Rachel, but there was a long way to go before I found her. I had no address for her. All I had was the knowledge my sister was enrolled in the school. I was prepared for the worst. I was aware I could be making this journey for no reason.

There were two more stops. Then I had three blocks to walk. My plan was to go straight to the art department where I would ask anyone and everyone if they knew Rachel. Not much of a plan, but it was all I had. That and my need to find my sister. If I failed…well, I couldn't think about that yet. I didn't have much time. I needed to be back in New York City by 5:15 to catch the train back to Philly.

The streets were noisy, dirty, and busy, but not as scary as I had feared. The art building was easy to find. What I hadn't counted on was a security guard who didn't want to let me through because I didn't have a photo ID. I was on the verge of panic, so I decided to tell him the truth. The short version. About how Rachel had run away and I hadn't seen her in nearly a year. I left out the part about being homeless.

When I stopped talking, he stared at me without speaking. Then he said, "You look harmless enough. Sign in. Go." He waved me through.

I thanked him three times.

"Good luck," I heard him say as I ran into the building.

There weren't many students in the building, but I stopped each one and asked if they knew Rachel Williams. I showed them a picture of her. I was beginning to realize the stupidity of my plan when an office door opened and a woman came out. She started to walk past me.

"Excuse me," I said. "I wonder if you can help me find someone. My sister. She's a student here."

She stared at me for a second and for some reason I thought about Joy Pierce, my social worker.

"You look young. Do you go here?" she asked.

"No."

"Why don't you know where your sister is?"

I was afraid she was going to call someone like social services and my fear was making me sweat, but I hadn't come all this way to run away scared. I told the same story I had told to the security guard.

When I stopped talking she said, "Come inside. What's your sister's name?"

We went inside the office she had come out of and she sat down behind a desk cluttered with folders. The small windowless room had bookshelves crammed with books going in every direction. I watched as she booted up the laptop on her desk and waited while she typed and looked at her screen. I was afraid to say a word.

"Ah," she said, raising her eyebrows. She picked up a pen, then rummaged around on her desk, until she found a pad under a pile of papers. She wrote on the pad, then tore off the page and handed it to me.

"Here. This is Rachel's address. If you are in reality a mad stalker and you get caught, don't tell anyone where you got this information."

I stared at her. She smiled. "I'm joking. Your story is too startling to be false. What's your name?"

I told her. She said, "Here, Cordelia. Take my card. Email me and let me know how things turn out."

~~

We stood staring at each other. All the things I had planned to say evaporated into the air like the early morning fog over tent city.

Rachel broke the silence. "Why did you come?" she asked. I knew then this reunion was different than the one I had envisioned. She didn't hug me nor was she happy to see me.

"Daddy died. Mommy's a mess. We're homeless. We...I...I needed to find you. I need you," I blurted out my words. Here was the one person who should understand everything I had gone through, the one person I thought could help me, and she didn't seem to care.

Rachel looked away from me. I wanted to hear her say how she felt, how her life was, how much she missed us. None of that happened. After asking me how I got there, Rachel told me I had to leave. She let me in her apartment long enough to use the bathroom.

I was thirteen years old. If I was lucky enough to live a long life, I was certain my heart would be broken many times. But nothing that will ever happen to me will hurt me in the same way that my sister hurt me that summer day.

As Rachel walked me back to the subway, she told me she knew about Daddy and she knew the house had been sold.

"I need to be apart from all that," she said.

"Why?" I asked.

"I can't be there. In that life. You wouldn't understand," she said.

"What's wrong with you? What do you want?"

"I'll write to mom," she said.

"Where? We live in a tent. Emily Williams care of Hardscrabble Road, Tent City, USA."

We didn't speak another word until we got to the station. We stood side by side on the platform as the subway screeched to a stop.

"Bye, Delia. Be careful." And Rachel turned her back to me and walked away.

On the ride home, I realized that I had imagined if I could find Rachel and bring her back to Emily, it would heal us. Make a whole again. In some way, it would save us. Now I knew better. Rachel was as lost as we were and, at least for now, she needed to stay lost. We had to save ourselves.

CHAPTER 7
August, 2012

I don't know what I was aware of first, the smoke or the uproar. By the time my eyes opened both were invasive. I'd been in such a deep sleep, I wasn't sure if I was dreaming.

"Get up," Emily was screaming, pulling me by my arm. I could hardly see. "Get up! Please! You have to get up!" She pulled as she yelled until I sat up. As soon as I did, I went into full panic mode.

"Oh my God!" I shrieked.

"Let's go." We threw open the tent flap. There were smoke and cinders everywhere. Off to our left we could see flames.

"This way," she said, grabbing my hand and pulling me to the right.

"I can't see! What about Gloria?" I screamed.

"We can't stop. She'll be okay." As scared as I was, I knew my mother was right. If everyone ran around looking for everyone else we'd all perish.

People were stumbling around and screams of "fire, fire, get out, get out" echoed through the confusion. I looked back over my shoulder as we ran. Nothing but smoke. I could feel intense heat coming from behind. Flames were high above us. I remember thinking it was strange they weren't red like they were in cartoons. The blaze was golden orange, yellow, blue, purple, gray, black. If the scene wasn't so frightening, it would have been beautiful. The fire seemed to be moving in the opposite direction, away from us. I heard sirens coming closer and closer. They got so loud I put my fingers over my ears. How could the fire trucks get in? The road we called Hardscrabble Way ended about five hundred yards from where the tents were. There was a lot of concrete on the other side of the overpass and there was nothing to burn. In the other direction, a path surrounded by woods and grass led to the tents.

My mother kept pulling me forward gripping my hand so hard it hurt. The smoke made it hard to breath. Where were

Denny and Daryl? We could hear voices up ahead and kept moving toward them.

When we got to a clearing away from the smoke and cinders, Cheyenne was there talking on his cell phone. A few others were with him. Gloria wasn't there. Neither were Denny, Daryl, Haysoos, Larry, Crazy Annie, or Sarge.

"Stay put, everyone," Cheyenne ordered, not bothering with his megaphone which was still hooked to his belt loop. The clip board was under his arm. "I've got Daryl on the phone. They went east. They're gonna circle around and meet us here. We're trying to get a head count. See if everyone made it out." He took the board out and started to make marks on it.

If Daryl got out then Denny must be with him.

"Who's with him?" Emily asked. "Gloria?"

Cheyenne held his finger up in the air, telling her to wait. He was listening to whatever Daryl was saying. Then, there was a commotion coming from the woods. We heard an otherworldly squeal and out of nowhere there was a flash of animal running towards us. It was too dark to see what it was. Everything happened at once. Cheyenne dropped his phone and the clip board. He reached in his safari vest, pulled out a pistol and aimed yelling, "Wild boar!"

I looked at the blur of animal.

"No!" I screamed as I ran forward. "Don't shoot. Don't shoot. It's Roberta!"

My mother screamed, "Delia, no!" and then there was an earsplitting *pop*. The gun went off just as I grabbed Roberta's collar.

I heard Cheyenne scream at my mother, "Are you insane grabbing my hand like that? Is everyone okay? Delia, are you alright?" I was crying, patting Roberta all over to see if she was hurt.

Then Haysoos came bounding out of the woods in hot pursuit of Roberta. He stopped dead in his run when he saw all of us. I started to shake. I realized what a stupid thing I had done. I could have been shot. But I had saved Roberta. And my mother had saved me. She'd grabbed Cheyenne's hand to stop him just as he'd pulled the trigger. Lucky for all of us, the shot went off into the sky.

"WHO THE HELL IS ROBERTA?" As soon as Cheyenne knew he hadn't shot me, he lost it. He turned and screamed at me, "You know this animal?"

"Don't yell at her, Chief. Roberta's mine," Haysoos said.

"Why. Do. You. Have. A. Pig?" Cheyenne stared at Haysoos. No one, but no one wanted to be Haysoos at that moment.

Then people started coming from different directions all at once. Gloria, Crazy Annie, Larry, Denny, Daryl, the two Jimmys, even Sarge. Everyone was hugging, some were crying. Roberta, for the moment, was forgotten.

"What are we gonna do Chief? We've lost everything," someone asked when the hugging stopped.

Cheyenne was quiet for a moment and then he shrugged. "We've already lost everything."

And the absurdity seemed to hit everyone at once, and out of relief that we were all unharmed, we started to laugh until we couldn't breathe.

"Wait. Where's Cher and John?" someone asked. I had forgotten about them. It had been ages since I'd even seen them.

We all grew silent. We waited while Cheyenne called the fire department and tried to find out what was happening. He explained who he was and someone told him to stay put, the fire chief in command would come and find us.

There wasn't much talking after that. We were all in shock, horrified at what could have happened to us in the fire, and worried about what had happened to Cher and John. After what seemed like an hour, the fire chief and a few firefighters came. The fire chief looked us over, a raggedy tribe in our pajamas with a potbellied pig who was now tied on a rope leash. He shook his head as though in disbelief.

"Evening folks. I'm Chief Jarvis. We've got the fire under control. I'm staking two firefighters out here for the rest of the night to make sure things don't spark up again. It's been pretty dry."

He cleared his throat. "I've got some bad news and some good news. The good news is, because the breeze was blowing away from your camp, most of the tents were unharmed."

I heard a sigh of relief. Then our Chief asked, "And the bad news?"

"We've got a couple of injuries and four tents were destroyed. But most of your group is safe. The rest gathered over near the Expressway. The Red Cross is coming and will make arrangements for all of you to spend the night someplace safe."

Chief Cheyenne argued with Chief Jarvis. He wanted to stay with the tents and guard our things. The argument went back and forth for a while. At first Chief Jarvis refused, but he finally relented and agreed to let Cheyenne, Denny, and Daryl stay on Hardscrabble Way with the two firefighters. Cheyenne agreed with the fire chief that it wasn't safe for all of us to go back tonight until the danger had passed. We needed to wait and make sure the fire was out for good.

The two injured were Cher and John. They were lucky. They didn't get burned, just overcome by smoke. But it was serious and both of them were in the hospital.

Cheyenne called Reverend Willy who came in the purple bus, bringing some food and blankets. He waited with us until the Red Cross showed up and told us where we could spend the night. They didn't have enough room in the Red Cross truck for all of us, so Reverend Willy drove some of us to a school where there were cots being set up for us in the gym. There was food, coffee, and hot chocolate. Everyone was really nice, but it was embarrassing to be there. The worst part of the whole event was the media attention we got. There were reporters and cameras everywhere. I was terrified about the publicity and kept to the back edge of the group as much as I could so no one could take my picture. Joy Pierce was never far from my mind.

The Red Cross volunteers rolled a television in to give us something to do. We watched the news about ourselves, which was pretty much an out-of-body experience. There were photos and film clips of the tents on Hardscrabble Way. The comments about the homeless enclave made us either look like pathetic victims or derelicts. It's hard to say which was worse. There was an interview with someone who said she was "an advocate for the homeless." I couldn't imagine what that meant. She ended by stating, "The homeless do not choose to be homeless."

The broadcast ended with the reporter blaming government officials and saying it was their shame for letting us live in "*those* conditions." Everyone agreed about one thing. It was sheer luck not a soul was killed. No one from our camp would talk to reporters, so the truth about who we actually were and how we all got to this point was never explained.

What the reporters did reveal was the reason John and Cher had kept to themselves. They were apparently growing marijuana and had buckets of it in their place. According to the reporters, they were so stoned the night of the fire, they had let a joint smolder. Somehow the cinders had caught fire. Everyone was surprised that no one had smelled the marijuana or guessed they were getting high. But apparently, John's construction of his plywood house was a devious way of concealing what was going on behind the wall of the homey looking *22 Paradise Lane.* They were incredibly lucky to have gotten out alive, but not so lucky in other ways. They were arrested on multiple charges including reckless endangerment and all kinds of drug charges.

John and Cher had endangered all of us in more ways than just the peril of the fire. The last thing the Hardscrabble Way residents needed was attention. All the exposure was bound to bring more bad news.

A few days after we were back living on Hardscrabble Way, Cheyenne called an emergency meeting. There was a man standing next to him when we arrived. Cheyenne had his calm face on, but I could tell he wasn't happy. Through his megaphone, he introduced the man.

"This is Councilman Perez. I'll let him tell you what he told me."

The Chief held out the megaphone to Mr. Perez. The man looked a bit surprised, then gestured that he didn't want it. The Councilman told us that thanks to all the publicity, there had been a hullabaloo of public outrage demanding that Philadelphia shut down the tent city and find housing for its residents. The city had responded by opposing that argument. Philadelphia wanted to reclaim the land and throw us out, but they didn't believe it was the city's responsibility to relocate us. Homeless advocates, such as the one we saw on the news, had organized a rally which had received much attention. The town council had responded by calling a special meeting to take action regarding our "situation." The meeting had resulted in a committee that was taking our options under consideration. Nothing had been finalized yet. Councilman Perez said he was just here to keep us "apprised."

He was bombarded with comments, concerns, and questions with everyone talking at once. Mr. Perez was patient and spoke in a kind voice. He stayed as long as people had questions. At first he didn't say much more than he had said at the beginning. After a while, he admitted that since it was already the end of August, he figured we wouldn't be forced out until October or November because "any time there's a committee, wheels tend to move slowly." We would be probably offered low income or subsidized housing and food stamps, if we weren't already on them. Because we were so much in the public eye, everyone might be offered job training and assistance in finding employment once they were trained. He promised there would be no stone unturned and everyone would "most likely" receive aid of some sort.

171

Cheyenne turned to him and asked, "So if I hear you correctly, either way, we are going to have to vacate Hardscrabble Way?"

"Most likely," he repeated.

When the questions stopped coming, Councilman Perez left. Cheyenne was quiet for a long time. His jaw was clenched and a vein on his forehead throbbed. I thought for sure when he did speak he would yell. We all waited for him to say something. Anything. No one said a word. It was like we were all afraid to breathe, never mind talk. Then Cheyenne took a deep breath and spoke in a voice so quiet you could barely hear him. For the first time, I wished he would use the megaphone.

"We brought this on ourselves. There were rules in this enclave and they were violated. The rules were in place for a reason, as all rules are. This is the result. We're now officially becoming a diaspora." He paused and his chin tilted toward the ground.

I wasn't clear on what he meant, but I got the gist from his tone. I wondered if that was all he was going to say. He was quiet for a few moments. He sighed and continued, "We're going to be displaced. Removed from the only home we know. Removed from each other. We're going to be separated. Do you understand?" He looked around at all of us.

"We've spiraled down the drain here, folks. The very thing I've been trying to avoid has fallen upon us now, and it is entirely our own doing. Failure to obey rules has brought us to this point." He didn't sound as angry as I'd expected. He was--well, the word I would choose is defeated.

"There's one more matter I have to deal with." He pointed at Haysoos.

"You."

Everyone looked at Haysoos. He looked down at the ground.

"You need to leave. Tonight. You broke the rules."

I waited for my turn. Was I in trouble, too? Maybe Cheyenne forgot I knew about Roberta and had helped Haysoos hide her.

"But Chief, I need time to find a place that will let me keep Roberta. We're leaving anyway," Haysoos pleaded.

"Rules are rules. Go."

Haysoos put his head down.

"C'mon Chief, let him stay," Crazy Annie said. "A few more days can't matter at this point. He didn't cause what happened." A chorus of voices chimed in, agreeing.

Cheyenne was quiet. He appeared to be thinking it over. Finally, he spoke. "You can stay on one condition."

Haysoos looked up, waiting.

"I've always loved roast pork. We'll have a huge pig roast for Labor Day."

Crazy Annie yelled, "That's disgusting. You're a heartless man. Which is redundant. All men are heartless."

People paired off and got in arguments about rules, pig roasts, and other topics that didn't seem to matter.

Haysoos walked off in tears. I followed him. I needed to see sweet Roberta, the innocent cause of this latest drama. Except even I knew she was just a distraction from the bigger issue. Where were we all going to live?

There was so much to digest. Over the next few weeks every conversation was an endless debate. No one was sure if this was a blessing or a curse. Some argued it was, after all, the government and they were known to screw things up, turn a blind eye, not follow through, and not really give a damn. On the other hand, if the public and the press were really watching, then maybe this could be the break everyone needed to get back on their feet.

The only good news was that Cheyenne went to see Haysoos the day after he yelled at him. Cheyenne apologized and let him stay. Cheyenne admitted he was taking out his frustration with the city on Haysoos and Roberta. Even though Haysoos *had* broken the rules that were put in place for everyone's good, it didn't matter anymore and Roberta had done no harm. They could both stay until Haysoos found a place for them to live. At least that worked out.

~~

It's hard to believe that so much could happen to me in one year. This time last year my biggest problems included training for my next competition, learning new routines for cheerleading, buying outfits for school, and what to wear to all the parties I was being invited to. To think. I actually thought those were problems.

I turned fourteen, at last. Everyone at Hardscrabble Way threw me a birthday barbeque. They lined up all the grills in the circle where we gather to watch movies and have meetings. It was like a giant block party with music, balloons, and dancing. Everybody brought a dish or cooked something on the grills. The smells of charcoal and different foods cooking drifted through the camp and were tantalizing. My mouth watered all day long. There were sausage and pepper sandwiches, hot dogs, burgers, corn on the cob, and Gloria's incredible potato salad. If you think it was easy to make potato salad in a tent city, think again. She boiled the water for the potatoes on one of the grills and used olive oil instead of mayonnaise for the dressing, since mayo spoils in the heat. Larry grilled something called kielbasa; a kind of sausage I'd never had, and he served it with sauerkraut. Haysoos brought chili and amazing little stuffed pastries called *empanadas* from the Spanish restaurant where he worked.

My mother, the queen of all things catered, was in charge of buying the cake. As resourceful as everyone here is, there was no one who would attempt baking on a grill. Emily went all princessy on me which was a tiny bit embarrassing, but was actually a lot of fun. When it was time for cake, she put a tiara on my head and gave me a sparkly wand like the fairy godmother in Cinderella.

"Close your eyes," she ordered. "I want you to get the full effect of the cake." I did as I was told.

In a few seconds I heard her say, "Okay!" and everyone started to sing.

When I opened my eyes, my cake had silver sparklers surrounding a 3-D castle and a tiny princess who was holding a wand just like mine. Everyone was wearing paper crowns with glittery gold stars stuck to them, and they looked as though they had never been to a better party. When the singing stopped Cheyenne said, "Make a good wish, Delia."

Who knows what I would have wished for on my fourteenth birthday if none of the things had happened to me that had happened this year; losing my father, losing our home, my sister disappearing. Maybe an iPad, a bigger TV, a new computer. Things. I tried, but couldn't remember what I had gotten for my thirteenth birthday. Lesson learned. Objects don't matter.

So I wished for the one thing I was missing in my life right now that did matter. I wished for Rachel. I had everything else I needed. Then I took a big breath, made my wish, and blew out fifteen sparklers.

"I know you're officially well into your teens now, but I'll never get another chance for a princess party, so I decided to go for it," Emily said. "Forgive me?" I had to laugh. I knew I wouldn't have thought this was funny if I was back in my old life. I would have been mortified and hated my mother for embarrassing me. Somehow here, it was just sweet.

No one had much, but they all gave me a present that meant something to them, or that they thought I'd like. I loved all my gifts, but there were a few favorites. Gloria gave me a generous gift certificate to her salon. I can get a haircut, even highlights if I want them, a mani and a pedi. I'm going to save it and wait for a special occasion. Maybe for the first day of school. Speaking of school, Denny and Daryl gave me a backpack.

Crazy Annie's gift blew me away. She gave me a framed quilt from the artist Kate, at the warehouse. It was a small square, around twelve inches, and Kate made it especially for me. Like her other quilts, it told a story. There was a girl, a cheerleader. She had a huge dark cloud over her. She stood looking down a path. At the end she could see a bit of golden light that seemed to be rays coming from a distant place. I would keep this forever. Of course, I still had the painting Rachel made that I kept when we moved. I didn't have a room to put my art in, but I had two pieces of original art. I was well on my way to being a collector.

The surprise of the night was that Sarge appeared. He didn't say a word, but he handed me a package that was wrapped in a piece of newspaper and tied with a string. I was pretty sure it was a book. I was touched by his thoughtfulness. I thanked him and offered to make him a plate of food. He nodded. I piled food onto a plate and looked around. I found him sitting on the ground, leaning against a tree.

"Here you go," I said. I wanted to ask him to come sit with us, but decided to leave him be. I couldn't imagine what was going to happen to him when we all had to leave.

"I hope you like the book, Delia." He picked up the burger I'd put on his plate and took a bite.

"I'll bring you some cake."

Later, when I looked for him he was gone. I removed the newspaper from his gift. The book looked like a journal. I flipped the pages. There were dozens of hand-written poems. I opened to the front page. Written there in beautiful handwriting it said: *War* by Sergeant Avery Mitchell. I closed the book. I'd save this for another day.

As if the poetry book wasn't amazing enough, hands down my favorite birthday present was from Larry. When I was done opening my gifts and everyone else had drifted off, he walked over to me and said, "Open your hand." When I did he reached down into his pants' pocket and pulled something out. He put the object in my hand, then closed my fingers over it.

"You've had a tough year, Delia. You have spirit and optimism. When life gets overwhelming, I want you to look at what I just gave you and remember that there's something greater than us in the universe. There's a plan of some sort.

We don't always like it or understand it, but we don't have to." He tapped my hand with his finger.

"I've carried that," he cleared his throat. He seemed to choke up. "I've carried that in my pocket to remind myself that we live in a world where something like that exists. It's perfect and not one human had anything to do with creating it. Things work out the way they are supposed to work out. Remember that."

He was smiling, but he had tears in his eyes. "You're going be fine, kid."

He walked away. I didn't quite understand what he was saying. I stood there for a few moments, then I opened my fist and looked at what was inside. The tiny hairs on my arms stood up as I stared at what was in my hand. I was holding a nautilus shell. A perfect shell. A perfect spiral. Just like the ones we used to collect in Sea Isle City. Just like the ones Rachel used to sign her paintings. I had never told Larry about the nautilus.

"Did you have a good birthday?" I hadn't noticed my mother come up to me.

"The best one I've ever had. Thank you so much."

"I didn't give you a present," she said.

"You don't have to give me anything."

"I've been saving money all summer to take you shopping for school clothes. It's a new school. You need some things."

I hugged her harder than I'd ever hugged her before. We'd been clothes shopping a million times. I had always taken it for granted. I had always gotten whatever I wanted, whenever I wanted it. Now, for the first time, it meant something.

"Do you want some help cleaning up?" I asked.

"No, birthday girl. Go to bed."

I was exhausted. I needed to go to sleep. I wanted to digest all I had eaten, and all the happiness I felt. I headed to our tent.

"Delia," she called after me. I turned to her.

"I'm so proud of you," Emily said.

I didn't know what to say. She had never said that to me before. I blew her a kiss. "Goodnight. I love you."

~~

Sometime that night, Larry died in his sleep. I never got to tell him what the nautilus meant to me.

I had kept my promise to him. I never told anyone else he was sick. When I heard he was gone, I went numb. Like when I used to go to Dr. Roy, our dentist, and he'd stick me with a needle filled with Novacane. I hated that I couldn't feel my tongue or my gums for hours. Once, when I was about ten, Daddy brought me to my appointment. When we left I was so hungry I talked Daddy into letting me have a slice of pizza before all the Novacane wore off. I bit a huge chunk off my tongue because I couldn't feel it. My tongue bled and bled, but I didn't feel a thing. I still have a dent in my tongue where I bit it. I sometimes wonder where it went. Did I swallow that piece of my tongue?

As strange as it seems, I was obsessed. I couldn't stop thinking about the dentist. What if I grew old on Hardscrabble Way and my teeth fell out like Irish Jimmy? He said they got knocked out, but who knows for sure? I cringed when I thought about how that must have hurt. What if his teeth rotted out of his head because he couldn't go the dentist? What if he made up the fall? Lots of people make things up. I don't know if they don't recognize the truth or if stories are easier to deal with. Maybe it's both.

I was lucky. My teeth were straight and white. It was hard to keep them healthy, living in a tent and sharing a bathroom with so many people. Every night before I went to sleep, I brushed with bottled water. To think, I once had my own bathroom. Good thing I didn't need braces like Margot did. I wondered if I went back, if she'd still be my friend. It was doubtful. But it didn't matter. We were never going back. I tried never to think about the past, or how hard it was to live like we did. But I had to think about something or I would have to think about Larry.

The morning after my party, it was Larry's turn to clean the latrine. If it wasn't, no one would have missed him so soon.

Crazy Annie found him. She went to his tent to yell at him because he hadn't cleaned yet, and it was past ten. She thought he was still asleep, she said, so she shook him. Poor Annie. I'm not embarrassed to admit I'm relieved it was Crazy Annie who found him and not me. I've had enough to deal with. Shaking dead bodies is more than I could handle.

The biggest problem was going to be getting him out of there. They couldn't bring an ambulance far enough inside to take him away. There were some druggies and losers living on the outer edges of Hardscrabble Way. There had been more and more of them coming lately. Maybe the publicity from the fire brought them. Cheyenne told us they were dangerous. He was worried. Hardscrabble Way was slipping out of his control. There was nothing anyone could do to keep people away. The newcomers didn't sign our agreement. Cheyenne started a night patrol to protect us from thieves or from being attacked. I always preferred not to think about the scariest parts of living in a tent city, but I never went anywhere by myself. It was a relief to Sarge was around if I needed to go anywhere.

A few days before Larry died, a girl on the outskirts overdosed. A teenager, maybe around Denny's age. She was a blissed out mess. You could tell just by looking at her. I saw her a couple of times just sitting and staring at her fingers. When she OD'd, an ambulance came and took her away. I didn't see them take her out, but everyone was talking about it. She was alive, but unconscious when they carried her to the ambulance on a stretcher. I was glad she was gone. I felt guilty for feeling that way, but when I saw her she made me think about Rachel. It made me sick. Even though when I saw her, she didn't seem to be high or using anything. I still hadn't told anyone I went to see her. I wanted to talk about it, but I couldn't find the words. Mostly I didn't want anyone to think badly of Rachel. I hoped the girl didn't die. Maybe she went home to her family, the family who had been worried sick about her.

179

As much as I tried not to think about Larry, I couldn't help myself. They would have to bring him out on a stretcher. I didn't want to be there when they came. Someone once told me bad things happen in threes. Three people had left me without saying goodbye. Rachel, Daddy, now Larry. I hoped there weren't going to be any more.

~~

"Awright y'all. Listen up. Heah's what we're gonna do."

Marvin Mullins was the first man I ever met face to face who had a southern drawl. A deep one. The more worked up he got, the more he drawled. And he did get worked up. Often. And often his drawl was so thick, I could barely understand him. Like when he told us he was going to help us find housing. He said, "I promise y'all, by the fall I'm gonna have y'all breathing rumair and not living outdoors." Rumair? I had no idea what rumair was. I thought maybe it was something like oxygen.

I asked my mother if she knew what he meant. "He's saying 'room air.' He'll have us breathing 'room air' instead of being outdoors." She smiled and shrugged her shoulders. "Southerners," she said, as if that explained everything.

Marvin was working as our advocate pro bono. I was learning a lot. Marvin was a lawyer and he was representing the community in Hardscrabble Way against the city of Philadelphia which was asserting their legal right to the land we were using. They wanted us off the property. Marvin was acting as our legal counsel. That was the advocate part. He was doing this free of charge. Which was the pro bono part. He worked for a civil liberties group that specialized in helping the homeless. He explained all of this to us the first time we met him. Marvin grew up poor in Louisiana. His single mom brought him up and most of the time they had barely scraped by. They lived on welfare off and on for years. He was passionate about "giving back" as he called it. That's why he was helping us. I loved listening to Marvin, especially when he told us things like, "My Mama Ella, may her soul rest in peace, believed in four things: gumbo, a paddling with a wooden spoon when necessary, education, and giving back. Not necessarily in that order." I think I would have liked Mama Ella.

"You good folks are in a precarious situation. I've seen these tent cities down south. There's more and more of them springing up. They can be dangerous places. You've been lucky here. So far. I heard about the fire and all, but even so..." Of course when Marvin said all of this, it was way more southern.

He was going to argue that the city wasn't using the property anyway and therefore should let us remain. He said there were other cases that preceded ours and the tent cities had won the right to stay. "Honestly though, I'm not optimistic about this case. But we'll use the case as an opportunity to get a ton of support for the plight of the homeless. If we lose, we'll make sure as shootin' ducks on a cool day in autumn, you folks will get outta here into some decent housing. You should be happy to be getting the heck outta here and I'm here to help you."

Marvin promised if we lost the battle against the city, he would help us to find places to live and jobs for those who needed work. He would also arrange for school or some kind of training for anyone who wanted to learn a skill. He swore on Mama Ella's grave he wasn't going to abandon us to "the system" as he called it, but was going to make the system work for us. He told us there were resources that most people didn't take advantage of because they didn't know about them or because there was too much red tape. Marvin was going to help everyone slice through the tape.

"I am your personal escort through the velvet rope, as it were."

After the first meeting, Marvin Mullins set up a make-shift office which consisted of a small folding table with his laptop and a bottle of water on it. Sitting next to his chair was a huge briefcase on wheels that was like a portable file cabinet. Marvin said he wasn't going to waste valuable time waiting for the court to decide if we had to move. He wanted everyone to have

181

a plan. Marvin came daily for a while and held individual meetings with everyone who lived in Hardscrabble Way. He asked an abundant number of questions and typed furiously the entire time. When he was finished asking questions, he would dig down deep into his bottomless briefcase and pull out a form to suit the needs of each person. Occasionally, Marvin would yank another water bottle out of the briefcase. Every few hours he'd reach down and a charged battery for the laptop would appear. One by one, Marvin helped people fill out the correct forms that would help them to get whatever they required. Or so he said.

There were Marvin doubters and there were Marvin believers. Some didn't care if we won the case that would enable us to stay on. As long as they could get housing and a job, they would be delighted to leave the tent city. A few, like Sarge, didn't show up at all. I worried about what would happen to Sarge. He was a fragile man.

Sarge's poems were painful to read. It was like looking at his soul, exposed. He wrote vivid descriptions of his experiences in Iraq. His poems didn't rhyme. Some were short. Fragments of thoughts that rambled and didn't always make sense. Many of the pages described long, hot days in the desert where nothing much happened. But his words made it clear, even the uneventful days brought unbearable anxiety. The expectation that something *might* happen was worse than the actual event. He could barely cope with never knowing what was going to happen next. His final entry was one line about two men in his unit who got blown up walking down the road. After that, he didn't write any more.

I couldn't read too much at one time. I needed to stop reading after every few poems. Actually, I didn't want to read it at all. The story was too real, too personal, and I didn't want to know what had happened to him. But I couldn't help myself, and after a day or so of trying to ignore the book, I'd start to read more. I was halfway through when I discovered Sarge had been married. He mentioned a woman in a few of the poems. At first, I didn't realize she was his wife. Until I read this.

Lila
My wife, my life.
I wait. I watch.
Powered by fear and longing.
Longing for…what?
Home. Unrecalled, unrealized memories.
What is home? You. Your lips,
Your thighs, the smell of your hair after you've washed it.
You in the kitchen, the bedroom, the car.

Luminescent sun, blinding sand
blur the horizon
until I can no longer tell what is real. Are you there?
Do I imagine the figures I see miles ahead of me in the dust?
Are you there? Were you ever there?
Will you know me if I come home without limbs, without a smile,
without my heart? Did you ever know me? Did I?

Until the Lila poem, Sarge never said Lila was his wife. In a later entry, he wrote about when he came home after his first tour of duty and Lila was visibly pregnant. Sarge hadn't been home in a year. He volunteered to go back to Iraq. The poems never mentioned Lila again.

Even I could see that it was unlikely Marvin would be able to help Sarge. He was the Tin Man in the *Wizard of Oz*. Only his heart wasn't missing; it was shattered. Sarge needed a lot more than Marvin carried in his briefcase.

If we were getting removed from Hardscrabble Way, our most basic requirement was a place to live. Some needed a job, and a few people wanted to go back to school. I worried about Haysoos. He had a job, but he needed a place to live where a pet pig was accepted. That, in itself, was a challenge. But I doubted he would ever fill out the paperwork. He was not an American citizen and was at risk of getting deported.

Everyone liked Marvin, but most people didn't believe that any good could come from the court battle. He was one lawyer against an entire city. He'd promised he could find affordable housing for all of us, but that was a tough promise to trust. I hoped it was true, but even I had my doubts. I knew we hadn't planned on staying through the winter, and I wasn't insane enough to want to spend Christmas freezing in a tent. Yet now I had to face the reality of *everyone* leaving our community. It was almost enough to make me break apart. I dreaded more unplanned change and my anxiety kept me awake most nights. One night when I finally fell asleep I dreamed I was alone, floating down a river in a kayak. The water was still, but I barely had to paddle, the flow of the current pulled me slowly along. When I needed to row, my oars barely made a ripple in the calm water. The river felt familiar, like I'd been on it many times before, and I recognized landmarks that helped me grasp exactly where I was going. I moved confidently, taking my time to appreciate the sights as I rowed to my destination. When I awoke, I couldn't remember the end of dream, if there was one, but I felt rested, and calmer than I'd felt in a long while. I reminded myself that the last big change in my life, moving to Hardscrabble Way, had worked out. After all, I'd met Denny, Larry, Crazy Annie, Haysoos, and even Roberta. It was upsetting me to know I wasn't going to see them every day when we moved. The future scared me, but the uncertainty of the move wasn't the only cause of my apprehension. As if that alone wasn't enough, school was starting in a week and I was terrified.

PART 3

CHAPTER 1
September, 2012

When I woke up at 5 a.m. it was dark and freezing. I had a new level of respect for Denny once I saw what he did every day just to show up for school. We had to take two different busses to get to Central. That's after walking twenty blocks to get to the first bus. When we did this in the summer, I was so nervous about getting into high school, I didn't think about the actual trip and what it involved. I don't know how Denny did this commute in the middle of winter. I was ready to cry by the time we got to the bus stop. I never thought getting to school could be an ordeal. School was yet another thing I took for granted before we lost everything. I realized I'd never be able to stay after for activities. It would mean I'd have to do the reverse trip all alone, in the dark. I couldn't expect Denny to wait around for me. He worked with Daryl after school so he wouldn't be able to wait even he was willing to be my chaperone.

When I got to school I had no idea how I was going to find all my classes. All schools are confusing. Corridors all look alike. Hallway walls are made of the same beige brick, and you can never tell which way you're facing. Central was no exception. As an added bonus, the halls were crowded, everyone was shoving everyone else, and white faces were the minority. I've never done well in a crowd. I'm too short. I clung to Denny's elbow as he steered me to my homeroom. He bent over, kissed me on the cheek, wished me luck, and told me where to meet him after school.

With sticky, wet armpits and a dry mouth, I went inside and found a seat in my already crowded homeroom. The bell rang. People still straggled in until there were no seats. The teacher looked exasperated and directed the latecomers to stand in the back. With no greeting or comforting words of welcome for the new school year, she called attendance, passed around a few handouts, read a few notices, and then started to shuffle some papers on her desk. She never said her name. She never smiled. She was more frazzled than any teacher I'd ever known. She could have at least tried to make us feel welcome. We were freshman. We were new to the school. We deserved some kind of greeting. I glanced around the room. Everyone else seemed to know someone. Nobody talked to me.

Just as the intercom started to crackle with an announcement, the teacher noticed another stack of papers. "Oh no!" She grabbed them, waved them in the air, and yelled, "No one leave until you sign these! I almost forgot." She drowned out the scratchy voice on the intercom and I wondered if we'd missed something important.

"Read this," she ordered, as she passed the papers down the aisles. "It's the new school anti-bullying policy. You have to sign it."

"What if I don't wanna sign it?" a voice called.

"The principal will bully you until you do," someone replied.

"I didn't get one," someone complained. The room was getting loud. It felt like everyone except me had someone to talk to.

I looked down at my schedule for the millionth time, pretending to study it intently so no one would think I cared that I was the loser who had no friends. I had Spanish first period in room 308. There was a map, but I had no idea how to get from where I was to where I needed to go. Map reading was not once of my strengths. I could never even figure out the map in the mall. The one that shows YOU ARE HERE. I was still staring at my map when the bell rang for first period. Everyone stood up and started to leave. How did they all know where to go? In a controlled panic, I went up to the desk. My homeroom teacher didn't even look up. I missed middle school. I missed kind teachers. I missed knowing everyone and feeling safe and solid in familiar surroundings. I stood there politely waiting for the teacher to look up. It took me a minute to realize she wasn't going to acknowledge me so I said, "Excuse me. Could you please tell me how to get to 308?"

She looked up at me. "I have no clue. Didn't you get a buddy and a walk-through?"

I stared at her. I had no idea what she was talking about.

She rolled her eyes. "I don't have time…you were supposed to get a letter to come to freshman orientation. Freshman all got buddies and a walk-through in August so you'd know where to go." She stared at me, staring at her. Sighing, she said, "Obviously, you don't know what I'm talking about."

I shook my head. No letter. No orientation.

She started writing. "Here. Here's a pass. Go to guidance. Tell them you need a buddy. They'll assign someone to you. I'd walk you down, but I'm overwhelmed… I've got to get ready…my class…" She waved her hand. Students were started to trickle in. Some were waiting by the door, not sure whether to come in or not. I stood there frozen, a sick feeling rolling in my stomach. She handed me the pass.

"Here. Go." I took the pass and started for the door. "Good luck! See you tomorrow," she called as I left.

Tomorrow? I doubted I'd survive.

I wandered a few hallways, made a few wrong turns, before I realized I was going in a circle. Somehow I managed to find my way to guidance where a secretary glared at me over half-glasses, pointed at the door and barked, "Leave." Sitting on her desk was a frame surrounding the inspirational words "The secret to my success is knowing who to blame for my failures."

I was frozen to the spot. I couldn't leave; I had barely found my way there. I was lost.

She peered at me again. "There are no schedule changes until next week. Come back then."

I stood there stuttering, explaining my problem. Maybe she felt sorry for me. She wrote down my name and told me a senior would find me and be my buddy. "In the meantime," she ordered, "get to class."

"If I could find the class I wouldn't *need* a buddy, would I?"

I was so stressed, I couldn't believe how snippy I was. It worked though. She found someone to walk me to class. Mortified, I felt like a kindergarten kid just starting school. To make matters worse, I interrupted the Spanish class with my late arrival. Everyone looked at me as I came in.

I lucked out with second period. The room was 300, so I figured I'd be able to find it. It couldn't be far from 308. I got to Honors English on time and sat towards the middle of the room knowing that if I sat in front the kids would think I was a suck-up, and if I sat in back the teacher would think I was a flunky who didn't care. I thought I had things under control. Little did I know I was about to suffer my greatest public disgrace. Ever.

English started out well. It was pretty routine stuff, not too different from my old school. The teacher, Ms. Lindsay, introduced herself and gave out her course of study. She turned on the LCD projector and told us to copy down a few rules and requirements. As we did, she took attendance. Then, in typical feel-good English teacher mode she called on students one by one and asked different questions so we could introduce ourselves. She asked a few general questions about hobbies, favorite movies, sports, and other interests.

This was familiar. I began to feel better. Maybe school wasn't going to be a disaster, after all. I never saw it coming. Ms. Lindsay called out my name, "Cordelia Williams." I raised my hand to identify myself. She asked if I had a nickname. Delia, I told her. She asked me to tell her about the most significant thing that happened to me last year in eighth grade. As soon as she said that I went cold. Freezing cold. The hair on the back of my neck stood up, I got goose bumps, and I started shivering. A clammy sweat formed on my face and my throat seemed to close. I couldn't speak. The entire horrendous year that I had blocked out, refused to think about, and tried to eliminate from my memory washed over me. Ms. Lindsay was staring me and waiting for an answer. I heard her say, "Delia, are you alright?" I opened my mouth to speak. That's when my dignity and my anonymity were lost forever at Central High School.

I threw up all over my desk. I barely remember what happened next. What I do remember is a chorus of "ewwws" and "gross" and Ms. Lindsay nervously asking me, "Was it something I said?" Someone walked me to the nurse's office. The nurse took my temperature and asked me stupid questions. She made me lay down with an ice pack on my head. I guess that is universal. School nurses give ice packs whether you have a bloody nose, a wound, a headache, cramps, a contagious disease, or have just puked in your English class.

After a while, the nurse came to check on me as I lay there quietly wishing for death. She wanted to call my mother and I jumped up and said, "No. I'm fine. Send me back to class." As much as I wanted to disappear, I couldn't let them call Emily. I couldn't upset her.

I was devastated. I couldn't go home, but I wasn't sure how I'd manage to show my face in English again. For the rest of my high school life I would be the girl who threw up in class on her very first day of high school.

I don't know how I made it through the rest of the day. I couldn't bring myself to go to the cafeteria during lunch period and sit down with a million people I didn't know. So I hid in a bathroom stall until lunch was over, sweating with fear, hoping no one would find me.

When I met Denny at the end of the day, he looked at me and, "What's the matter? Did something happen?"

I shook my head no.

He raised his voice. "Are you sure? Did someone start something with you? Tell me."

"I had a bad day," I said. My voice sounded small.

"What kind of bad day?"

"I threw up. On my desk. In English. I can't go back."

Denny stared at me. And of all the reactions I would have expected, he had the one I never would have thought he'd have in a million years. He laughed. Hysterically.

"That was *you?*" he said when he could finally speak. "I heard about that in lunch."

I couldn't even speak. I didn't know if I was furious with him or just out and out hated him. I walked away.

"Wait. Wait up. I'm sorry...I didn't mean...you have to admit, it's pretty funny. Well, it was until I found out it was you."

"Leave me alone."

We walked to our bus in silence. On the two bus rides home, Denny did his homework. He needed to get it done so he could go to work for a few hours with Daryl. Every once in a while, I caught him looking at me as if he wanted to say something. He didn't, which was just as well since I had no words. I was crushed. Dropping out seemed like my only option. All the way home I thought about why I had become the unluckiest girl on the planet. It didn't seem possible that I could ever feel better again. I thought about Larry's nautilus shell and what he had told me about the universe. Whatever the plan was for me, I didn't think I could handle it.

By that night, everything looked different. Larry was right. Just when things seemed so dark, like there could never be light again, magically something shifted. And the last thing I expected was that the light would come from Emily.

My mother was waiting for me when I got home from school. She looked, well, radiant. Glowing. I had been noticing differences in my mother for a while. Ever since the fire when she grabbed me by the hand and led me away to safety, she was more in control, more confident than I had seen her in a long while.

"Tell me everything," she said, handing me a chocolate chip cookie and a juice box. "I want to hear all about your day."

I had never heard those words come out of Emily's mouth before. Oh, maybe she'd asked me how school was or how cheerleading practice went, but she never listened when I answered. She was listening now. She was looking right at me, waiting for me to speak. Now. Now that I had nothing good to say. I didn't want to upset her and tell her the truth about the horror that had been my day, so I sat there not knowing what to say.

"What's the matter?" she asked. "Did something happen to you?"

"It was the worst first day of school in the entire history of first days," I blurted out. I couldn't help it. I told her everything. I even told her how I'd hid in the bathroom so I didn't have to face the lunchroom alone.

When I was done, one tear rolled down my mother's face. Reaching out her arms, she wrapped them around me.

There was one more thing I needed to say out loud. "And I'll never be able to stay after for activities. I could never make this trip without Denny and walk home all that way alone in the dark."

She beamed at me. "You won't have to. Marvin Mullins found us an apartment today. A decent place in a safe neighborhood. We're not waiting for the court case. We're moving. You, me, and Gloria." Before her news could even sink in she added, "And that's not all. I got a job."

Just like that, things turned around. My mother was going to be a yoga teacher in a studio not far from Gloria's salon. I guess I was just as guilty as my mother when it came to not listening to her when she talked to me, because I'd never bothered to pay attention when she used to talk about her yoga and Pilates classes. They had always just seemed like frivolous hobbies. If I had paid more attention, I'd have known that she was certified to teach both. One of Gloria's clients was the owner of a yoga studio and happened to mention to Gloria that she was losing her best teacher. The woman was pregnant with twins and was going to stay home to take care of them. Gloria told her about Emily, which led to my mother getting the job. My mother was going to work!

Getting an apartment was a dream come true, but oddly it made me feel homesick even before we moved. Homesick seemed like a strange word. How could I be homesick when we were homeless? We may not have had a house, yet I didn't feel like I didn't have a home. Hardscrabble Way had become my home and I'd come to love all the people there. I thought of them as my family. As excited as I was about moving to our apartment, I couldn't bear the thought of leaving Haysoos and Roberta, or Crazy Annie, the Chief, and even Sarge. Not to mention Denny and Daryl. Moving was going to mean not seeing them every single day. I knew I had to find a way to keep them all in my life. I wasn't going to let go of the people I'd learned to trust and depend on. I felt worse about leaving here than I remembered feeling when we left our house. Back then I'd been too numb to feel anything.

On the other hand, it was such a relief to know we were not going to have to spend the winter living in a tent. We would be able to shower whenever we wanted. We'd have a refrigerator and electricity. We still wouldn't have a washer or a dryer, but the laundromat would be closer to where we lived. Maybe I could even get the internet again and do my homework without having to go to the public library. I hadn't let myself miss all these things, but now the idea of getting these luxuries back made me so excited I wanted to do flips. And maybe, maybe I could try out for cheerleading. Now that we were moving closer to Central, staying after school would be manageable.

We were one of the first to find a place to live. Because we were going to live with Gloria, we had more money than the others had. And, thanks to Marvin, my mother and I were going to get Social Security checks because daddy died. We never would have known about that if it wasn't for Marvin. With Emily's new job and our checks, we wouldn't need to be on welfare any more. And Marvin was helping Gloria to research small business loans. That was going to be tough, he said. There wasn't much money out there because of the overall economy, but he was going to keep trying.

I'd known all along we couldn't stay on Hardscrabble Way forever. Not that I wanted to. But spending the summer there had turned out so much better than I had expected. Moving on was scary, but the future was always going to be an unknown. I had no idea what to expect next. All I knew for sure is that I had my mother and Gloria and that we had a new apartment. I wasn't going to worry about anything else for now. Except facing my English class. In an odd way, I felt selfish leaving the others behind. We were lucky to be getting out. Everything was changing. Hardscrabble Way was getting attention from everywhere and no one liked what was happening.

The publicity had gone over the top when an argument broke out at a town council meeting. When the topic of what to do about the homeless situation came up as a question from the audience, a council member said she was tired of the subject. They quoted her as saying "We don't have a homeless problem. The homeless *are* the problem. Mostly, the homeless are welfare addicts, drug addicts, and dregs of society who simply won't help themselves."

That set off quite an uproar at the meeting. After, the quote was played repeatedly on TV news. A few days later, cameras and reporters appeared on Hardscrabble Way asking people for comments, filming how we lived, and taking still photos of our "lifestyle." One newspaper article had a headline "A Hardscrabble Way filled with Run-a-mucks."

The publicity generated interest from groups who came wanting to help. It was hard to tell who was worse. A group called The Philadelphia Committee for the Homeless offered to help. They did bring us a ton of supplies. So did another group called Project Winter Heat. They all meant well, but the attention was embarrassing. We lost our privacy as well as our dignity. Everything Chief Cheyenne had tried to avoid was

193

right there in his face. I didn't see him much, but when I did he looked miserable.

I guess the only one more miserable than the Chief, was Sarge. He disappeared from Hardscrabble Way without telling anyone he was leaving. The worst part was, he kept to himself so much, it was days before anyone realized he was gone.

When I was sure there were no photographers, I went to the chapel tent to spend time being thankful for our good luck and pray for everyone else to be as lucky as we were. I looked at the collection of porcelain figurines. I would never know who had put them there. I'd grown fond of the hedgehog and wondered if it would be missed if I took it with me. I decided to leave it. Someone else might need it more than I did.

The best thing about teenagers is they have extraordinarily short memories and even shorter attention spans. I was the talk of the school for the first two days. But outside of my English class, no one knew who I was. All they knew was some pathetic girl barfed in class. The kids in my class were pretty cool about it. If they said anything at all, it was just to ask me if I was alright. If anyone mocked me, they did it behind my back and I never knew.

I was sitting in Social Studies class writing a short essay and something hit me on the shoulder. I turned around to see what it was and I saw a dark, pretty face surrounded by a halo of curls grinning at me. She gestured with her chin for me to look down and I saw a folded piece of paper. Checking to see if the teacher was looking, I leaned down and picked up the note. Unfolding it, I tried not to smile. I hadn't gotten a note from anyone since I left middle school and my old friends.

I read the curvy handwriting. *Matteo says hi! He's been looking for you. Meet me after class. Stephanie.*

Matteo. I'd almost forgotten about him. I tried to forget about his sister Sheba, but I couldn't. Frequently, I found myself wondering if Denny was seeing Sheba now that they were back in school. I didn't dare ask him. He didn't have much time to hang out, I consoled myself.

Stephanie was waiting for me outside the classroom door. "I'm Steph and I'm starving," she said. "What period do you have lunch?"

"Next period." I still hadn't made it to the cafeteria. I couldn't bear going in by myself. This was the third day of school and I was still spending lunchtime in the bathroom.

"Me too. Let's go. Do you need to stop at your locker?"

"No. I'm good." That was another thing. I was still shaky on where I was going, so rather than risk getting lost I never went to my locker. I carried everything with me all day. Needless to say, my backpack weighed a ton.

"K. I'm just gonna stop for a sec." She plowed her way through the overcrowded hall. I admired her pluck. I felt like grabbing her elbow and hanging on so I wouldn't lose her, but I just kept shoving my way through the sea of people. Of course, all of them were taller than me. I come right up to a lot of people's armpits. It sucks being short in a crowd.

When we finally got to the cafeteria, it was a noisy, smelly, chaotic space. Teachers with whistles stood along the sides looking like police guards. It did look more like a prison than a place to eat.

Stephanie said, "I'm getting in the sandwich line. You?"

Nodding, I followed her through the line. I grabbed a tuna sandwich and a water bottle. I was grateful for the swipe cards that all students used to pay for their meals. No one had to know I was getting free lunches, since every student used a card whether they paid or not.

I continued to glue myself to Stephanie's rear end. "I'm still getting used to the size of this place," she said. "It's so much bigger than my middle school. How about you?"

"This is crazy big compared to my school," I said as she stopped at a table and squeezed in on the bench next to some girls who waved at her. One of them asked, "Who's this?" and looked at me. I forced a smile as I sat on the edge of the bench.

Even my tiny butt barely fit on the leftover space. No one moved over. I wondered if my old friends would have scootched over for a new girl.

"Delia is a friend of Matteo's. She's new," Stephanie looked at me. I felt like I was supposed to say something.

"Delia Williams," I said. Awkward.

"That's Queenie, Jervais, Marie Elena, and Rosa," Stephanie said. "Where's Filippa?"

"She skipped school," Rosa answered.

"Where did you go to school last year?" Queenie asked me.

I was embarrassed to tell them I'd come from the Main Line. I felt like it would make me a freak. Stephanie saved me from having to answer. "Filippa's skipping already?" she asked. "That's not good. This isn't middle school. They're not gonna pass her just to get her out of here." Stephanie turned to me.

"So Matteo's looking for you. He asked me if I knew you."

"How do you know Matteo? He's a senior," I said.

"He's best friends with my brother Chris. I've known him all my life, practically."

"So you must know his sister Sheba," I said.

Stephanie scrunched her face. I couldn't decode the scrunch.

"How do you know Sheba?" she asked.

"I met her this summer. I was swimming at a creek with Denny Jaxson." I couldn't help myself. I had to ask. "Are they going out?"

Stephanie shrugged. "Denny's a fox. Where did you meet him?"

This lunch was making me uncomfortable. I did not want to talk about my homelessness in the first five minutes of what might be a new friendship. "We've been friends for a while." I changed the subject. "What did you write about in class today?"

"I hate writing. My mother would kill me if she heard me say that. She's a teacher. Wanna come over after school some time?"

I couldn't believe it. Three days in high school and I had found a lunch group to eat with and I'd been invited to hang out at a new friend's house. But the homeless thing was a problem. At least until we moved. I was afraid to get my hopes up, but maybe things were starting to work out.

At the end of my first week at Central, Mr. St. Clair, the counselor who helped me in the summer, called me down to his office to see how I was doing. I told him about my upsetting first day. He'd heard about the girl who got sick, but didn't know it had been me. He was so sweet and sympathetic. He asked me if I was getting involved in activities. I told him I hadn't been able to find out anything about cheerleading tryouts, so he walked me down to the gym to talk to the coach. Mr. St. Clair introduced me to Coach Bender. It was upsetting to find out they had started the whole process in the summertime to give the in-coming freshman girls time to learn routines. Mr. St. Clair told the coach an abbreviated version of my story. When he was done, she said, "You're getting a late start, but here." Coach Bender pulled a file from her desk drawer. She opened it and gave me a piece of paper.

"You need to learn any three cheers that we already use and you need to do one original routine incorporating the mandatory moves. They're listed on this handout." I looked down at the paper. "You can go beyond them, of course. Tryouts start Wednesday." This was Friday.

I looked up at the Coach. "How can I learn the cheers? I've never seen the squad." This seemed hopeless.

Coach smiled. "YouTube. We've posted them on YouTube."

Mr. St. Clair looked at me. "Delia, I'm sorry. I should have thought of this in the summer. Well, there's always next year."

"Thanks, Mr. St. Clair. I'll be fine." I looked at the Coach. "Thank you, Coach. I'll see you Wednesday."

Coach Bender tilted her head and looked me over. "There'll be four judges. Me, the two senior captains, and one of the

197

other PE teachers. Wednesday's round one. Callbacks will be the following week." She put her hand out to shake mine. I put my hand in hers. "Good luck, Delia."

I had four days to watch and learn three routines and make-up one of my own. I was pumped. This was the toughest challenge I'd ever given myself, but my competitive nature was kicking in. There was a difference though. This time, I was doing this because I wanted to prove something to myself. As luck would have it, I ran into Matteo as I was leaving the Coach's office. He walked me to my next class and I quickly told him about tryouts. He offered to help me learn the routines and find a place to practice. I was so excited, I stood on my tiptoes and kissed him on the cheek.

"Finally!" he said. "I knew there'd be a payoff if I hung around the gym enough." He told me to meet him in the library after school, then he grinned and waved at me as he ran down the hall to his class. I'd use the internet in the library to look at the team cheers. Then I'd get to work.

Their style of cheering was different than I was used to. It was more physical and less stylized. But I had been taking gymnastic classes since I was four and there weren't any moves I didn't already know. It was just a matter of learning their routines and developing one that was unique. Matteo showed me a gym where I could practice. It was tucked way in the back of the weight-lifting rooms. The gym was open all weekend for kids to come in and work out. There was a PE teacher there to supervise. One of the advantages of being an inner city school was they really tried everything to keeps kids busy and off the streets.

My usual advantage was being tiny and being used as the flier. But I had no one to be my base; the girls who spot and catch me. I'd have to rely on the strength of my floor work. I worked up a routine to a mash-up of Michael Jackson songs that I downloaded onto my iPod. I choreographed in the mandatory moves first; a split, handspring, and a cartwheel, then I got elaborate with my jumps.

I incorporated a round-off without hands, a one-handed cartwheel, and then a few basic moves to transition. I hoped that the judges would think the basic moves were my finish, because then I would surprise them. I saved my best moves for a spectacular finale. It was the trifecta of my finest stunts. First, I'd perform a salto--a somersault with my feet coming up over my head and my body rotating around my waist. I'd land on my feet and immediately launch a series of handsprings across the floor. Finally, I would conclude with a double salto with a half twist on the first and second salto. If I could pull it off. The double is exceptionally challenging and I was rusty. More significantly, because it was coming at the end of a grueling routine, I needed a tremendous amount of strength just at the point when I'd probably be ready to crumble. I was counting heavily on my years of experience to carry me through. And adrenaline.

~~

I've performed and competed in dozens of gymnasiums. There's an atmosphere in a gym that compares to nowhere else. If I were stricken blind and left in a gym I would know exactly where I was. There's a smell that's part sweat, part floor wax, and part energy that's so familiar to me it's like I've come home. Even so, I have never felt as downright scared as I was in Central's gym before cheerleading tryouts. I was so regretting that I had stopped going to practice last year when all hell broke loose in my life. I couldn't change the past, but there's no question that I was not at the top of my form. My flexibility was still there, but my execution was shaky. I got through the mandatory cheers. Now all I had left to perform was my individual.

I tried to stay focused and in my own head while the other girls did their routines. I didn't want to watch them and get rattled. As soon as you start to compare yourself to someone else, you can lose your self-assurance. I heard my name called

199

and I took my spot on the floor. My heart felt like it would bounce right out of my chest. Central's gym is huge and as I stood alone on the gleaming, wooden surface waiting for my music, I wished I still had my old confidence.

The opening notes of *Thriller* blasted through the gym and I assumed my position and waited, smiling, for my cue. I had a hundred and twenty seconds to show what I could do.

As the final notes of *Got to be Starting Something* pounded in my ears, my feet planted perfectly after nailing my double salto. My hands in a V in the air, I paused a second to catch my breath and appreciate the rush I got from completing what I had set out to do. Even if I didn't make the squad, I had tried.

I smiled at the judges as, hands to hips, I ran off the floor. There were girls on the side who had been watching me. I looked at them, hoping someone would give me feedback on how I'd done. They started whispering to each other, but no one looked at me. I turned and looked back at the judges' table, hoping I could sense a reaction, just as I used to do after a competition. They were leaning forward and talking to one another. Their body language was impossible to read. Just as I was going to turn and walk away, Coach Bender happened to look up and glance my way. Our eyes met for one long moment. Then, she raised her eyebrows and smiled at me. Music began to play. Another girl was on the floor. The Coach immediately turned her attention to the next candidate.

I had no clue how to interpret her smile and I wasn't about to read anything into it. She was probably just being nice to the new girl. No matter. It was all out of my hands. I'd done the best I could do given the circumstances. All I could do now was wait and find out if I'd made it to the next round.

By some miracle I survived the first cut of freshman cheerleading tryouts. I was too nervous to check the list so Stephanie did it for me. She was nearly as excited as I was. For the next phase I got to practice with the junior varsity squad for a week before the second round. There were twenty finalists and we had to learn a new cheer. This time, I was able to use a few of the girls as a base for a lift and a cradle catch, so I performed a flier stunt. Nothing fancy. Just a pose. But it highlighted my timing and that I was willing to fly. The final results would be posted in the gym on Friday. I knew I performed well, but I was up against some truly talented girls. Their athleticism was impressive, especially since I knew these girls couldn't have had all the advantages I had. I'd been taking lessons since pre-school. When I got off the floor, this time some of the girls came over and asked me if I'd show them how to do some stunts. I told them I would but only if they showed me some of theirs. That moment capped off the tryouts for me. I was good enough to get the attention of Central girls. But what mattered wasn't that I got their attention, what mattered to me was I gave that tryout everything I had. I felt good about myself, no matter what the outcome was. I was still one of the tiniest girls, so I had a shot at being a flier. There was nothing left to do except wait until Friday when the final results would be posted.

~~

I loved hanging out with Stephanie at her house. Her family was...well, it was such a *family*. The Browns had an apartment that was small, but homey. They had the kind of life I always wanted without even knowing I wanted it. Her dad was African American and he worked for the Post Office. Her mom was Dominican and was a first grade teacher in Philly. Stephanie was in the middle of two brothers; Chris, the senior who was friends with Matteo, and Stevie, a fifth grader who was so cute. I loved how close Stephanie was to her brothers. She sat down with Stevie and helped him with his homework before she did her own.

It didn't hurt that Mrs. Brown was an awesome cook. I wonder if everyone's mom cooks except mine or if I gravitated towards friends who had moms who cook. Mrs. Brown made these Dominican dishes I'd never heard of before and I couldn't get enough of them. She sent me home with doggie bags. She said it was because I loved her food, but I think she was afraid I didn't get enough to eat.

"Why are you so skinny? You eat?" she asked me when we first met. Everyone in the Brown family was on the robust side. In a good way. I loved that Steph was curvy and she didn't seem to mind a bit. After my years at Bala Cynwyd Middle School watching girls eat lettuce and calling it lunch, that was so refreshing to me.

The first time Steph asked me to hang out I made a lame excuse. I didn't know how to deal with getting back home to tent city. The second time she asked me, I told her everything. The whole truth. It was such a relief not hiding things. I never felt like I could tell Margot or my other friends about what I was going through. Maybe I underestimated them. It's possible they would have understood, but they had always been quick to gossip and be judgmental. To be fair, if Margot or Alexa had become homeless instead of me, I wouldn't have known how to how to act or what to say, either.

I told Stephanie she could tell her parents, so the Browns knew my story and knew that I was homeless. Mrs. Brown said she would drive me home if I came over. She was so nice about everything. She met my mother and Gloria the first time she brought me back to Hardscrabble Way. If she was shocked or upset about where we lived, she didn't show it.

I told Stephanie about my sister and how Rachel went missing. When I got to the part when I found her in Harlem and Rachel sent me away, Stephanie was so upset she almost cried. She told me she thought that maybe Rachel had to handle things in her own way and that I just had to be patient. "She'll be back," Stephanie said, trying to console me. I wasn't sure.

~~

So much happened in a few weeks. First off, I didn't make the squad. Even before the results were posted on Friday the coach came to find me and told me how impressive she thought I was. I knew as soon as I saw her that I didn't make it. I had wanted to cheer again so badly I thought I'd be more upset. But the girls who had been there all summer knew the cheers and they were talented. The coach apologized that she couldn't put me on the squad, especially after everything I'd been through. She did make me an alternate though, and I got to practice with the squad. I was happy about the way things turned out. It was way more than I ever expected. I was satisfied with the fact that I had gone after what I wanted. And it wasn't because I was trying to get anyone's approval.

I didn't see Denny as much as I would have liked. I saw him in school, but after school he had work and I had practice or games and then homework. Denny had been right about Central being safe enough, but it did have a rough crowd. I was surrounded one day as I was leaving cheerleading practice.

I had just left the school property and said goodbye to a couple of girls who walk in the opposite direction from me, when some boys I didn't know appeared. Before I could escape they made a circle around me. One of them recognized me and said, "Aren't you Delia? The girl on top?"

Another one said, "On top of who? Is she a porn star?"

"Delia, I'll let you get on top."

I was starting to panic when I heard a voice behind them say, "Back off. Now."

The boys turned around.

"You don't mess with her. You understand? And you spread that word. You mess with her and you mess with me. You got it?"

The boys started to scatter. "Sure, Matteo. No problem. We were just fooling with her, that's all. Didn't know she was a friend of yours."

He stood, arms crossed, watching them leave. He didn't act at all like the Matteo I had met last summer at the creek. He was, at this moment, scary.

When they were gone he said, "You okay? They didn't touch you, did they?"

"I'm really glad you showed up. They were more afraid of you than I was of them. Almost."

"I wrestle. I'm undefeated. On the mats you have to psyche people out even before the take-down. People don't tend to mess with me." He grinned. "I can be quite the bad-ass."

"Undefeated? Impressive."

"I made it to State finals last year. I'm hoping it'll help me get some scholarship money."

"I can't wait to see you wrestle."

"I heard you made the team," he said. "I meant to track you down and congratulate you. I've been super busy."

"I didn't make the squad. I'm an alternate."

"Still. A big deal. Good for you!"

We hadn't moved yet and I still had to walk to the bus. "I better get going," I said.

"Will you go to the Harvest Ball with me?"

I looked at him. "But…" I stopped.

"But what?"

"But you're a senior."

"And?"

"And why would you want to take me?"

"You're different from the girls at Central. They're all in your face and you…just *get* things."

I needed a minute. No one had ever said anything like that to me before.

"No strings," he said. "We'll have fun. I like hangin' with you. What do you say?"

"I've never gone to a high school dance before. With a senior, yet." I poked him in the side, teasing him.

As soon as he left I called Stephanie. "What do you wear to a Harvest Ball?"

She said, "It's like a prom only not so much. I think. Why?"

I told her about Matteo and my dramatic rescue.

"I'll ask my brother Chris, but you know. Guys are useless. Um. We could ask Sheba."

"She shops at 'Hoes R Us.' I'd never take her fashion advice." Then I had an awful thought. What if Sheba was going with Denny?

I needed a dress. I didn't want to ask my mother to spend money. I didn't know what I was going to do. That night, I lay on my cot unable to sleep, when I realized the answer. I still had Rachel's blue prom dress and her silver sandals. The most impractical thing I had kept from our old life, now had a purpose.

"I'm so emotional. It's your first high school dance," Gloria said, when I tried the dress on for her and Emily.

Emily weighed in. "I'm so glad you're going to a dance, Delia. You don't know how badly I've felt about you missing your eighth grade dance and your graduation. The party we would have had…This doesn't begin to make up for all of that, but…" My mother's eyes sparkled like the little diamonds in my ears.

"Stop!" I said. "None of that matters now."

"You're right," Gloria said. "Let's enjoy what we have. This dress looks perfect on you. I'll do your hair and you are going to be one gorgeous little mama at that Ball."

I looked over at my mother. She was smiling, but she looked a little sad. I suspected she was thinking of Rachel wearing the same outfit a lifetime ago. I had a twinge of guilt. Lately I had been thinking that maybe I should tell my mother that I knew where Rachel was.

I never mentioned to Denny I was going to the Ball. I told myself it just never came up, but I knew Denny would never bring up a dance in a million years. No guy would. I didn't want to bring it up. I didn't want to hear him lecture me about Matteo, for one thing. Besides, I was afraid to ask him if he was going. I just couldn't stand to hear he was taking Sheba. I wished I didn't feel this way about him.

After the incident with the boys, Matteo met me after practice every day and walked me to Stephanie's. The whole ordeal of getting to tent city on my own after practice was too much for me. We would be moving soon but until then, Mrs. Brown was driving me home after practice every day. She swore she didn't mind and I never felt like she did. Sometimes she sent me home with a hot meal for Emily and me.

I teased Matteo the first time he walked me to Steph's. "You worried about me?" I asked.

"A little. I know you're scrappy, but this can be a rough neighborhood. Doesn't hurt for people to know you're with me."

On the walk to Stephanie's, I decided to tell him why I went to the Browns instead of to my own home. To my relief and surprise he already knew.

"I know Denny for a long time. And his situation. He told me you live in the tent city, too."

I had to ask. "Do Sheba and her friends know?"

"No. I would never…it's not my story to tell."

Emily wanted to meet Matteo before the Harvest Ball. I had no idea how to manage the meeting. I couldn't imagine asking Matteo to visit me on Hardscrabble Way. I told Mrs. Brown my dilemma on our way home one night. That night, she asked Emily to come to dinner on Thursday and told me to invite Matteo. I was kind of embarrassed to ask him. I thought he'd think me such a freshman, but he was cool about everything.

We had meatballs and spaghetti and everyone was loud and it was like one rowdy family. Emily fit right in and even helped with homework, since we had already prepared the Browns for the fact that she was useless in the kitchen.

After Matteo left, Emily and I helped Mrs. Brown clean up the kitchen. "You have a wonderful family," Emily said. "I don't know where to begin to thank you."

"Don't even go there," Mrs. Brown said. "We are all one small step away from where you have been."

"I love your friends. Matteo seems nice," Emily said when Mrs. Brown dropped us off and we were walking to our tent. "He caught me by surprise, though."

"How?"

"You never mentioned he's African American."

"Oh! I just...I just think of him as a guy," I said. "It didn't occur to me to mention it." I looked at her.

"Are you upset?" I asked her.

"Not at all. You're an impressive young woman."

The night of the dance I was more nervous than I expected to be. Gloria put my hair up and then Mrs. Brown picked me up. I was going to get dressed at the Brown's house and spend the night there. When I put my dress on, even I could see I looked a lot older than 14. I didn't look as beautiful as my sister had looked, but when I looked in the mirror I liked what I saw. Matteo teased me when he saw me.

"For a jock, you clean up good, girl." He told me that he wasn't sorry he'd asked me, even if I was a mere freshman. He cleaned up well himself. His broad shoulders filled out his jacket.

I just wished I could *like him* like him. Not just as a friend. But the first thing I did when we got inside the Harvest Ball was to look around for Denny. I pretended to be looking over the decorations. I didn't like myself for it, but feelings are feelings and I couldn't make mine go away.

Seeing police at the dance startled me. I'd never been to any school event before where they needed police to patrol. Instead of making me feel safe, it scared me. I felt so stupid. Were there fights at these dances? Drugs? I hoped Matteo didn't leave me alone.

He didn't. There was a DJ and we danced almost every dance. I forgot all about Denny. We'd been there for at least an hour when I spotted Sheba dancing with some girls. Matteo saw her too. Over the music, he said, "There's my sister. Let's say 'hi.'" We walked over to Sheba and he tickled her from behind. She spun around to see who it was. The smile she had for her brother slid down her face when she saw me standing next to him. Clearly, Matteo hadn't told her who he was bringing.

"Shebe, hang with Delia a minute, will you? I don't want to leave her alone. Be back in two secs." Before I could ask him where he was going, he was gone.

Sheba and I stared at each other for a second. We both spoke at the same time.

"I didn't know you were hooking up with my brother," she said.

"I thought you'd be here with Denny," I said, hating myself.

She smiled. I couldn't interpret the meaning.

"Your brother and I are friends," I said. "That's all."

"Does Matteo know that?" she asked. Then she added, "Denny doesn't do dances." I wanted to ask her if she meant she was seeing him, but he didn't come to dances. But I didn't. I was afraid to find out, for one thing. And I was afraid she'd tell her brother I asked about Denny. The last thing I wanted was to hurt Matteo's feelings.

Later that night, back at the Brown's front door, he said, "I'm glad you came."

He leaned down and kissed me. It was a good kiss. Not like the time I kissed Denny, but it was a respectable kiss. He lingered just enough to make me wish the kiss had lasted longer.

"See you, Monday," he said, and he waited until I was inside the door before he left the stoop.

~~

I was taking a test in Spanish when my name came over the intercom. I wasn't sure I heard right, at first. I looked up. Ms. Arbora, my teacher, was looking at me. She'd heard it, too. "Senorita Williams, do you know what this is?" she asked.

I shook my head. No. My insides were in a turmoil. The last time I'd gotten called down to the office was when Daddy died.

Nothing in my life was ever the same again. I told myself I needed to stay calm. Nothing bad was going to happen.

"Should I finish my test before I go?" I asked.

"No. It might be important," she said. "I would call the office for you, but the intercom doesn't work on this end."

I handed in my paper. Just as I did, my name was called again along with a string of about five other names. I walked slowly into the main office, trying to figure out what they could want.

I went inside and the secretary looked at me. "Yes?"

"I was paged. Cordelia Williams."

"Not by us," she said. "Try guidance."

I walked around the corner to the guidance office and went up to the desk. The office was crowded with students waiting to see someone, so I barely noticed a woman sitting with a brief case in her lap. The secretary was talking on the phone. I stood by her desk, waiting. She looked at me when she hung up.

"I think you paged me. Cordelia Williams."

From behind me I heard a voice say, "There you are. Finally."

I turned around to face Joy Pierce.

~~

Mr. St. Clair was waiting for me to say something. He repeated the question. "Can you help me to understand, Delia? Ms. Pierce claims you ran away. That your mother is mentally ill and needs to be hospitalized."

Joy Pierce and I were practically knee to knee in front of Mr. St. Clair's desk. Her long legs had nowhere to go and I couldn't let her touch me, so I pulled into myself like a turtle and tried to make myself as small as possible.

I forced myself to appear calm. "My mother is fine, Mr. St. Clair. She just got a job. You know my story. Things were tough for a while. We're fine now. She's fine." I looked at Joy. Even sitting, she was an intimidating woman. "I know Emily didn't seem fine when you met her. We had just lost everything and…things were bad. But we're good now. We don't need your help anymore."

209

Joy stared at me. She tapped one finger on a manila folder she had in her lap. Her finger tapped as quickly as my heart was beating. I hoped my heart wasn't as loud as the sound that one finger was making. She smiled and her smile was small and forced, not showing any teeth. Then, she tilted her head and said, "I'm afraid it's not so simple, dear. Cordelia, I know you've been through a great deal. But you and your mother have caused a great deal of trouble. Wheels have been set in motion. For your own good, of course."

"What exactly are you trying to say, Ms. Pierce?" Mr. St. Clair asked in his charming accent. I still didn't know where he was from. Wherever it was, I wished I was there.

Joy ignored him. "Where are you living, Cordelia? Not at the address you gave when you registered for school. I went there." She leaned in closer to me.

My courage and bravado melted away. Only one week from today I would have an actual address. I knew that wouldn't matter to Joy. Once she found out I was living in a tent city she would take me away. "How did you find me?" I asked.

She smiled again, and her face was smug. "All it took was time and patience. I went back to your old school to see if you had requested your transcripts. Your principal Mr. Rose had to tell me where he sent them." Her face changed visibly. "He was rather unpleasant. He blamed me for letting you disappear. After I left he called my supervisor and told her how upset he was that I didn't register you in a school. I was placed on probation because of the stunt you and your mother pulled. So you see..." she held up the folder as if it were a victory flag. "I can't let this go. These are court papers ordering you placed in a foster home. Your mother will have to prove competency in order to restore her parental rights."

"Wait a minute! Why don't you have to prove her mother is incompetent?" Mr. St. Clair sounded furious. "It seems to me *you* are one who showed incompetence."

"There will be due process in court, Mr. St. Clair. In the meanwhile, this authorizes me to take Cordelia."

"Based on what?"

"My professional judgment. My evidence was the condition Emily Williams was in when I saw her last. I did my due diligence insofar as the court is concerned. They are allowing me to remove Cordelia temporarily from her mother's custody. She will have the opportunity to prove her fitness as a mother at a hearing. Surely, Mr. St. Clair, you can see this is in the child's best interest."

I'd heard enough. I weighed my options. If I stood up and left, would they have time to have the security guards stop me before I exited the building? I decided to take my chances.

"Excuse me," I said. My voice trembled, which wasn't an act. "I'm going to be sick. I need to go to the bathroom." I counted on my history of throwing up to convince Mr. St. Clair I wasn't lying. All I needed was enough time to get out of the school.

As I spoke, I stood up, covered my mouth, and bolted for the door. I heard Ms. Pierce say, "Don't let her go!" By that time I'd made it out of the office. I flew down the hall to the nearest exit, pushed on the horizontal metal bar, praying it wasn't locked. I hit the street running. I was free for now.

I headed straight to Center City to find Gloria. She almost dropped her scissors when she saw me in the salon. I told her what happened. "I came here. I didn't know what else to do."

Gloria called Marvin Mullins who was there within an hour. Marvin's drawl and Southern way of speaking might be as slow as ketchup pouring out of a bottle when you're dying for a bite of hamburger, but he moved faster than ice cream melts on a humid day in August.

Before closing time at the salon, he filed for temporary custody as my guardian. He reached out to Joy Pierce's supervisor and told her what had happened. He let the supervisor know I was safe and in his protective custody and he faxed over the paperwork to prove it. He informed the supervisor he was filing harassment charges against Joy and she needed to back off. Then he went to family court and filed a motion for a hearing date. He would argue my case. We'd fight family services and establish my mother was not unfit and could remain my legal guardian. All this and Emily still had no idea anything was going on.

At closing time, Gloria and I went to meet Emily at the yoga studio. On the bus back to Hardscrabble Way, we told her everything we knew up to that point. Marvin was coming to meet us later that night to fill us in on the rest. Emily put her hands to her face. "I should have known better. I knew she'd be back. We should have contacted her, got in front of the whole mess."

Emily said the same thing to Marvin later that night. He patted her hand and said, "There, there, Ms. Emily. As my mama Ella would say, if the egg is already cracked, there's no patchin' it. Just move on to the stove and make an omelet." Even Emily had to smile. He had such a way with words.

We were going to family court on Friday. He would be there to plead our case to the judge. One of two things could happen. The whole thing could be dismissed, or I could be sent into foster care with Emily being declared an unfit mother. That could last as long as six months, after which we could go back to court and file again. Marvin offered no predictions about what would happen.

"There are too many variables. On the surface, the story sounds sordid. We're going to have to be upfront with the judge about where y'all have been living. Recent developments—your job, the apartment—will have to be taken into consideration. In our favor is the fact that the job of the legal system is to try to keep families intact." He looked at me. "You will have a home by next week, Miss Emily has a job, and you, Miss Cordelia, took it upon yourself to get back in school. No thanks to Ms. Pierce. We got a lot going for us, but I make no promises except I'll do my best."

I trusted Marvin, but that wasn't good enough. I knew what I needed to do.

CHAPTER 2
September, 2012

We moved into our new place. It's tiny compared to our old house, but our apartment's got three bedrooms. Gloria, my mother, and I each have a room and I am over the moon excited to have my own private space. It's the size of a closet, but I'm not complaining. I unpacked my trophies and lined them up on the floor, since I don't have any shelves. Then I hung Rachel's painting across the room where I can look at it all the time. I was drawn to the colors and the whimsical figures. Looking at the image made me feel light-headed, carefree, a little like a kid again. There was something magical about her images. Of course, there in the lower right hand corner was a perfect nautilus shell. Contained within the heart of the shell, in the center of the spiral, was the distinct, Rachel *R* .

I hung the quilted piece that Crazy Annie gave me for my birthday over my bed. I have a night stand next to my bed where I placed Larry's nautilus so it's the first thing I see in the morning. Next to the shell, I put Sarge's book of poems.

The court hearing went in our favor, although the episode will always be dreadful for me to relive. The outcome could have turned against us so easily. So much could have gone wrong.

Joy Pierce made the facts--as she saw them--sound so believable. I still struggle to remind myself she was doing her job and in all likelihood, she believed what she said was the truth. There were slivers of truth, but she didn't know us. She turned our lives, mine and my mother's, into devastatingly simple, harsh-sounding statements she twisted to sound like facts.

I'd never been to court before so I had no idea what to expect. The hearing was held in the Judge's chamber, which is really just an office with a long conference table and high-back leather chairs that swiveled. There was a court stenographer typing on a machine and everything we said was recorded. The Judge told us a hearing was a legal proceeding just the same as being in a regular court, so we had to swear to tell the truth. Much later when it was all over, I realized there could be many versions of truth.

Before the hearing, just as we were entering the judge's chamber Marvin pulled me aside and talked to me alone. He told me not to be afraid and "no matter what, just tell the truth."

"What if the judge asks where we went when we left the motel?" I asked Marvin.

"That is an excellent question, young lady. You must answer honestly."

I looked Marvin, feeling hopeless. "It's sounds so awful."

"I know," he said. "Let's go inside." He signaled for my mother and Gloria to come over. He pulled the door open and held it as they walked in. As I walked past him, he touched my arm. I looked up at him. "Only answer the specific questions you are asked. Nothing more. Do you understand?" I nodded. We went inside.

Joy Pierce looked taller and skinnier than ever. Maybe it was the black pantsuit she wore. She got to tell her side first. There were times when she was speaking I wanted to stand up and yell, "I object," like you see on TV. Other times I wanted to call out "Liar!" because of the way she distorted what had happened. Mostly, I just wanted to disappear. I was afraid to look at my mother during Joy's testimony. I tried to sit still and not swivel in my leather chair. I knew it made no sense, but I felt as though if I moved the judge wouldn't take me seriously.

Judge Gooden listened attentively to whoever was speaking. Sometimes he looked down and wrote something on a pad he had in front of him. He wore a black robe, but otherwise he didn't look like a judge. Since I'd never seen a judge before, I had no one to compare him to except the judges I'd seen on TV when we were living in Motel Hell and all I had to do all day was watch endless hours of television. No matter what happened to me in court, I still had no regrets about not going to school back then. I couldn't have left my mother alone.

Joy elaborated about how neglectful my mother was to allow me to miss school during those weeks. What nerve she had. She was the one who had forgotten to come back to enroll me. The ultimate low blow was when Joy told the judge that Emily had another daughter. A runaway she hadn't seen in a year. I looked over at Marvin, who was watching Joy and listening with a calm face that I couldn't read. When Joy was finished, she requested that the court remove me from my mother's custody for a minimum of six months during which time she recommended Emily get appropriate counseling and seek employment. Joy suggested my mother be allowed supervised visitation for those six months. Then she could be granted another hearing to determine if she had rehabilitated herself enough to regain custody. Joy finished with what I suppose she thought was a heart-wrenching plea for the judge to act in the best interest of the child; meaning me. I didn't have a glimmer of hope left by the time she concluded.

Marvin had the job of countering Joy's accusations. He began slowly, with his lovely Southern drawl that moved at a pace which deceived you into thinking his brain moved as gradually as his speech. The longer he spoke, the more impressive he became. He began by reading a statement from Mr. St. Clair.

Mr. St. Clair explained how I'd come to school in the summer and registered on my own, even though my social worker had neglected to ensure I was registered. He politely, but assertively criticized Joy. He attached my grades, and he explained how I'd tried out for cheerleading even though I had less than a week to prepare. He said I showed "great promise" and he recommended I stay with my mother and be allowed to continue at Central. He concluded by saying I'd been through enough and he feared I would be harmed by another change.

Next, Gloria testified as a character witness for Emily. Marvin said she made a credible witness because of her background and the fact that she was now employed at a prestigious salon in the city. She had the job of telling the judge that Emily was never an unfit mother.

The judge questioned Gloria about how and where she met Emily and me. He was specific and to the point. When he asked, "At any time did you think Mrs. Williams was unfit to care for her daughter?" I held my breath. I knew Gloria wouldn't lie. She couldn't. It was court.

She waited a long moment before she answered. "Emily was clearly in distress. She was a young widow who had not only lost her husband, but lost her home and all of her resources. She had a teenaged daughter to care for and absolutely no way to do so." Gloria then looked directly at Joy for a long moment. She shifted her gaze back to Judge Gooden. "Your Honor, you know I would not be telling the truth if I said that Emily Williams was a capable human being or mother when I first met her. But I don't think you or I would have been in better shape than she was if we had experienced what she had been through. That does not make her an unfit mother. If I know anything, I know that Emily loves her daughter and would do anything for her."

I was next. The Judge spoke gently to me. He told me he was going to ask me three questions. First, he asked me to tell him what happened when we met Joy. I described what happened when she first came to our house. Next, he asked me why I had stopped going to school. I glanced at Marvin, who nodded his head at me. I told the whole truth. How Joy had said she would get me into school and she would call to tell me where I was registered and how I would get to school. I explained that when she didn't show up, I was not motivated to leave my mother alone in a motel and go off to find a new, strange school. The third question was the hardest and the one I was certain would defeat us.

"How would you describe your mother at this time, Ms. Williams?"

I did not want to go back to that time, but I had to. I had to find a way to capture how bad things were but how, as soon as we met Gloria, Emily started to improve and get the help she needed. All she needed was a friend to help guide her through a terrible time. Somehow, I got through the questions. I could only hope the Judge would understand what I was telling him about my mother. Just as I was finishing my statement, the door opened and a police officer came into the room. I had seen him earlier in the hall before we came in. He said, "Excuse me, your honor, but I have an important message for Mr. Mullins."

The judge nodded and Marvin excused himself and got up to speak to the officer. They spoke for a moment in low voices. Then Marvin turned to the judge and said, "Your honor, may I have a word with you privately?"

Judge Gooden and Marvin left the room. Their presence was replaced with a silence that was a deep hole of discomfort. Joy Pierce kept her eyes down and shuffled through some papers, pretending to read them. Maybe she really was reading them. No one spoke. No one knew where to look.

When the door finally opened, everyone's head turned. I hoped they were returning and that it wasn't the officer or another messenger coming in to tell us to be patient. With relief, I saw the Judge enter followed by Marvin. Behind them was a young woman with very short hair.

A second later I heard my mother gasp. "Oh my God." I followed her gaze and experienced a flash of recognition. I took a good look at the woman and realized she wasn't a woman at all. It was Rachel looking so grown up and beautiful I hadn't recognized my own sister. My mother reached over and grabbed my hand. She squeezed my hand, hurting it as she snapped at me, "Did you know she was coming here?"

I stared at her in disbelief. "You're not...are you still mad at her?" I sputtered.

I was scared and desperate when Joy found me again. When I learned we had to go to court I confided in Marvin and told him I knew where Rachel was. I told him I wanted to reach out to Rachel and ask her to come and be there for Emily.

"Well, Miss Delia, I don't see as to how it could hurt," he'd replied in that drawl I'd come to love.

After the encounter in Harlem, I didn't expect Rachel to respond so I wasn't at all surprised when I didn't hear from her. I had given her the details of the hearing, but since she hadn't answered my email it never occurred to me she would show up. Now that I saw the panic on my mother's face, I realized Emily was afraid of what Rachel might say. How stupid of me. Rachel might not be on our side.

Judge Gooden started by asking my sister to describe what Emily was like before Rachel ran away. When Rachel began by saying, "Being Emily Williams' daughter wasn't easy," I thought I had made the biggest mistake of my life by reaching out to her.

"All my friends wanted to be Emily's daughter. Emily was…is…perfect. Beautiful, smart, charming…there were never enough adjectives to describe my mother. My friends all envied me. They wanted to be me." She looked directly at my mother. "Only I didn't want to be me. I…I was a mess. I couldn't live up to my parent's expectations of me. That wasn't my mother's fault. That was on me."

The Judge asked Rachel a few more questions. He concluded by asking if Rachel ever thought Emily was unstable. Rachel said no.

When the judge finished questioning Rachel, he thanked her for coming. He told her how brave he thought she was to go off on her own at such a young age. He said he hoped she would reconcile with her family. "Families aren't perfect, as I well know." he said. "But they love you just for being yourself." Rachel's eyes were down. I couldn't tell what effect the judge's words had on her. My own eyes filled until I was afraid they would spill over and I would cry right there in front of everyone.

I had been afraid to look at Emily until it was her turn to speak. I was terrified she would unravel and become too shaken

219

or upset by everything she'd heard to speak to the judge. Instead, her face looked composed. She appeared steady and strong.

"I'm terribly sorry for the misfortunes which bring us here today, Mrs. Williams," Judge Gooden began. "Would you like to make a statement on your own behalf to counter the complaints Ms. Pierce has raised on behalf of the Division of Family Services."

"Thank you, Your Honor. I would. As you might imagine, it's painful to sit here and listen to the accusations Ms. Pierce has filed against me. Yet they're mild in comparison to the ones I have aimed at myself. Yes, I have had many harsh experiences this year. I had many privileges prior to my husband's death. But I neither appreciated what I had, nor did I use my privileges in ways that I'm proud of. I hope that Your Honor will not confuse the fact that I had money to buy things for my children, with being a good mother. I'm a better mother now that I lost everything." She went on to explain how she had found a job and about all the lessons she had learned since Daddy died last January. She ended by saying, "Being a good parent is not about what material things you give your children, Your Honor. It's about valuing them for who they are."

My mother has always had charisma and the knack of charming anyone who met her. Now, she had added another dimension to her appeal. Her sincerity shone through as she spoke and no one hearing her should have doubted her ability to take care of me.

Finally, it was Marvin's turn to cap off the hearing. By the time he summed up the arguments for not removing me from Emily's care, I'm certain even Joy Pierce could tell she had lost the case long before Judge Gooden gave his decision. As I listened to Marvin give his eloquent final statement, I decided that maybe I'd become a lawyer someday. Lawyers like him might not make much money, but he saved me from the one thing that I don't think I would have survived; being apart from my mother.

We left the court after what seemed like the longest day of my life. When we were outside, Emily turned to Marvin and took his hand in both of hers. "Thank you for giving me another chance to be a better mother to my daughters." Her hair was shining in the sunlight, her eyes were sparkling with tears.

"My pleasure, Ms. Emily. Any mother who has a daughter like Miss Delia who would run away not once, but twice to be with her must have done something right. And Miss Rachel is a fine young woman. You should be proud."

"I am," she said. "Your mama Ella must have been very proud of you. I wish there was some way I could repay you for all you've done for us."

"I'll tell you what. I am a simple man who loves a good, home-cooked meal. Why not invite me to dinner when you're in your new place, cook me up somethin' delicious and we'll call it even?"

I wish I had a photograph of the look of horror on Emily's face. I burst out laughing. My mother looked at me and she too, started to roar. We laughed so long and so hard my sides ached. Poor Marvin had no idea what was so funny. There was no way we could deny Marvin his request. We'd have to find some really good take-out food.

When he left, Gloria went to find Cheyenne and Crazy Annie who were waiting for us in Cheyenne's trailer. He had opted out of an apartment. Instead, he had purchased a used mobile home to live in. It was kind of cool, actually. He named it The Silver Bullet because that's exactly what it looked like on the outside. Inside it was roomier than you would expect and it came complete with all the basics; a small stove, a refrigerator, a TV, and even a shower.

Rachel, my mother, and I stood alone on the sidewalk.

"You cut your hair. Just like I dreamed," my mother said, staring at Rachel.

"I don't know what to say," Rachel and I said at the same time.

"I'm sorry about Daddy," Rachel said. "Sorry I was so mean when you found me, Delia." She covered her eyes, crying. Emily reached for her. All the tears I held in for so long poured down my face. The one thing I had wished and prayed for was happening. My family was together again and it was breaking my heart more than anything else had since this all began.

Emily abruptly stopped hugging my sister and turned to me, "You knew where she was? I can't believe you kept this from me. How long have you known where your sister was?"

"Emily! This is the best news!" Cheyenne arrived and hugged Emily first, then me and then Rachel, who he didn't even know. For the moment I was saved from having to confess my journey to Harlem.

"Come on. You three have a lot of catching up to do. Let's go to The Silver Bullet," Cheyenne said. "Gloria, Crazy Annie and I will go for coffee. You need some time to catch up."

We did some quick introductions, then Cheyenne walked us the few blocks to where he'd parked the mobile home. He let us in and put the coffee pot on. "I'm meeting Crazy Annie and Gloria down the street at the deli. I'll be back."

"He seems like a good guy," Rachel said.

"He saved us," I said. Thinking about everything that had happened since I last saw Rachel, I didn't know if we could ever catch up.

Rachel told us she had come back from California just after we'd lost the house. She didn't know where to start to look for us. We told her about Motel Hell and about Hardscrabble Way.

"You lived in a tent," she said, as if saying it out loud would help her believe it. "Was it awful?"

"Yes," Emily said at exactly the same time I said, "No. Not all of it." My head snapped sideways to look at my mother. She tilted her head and looked at me, raising her eyebrows.

When Rachel came back east, she'd gone home to our old house. She found it not only empty, but with the windows boarded up and a **For Sale: Foreclosure** sign on the lawn.

Stunned and alone, she had no idea where to start looking for us. She called one of her old friends who told her about Daddy. She reached out to my middle school to try to find us, which was useless. They didn't have a clue where I was at that point. Finally, she called Uncle Arthur. Of course he didn't know where we were either. She had no other way to find us.

"When you first left, Daddy hired a private detective. He traced you to California and then lost you," my mother said.

"I tried to find you, too, Rach. There was a page on Facebook," I told her. "Even before Molly sent me your email."

"I never looked at Facebook. I couldn't stand to hear about the people who knew us before. It was too painful."

I knew exactly what she meant. We weren't part of that life anymore and it was excruciating to be reminded of the past.

"What email?" Emily asked. "Delia, how long have you known where Rachel was?" she asked for the second time that day.

I ignored my mother's question. I had a question of my own that I needed answered.

"If you were trying to find us, then why did you send me away when I found you?" I asked.

"When did you see her?" Emily demanded.

"Was it because of what I did to you? I'm so sorry..." I said.

"No. Not that. I was stunned to see you. I hadn't come to terms with anything. I'd shut it all down. I moved on once I got into CUNY. Well...I pretended I'd moved on."

Emily interrupted. "At some point you two are going to have to fill in some blanks for me."

Rachel nodded. She looked at me and continued. "I was so ashamed. I'd been awful to you, to Daddy. She looked at Emily. "And to you. When you appeared at my door Delia, I just couldn't face you. I hadn't forgiven myself for letting the family down. I needed to break away. Be independent. I know that doesn't make sense. Can you forgive me?"

Rachel told us she had made a decent amount of money in California selling her art on the boardwalk. She'd finished high school out there in an adult night program. When she decided to come back east, she applied to CUNY. She not only got accepted, she received a scholarship and a work study program. Working part-time and using the money she'd saved from selling her work, she now lived with two roommates in student housing in the apartment where I'd found her just a few blocks away from the school.

"I was so worried about you. I felt so guilty..." Emily started, but Rachel cut her off.

"Don't! Nothing was your fault. When I left I didn't know what I wanted."

"You always knew what you wanted. I wasn't listening," Emily said.

"I wanted to work on my art," Rachel said. "I didn't fit in anywhere else."

"You knew how to take care of yourself," Emily said. "Better than I did. If it wasn't for Delia..."

"No. I didn't. Not in the beginning. I've edited out the rough parts. Someday, maybe I'll tell you everything." Rachel got quiet. We'd all been through so much.

"Homeless," Rachel said. Hearing her say it made it worse. "We went from living the American dream to being homeless. I was rebelling against how much we had. But I never thought we could lose everything. Even when I ran away, I believed I could come safely home again and somehow things would be alright." She looked at our mother, as if she was pleading with Emily to somehow make sense of it all. Emily looked away, as if she couldn't look at Rachel. Maybe she couldn't endure remembering the losses. She'd lost her husband, her home, and a year of being a part of her oldest daughter's life. She'd nearly lost me, as well. Not to mention she almost lost her sanity.

Cheyenne's megaphone was sitting on a small table next to the couch. Emily reached for it and held it in her hand. She looked at for a while.

"Did you ever think this could happen to us?" Rachel asked. She was looking at Emily, really looking at her, waiting for her to say something. Even with her short hair, her face looked very young.

Emily stood up, moved around the inside of Cheyenne's mobile home. She set the megaphone back in its place. Dreamily, her hand reached out and touched the curtain on the window. Rachel had asked the question, but I too needed her to say something. I don't know what. Consoling words. Something that would help make some sense of the experiences we survived. I was lost in that space just beyond childhood where you still want your parents to have answers, even though in your heart you know they don't. I had always worried about what would happen to Emily if we never found Rachel. Now, I was afraid this had all been too much for her. Had finding my sister pushed my mother to the brink, again? Just when I thought my mother wasn't going to say anything at all, she turned around and faced us. She came closer and gathered us both in her arms. I felt her hand smoothing my hair. When she spoke, her voice was filled with acceptance.

"Anything can happen to us. We're no different than anyone else. We only thought we were."

~~

Marvin wasn't as lucky two weeks later when he lost the case against the city and everyone was ordered to leave Hardscrabble Way. But he remained true to his promise to help everyone find housing. Denny and Daryl moved to an apartment a few blocks away from us. Crazy Annie lives in the same apartment building as them. I was especially relieved when Haysoos and Roberta found a place with a small yard and a landlady who lives upstairs by herself. She loves animals. Even pot-bellied pigs. She offered to take care of Roberta when Haysoos was working. We were making plans to celebrate Thanksgiving together and Gloria and Emily were going to host the dinner at our place.

CHAPTER 3
November, 2012

This was the Thanksgiving when I truly understood what the holiday was about. I was in the kitchen helping my mother. I could hear Denny in the other room playing guitar and singing. Emily was taking an apple pie out of the oven. She bought it frozen, but still. Last Thanksgiving, I never would have believed that even having an oven would seem like a luxury. There is nothing homier than the aroma of warm apple pie.

I walked out of the kitchen. In the living room, Gloria was dressed in a chunky sweater the color of apricots, and a long floaty skirt. Her wonderful red hair was curled and circled her face like a halo. She was laughing at something Crazy Annie had said. Haysoos was feeding bits of turkey to Roberta. I sat on the loveseat we'd gotten out of our storage unit. I was hugging my knees, taking it all in, and feeling like the luckiest girl in Philadelphia. Sure there were people missing from this Norman Rockwell scene. My dad. Larry. Crazy that Daddy was still here last Thanksgiving and that I didn't even know Larry. But I was thankful for what I had now, and I wasn't going to let what I was missing ruin everything. My mother caught my eye and smiled at me. I sensed she felt the same way I did. Grateful.

She's doing well. She loves her job and is even talking about starting her own yoga studio someday. If she hadn't met Gloria I doubt she would have ever been inspired to feel like she could accomplish running a business of her own. She and Gloria have been to see me cheer whenever they could get off work. One of the girls twisted her ankle and I've been filling in for her on the squad. No one yells louder at the games than my mother, although she makes it clear that she still hates football and really, really hates seeing me fly. I love how she's there for me.

Although the past is still painful, I posted on my Facebook page recently. I heard from people who knew me from my old life. They were relieved to know that I was alive and doing well. Margot was one of the first to message me. I apologized to her for disappearing. She wrote back and told me she understood. We're planning to get together after the holidays. Sometimes it feels like I dreamed my other life. The one where I lived on the Main Line, went to Bala Cynwyd Middle School, and had a father and way too many pairs of boots.

"Delia, are you ready for tomorrow? We have to leave early," Crazy Annie called to me from across the room.

"Of course I am," I said. "You know I wouldn't miss your show." Crazy Annie's work got accepted in the PAFA show. The actual show started December first, but the artists who were showing could start mounting their work the day after Thanksgiving. Since there was no school the day after Thanksgiving, I was going to PAFA to help hang her work. And Rachel was coming with us. She was here for the long weekend and we were sharing my room.

I walked over and sat down next to Denny, who was on the floor strumming his guitar.

"You're quiet," I said.

"Where's Matteo today?"

I looked at him, eyebrows raised.

"I heard you went to the dance with him," he said. "Are you two a thing?"

I shrugged. I didn't know what we were. We'd hung out a few more times since the dance.

"He's too old for you. You need to watch out."

"He's very sweet."

"He's a guy. I know guys."

"What are you saying?"

"Look, forget it. Forget I said anything. Let's have pie." He stood up.

"We haven't eaten yet," I reminded him.

"There are no rules on Thanksgiving," he grinned, and he walked into the kitchen.

I followed him. After I sliced him a huge piece of apple pie, I opened the freezer. I scooped a blob of creamy vanilla ice cream and plopped the ice cream on top of the pie. The pie was still warm and the ice cream started to melt, just the way I like it. I held the plate out to Denny.

"I know you mean well," I said, as I handed him the dessert. "But you don't…"

"You know I always wanted a little sister," Denny interrupted me. I watched him stick his fork into the pie and slide some ice cream on top.

"You're not my big brother," I said, not in a mean way.

He lifted the fork and pushed it towards my mouth. "Ssh. Eat." He smiled at me and my heart melted faster than the ice cream in my mouth.

"No? Then what am I?" he asked. He was looking straight into my eyes.

My first love, I wanted to say. But I didn't want to ruin what we had, so I simply said, "My best friend." Then, not feeling very sisterly, I reached over and touched his cheek with the back of my hand like I'd seen someone do in a movie once. I swear I could feel myself vibrate. I took my hand back. I leaned in, tilted my head up and kissed him on the cheek. "I'm having a happy Thanksgiving."

"Me too," he said, putting his arm around my shoulder. There it was again. I could feel the electric that zoomed through me when Denny touched me.

Maybe Denny and I aren't meant to be together. Maybe there would be other boys I would care about. But I remembered what my mother had said about no one had ever made her vibrate and I had a feeling this was special. Like Gloria after Cooper, I would date others, but I would have a hard time settling for someone else if that indescribable spark wasn't there.

"Where's Daryl?" Gloria asked us when we came back in the living room.

"He'll be here. He had a late delivery he had to make." The doorbell rang as Denny spoke. "Maybe that's him."

Daryl came in and kissed me on the cheek. "Can I eat something? I'm starving."

I took his coat. "I'll hang this in the closet." I now appreciate little things like having a closet so much that it gives me pleasure to say it out loud.

"We waited for you. Come on," I said. "You have to meet my sister. Then we'll eat."

Rachel was talking with Crazy Annie. As I had hoped, the two hit it off. They had so much in common. "Rach, I want you to meet one of my favorite people in the world. This is Denny's brother Daryl Jaxson. They were my first friends when we moved to Hardscrabble Way."

"I thought I was your only friend," Denny teased. I was so fascinated by what was happening between Rachel and Daryl that it was one of the few times I let Denny tease me without giving it right back.

"Your sister talked about you all the time. You're even prettier than she said," Daryl said.

Rachel's eyes were glued to Daryl. I turned to look at him. He had a hang dog look on his face and was staring right back at Rachel. This continued for a long moment that soon began to get awkward. I wondered if either of them was capable of speech.

"I'm Daryl," he said at last.

"I know," Rachel said. Everything went quiet again. I looked at each of their faces and I recognized this scene. Rachel was having a watermelon moment. It was *Dirty Dancing* all over again. I missed Larry.

"Come on, guys. I'll show you where the food is," I said, breaking the silent staring phenomenon that was traveling past awkward and becoming uncomfortable.

Denny made a snort sound. "I think we can find food. We've been here before. Come on, Dar," He and Daryl walked across the room to the buffet table.

I looked at Rachel and grinned. "What are you so cheery about?" Rachel asked.

"Are you vibrating?" I asked her.

"You're fourteen. What do you know about vibrating?" There was a touch of the old Rachel sarcasm in her voice. Then she smiled at me, embarrassed. "Yeh. I am. He's...he's so..." she stopped.

"I know," I said. "He is." She nodded her head. We didn't need words. We were, after all, sisters.

"I envy you," my sister said.

"Me? Why?"

"Look at you. You found your place in the world. You belong here, with your friends. I'm still searching for who I am, where I fit in."

I took Rachel's hand in mine. Our fingers intertwined.

She was right. I had everything I needed right here in this room. My family, friends, a home. And the feeling that anything was possible. I didn't need anything else. I had what I had been yearning for. I squeezed my sister's hand. Rachel looked at me with tears in her eyes. From across the room I saw Emily looking at us. She was smiling her beautiful smile. The three of us stood there looking at each other like a trifecta of grinning fools. Families aren't perfect. They fight. They make mistakes. If you are lucky enough to have a family, you need to hold on tight no matter what. We didn't understand that before. Not completely. We did now.

The End